WOMEN ON THE EDGE

I0592958

WELLESLEY STUDIES IN CRITICAL THEORY, LITERARY HISTORY,
AND CULTURE
VOLUME 19
GARLAND REFERENCE LIBRARY OF THE HUMANITIES
VOLUME 2124

WELLESLEY STUDIES IN CRITICAL THEORY, LITERARY HISTORY, AND CULTURE

WILLIAM E. CAIN, *General Editor*

MAKING FEMINIST HISTORY
*The Literary Scholarship
of Sandra M. Gilbert
and Susan Gubar*
edited by William E. Cain

TEACHING THE CONFLICTS
*Gerald Graff, Curricular
Reform, and the Culture Wars*
edited by William E. Cain

THE CANON IN THE CLASSROOM
*The Pedagogical Implications
of Canon Revision
in American Literature*
edited by John Alberti

REGIONALISM RECONSIDERED
New Approaches to the Field
edited by David M. Jordan

AMERICAN WOMEN
SHORT STORY WRITERS
A Collection of Critical Essays
edited by Julie Brown

LITERARY INFLUENCE AND
AFRICAN-AMERICAN WRITERS
Collected Essays
edited by Tracy Mishkin

MODERNISM, GENDER,
AND CULTURE
A Cultural Studies Approach
edited with an introduction by
Lisa Rado

RECONCEPTUALIZING
AMERICAN LITERARY/
CULTURAL STUDIES
*Rhetoric, History, and Politics
in the Humanities*
edited by William E. Cain

TEXTS AND TEXTUALITY
*Textual Instability, Theory,
and Interpretation*
edited by Philip Cohen

THE NEW NINETEENTH CENTURY
*Feminist Readings of
Underread Victorian Fiction*
edited by Barbara Leah Harman
and Susan Meyer

ETHNICITY AND THE
AMERICAN SHORT STORY
edited by Julie Brown

NEW DEFINITIONS OF LYRIC
Theory, Technology, and Culture
edited by Mark Jeffreys

BLAKE, POLITICS, AND HISTORY
edited by Jackie DiSalvo, G.A. Rosso,
and Christopher Z. Hobson

RACE AND THE PRODUCTION
OF MODERN AMERICAN
NATIONALISM
edited by Reynolds J. Scott-Childress

WOMEN ON THE EDGE
*Ethnicity and Gender in Short
Stories by American Women*
edited by Corinne H. Dale
and J.H.E. Paine

WOMEN ON THE EDGE
ETHNICITY AND GENDER
IN SHORT STORIES
BY AMERICAN WOMEN

EDITED BY
CORINNE H. DALE AND J.H.E. PAINE

Routledge
Taylor & Francis Group
New York   London

First published 1999 by Garland Publishing Inc.

This edition Published 2014 by Routledge
711 Third Avenue, New York, NY 10017
2 Park Square, Milton Park, Abingdon, Oxfordshire OX14 4RN

First issued in paperback 2014

*Routledge is an imprint of the Taylor and Francis Group,
an informa business*

Library of Congress Cataloging-in-Publication Data

Women on the edge : ethnicity and gender in short stories by American
    women / edited by Corinne II. Dale and J.II.E. Paine.
            p.   cm. — (Garland reference library of the humanities ; vol.
2124. Wellesley studies in critical theory, literary history, and culture ; vol.
19)
        Includes bibliographical references and index.
        ISBN 0-8153-3247-5 (alk. paper)
        1. Short stories, American—Women authors—History and criticism.
2. Women and literature—United States—History.   3. Gender identity in
literature.   4. Ethnicity in literature.   5. Sex role in literature.   I. Dale,
Corinne H.   II. Paine, J. H. E.   III. Series: Garland reference library of the
humanities ; vol. 2124.   IV. Series: Garland reference library of the
humanities. Wellesley studies in critical theory, literary history, and
culture ; vol. 19.
    PS374.S5W58   1999
    813'.01089287—dc21   98–38847
                                                                                    CIP
ISBN 13: 978-1-138-86442-9 (pbk)
ISBN 13: 978-0-8153-3247-3 (hbk)

Cover photograph: *A Beginning* by Andrew Shmerling.

General Editor's Preface

The volumes in this series, Wellesley Studies in Critical Theory, Literary History, and Culture, are designed to reflect, develop, and extend important trends and tendencies in contemporary criticism. The careful scrutiny of literary texts in their own right of course remains a crucial part of the work that critics and teachers perform: this traditional task has not been devalued or neglected. But other types of interdisciplinary and contextual work are now being done, in large measure as a result of the emphasis on "theory" that began in the late 1960s and early 1970s and that has accelerated since that time. Critics and teachers now examine texts of all sorts—literary and non-literary alike—and, more generally, have taken the entire complex, multifaceted field of culture as the object for their analytical attention. The discipline of literary studies has radically changed, and the scale and scope of this series is intended to illustrate this challenging fact.

Theory has signified many things, but one of the most crucial has been the insistent questioning of familiar categories and distinctions. As theory has grown in its scope and intensified in importance, it has reoriented the idea of the literary canon: there is no longer a single canon, but many canons. It has also opened up and complicated the meanings of history, and the materials and forms that constitute it. Literary history continues to be vigorously written, but now as a kind of history that intersects with other histories that involve politics, economics, race relations, the role of women in society, and many more. And the breadth of this historical inquiry has impelled many in literary studies to view themselves more as cultural critics and general intellectuals than as literary scholars.

Theory, history, culture: these are the formidable terms around which the volumes in this series have been organized. A number of these volumes will be the product of a single author or editor. But perhaps even more of them will be collaborative ventures, emerging from the joint enterprise of editors, essayists, and respondents or commentators. In each volume, and as a whole, the series will aim to highlight both distinctive contributions to knowledge and a process of exchange, discussion, and debate. It will make available new kinds of work, as well as fresh approaches to criticism's traditional tasks, and indicate new ways through which such work can be done.

William E. Cain
Wellesley College

Contents

Preface and Acknowledgments   vii

Introduction
    Corinne H. Dale and J.H.E. Paine   ix

Chapter 1: (Dis)Continuous Narrative: The Articulation of a
    Chicana Feminist Voice in Sandra Cisneros's *The
    House on Mango Street*
    Deborah L. Madsen   3

Chapter 2: Beyond Otherness: Negotiated Identities and
    Viramontes' "The Cariboo Cafe"
    Marta Caminero-Santangelo   19

Chapter 3: Judith Ortiz Cofer's *Silent Dancing*: Making More
    Room for Puerto Rican Womanhood
    Nancy L. Chick   35

Chapter 4: Flight and Arrival: A Study of Padma Hejmadi's
    Short Story, "Weather Report"
    Lakshmi Holmström   53

Chapter 5: Subversive Extravagance: Women in Hisaye
    Yamamoto's "Seventeen Syllables" and "The Legend
    of Miss Sasagawara"
    Veronica C. Wang   67

Chapter 6: Afrekete Rising: Two Coming-out Stories by
    African-American Lesbians: Pat Suncircle's "A Day's
    Growth" and Audre Lorde's "The Beginning"
    M. Charlene Ball   81

Chapter 7: Race/[Gender]: Toni Morrison's "Recitatif"
    David Goldstein-Shirley   97

Chapter 8: Playing in the Light: White Girls Dreaming in
    Eudora Welty's "Moon Lake"
    Elaine Orr   111

Chapter 9: Ruth's Journey into the Fields: Feminism in
    Ozick's "The Pagan Rabbi"
    Kathy Rugoff   129

Chapter 10 Reconstructing the Native-American Woman:
    Louise Erdrich's "Fleur"
    Corinne H. Dale   143

Contributors' Notes   161
Index   165

Preface and Acknowledgments

The purpose of this collection is to explore the intertwining social conditions of ethnicity and gender as they are represented in short stories by contemporary American women. The collection brings together analyses of short stories that focus on major ethnic cultures in the United States: Mexican American, Puerto Rican, Japanese American, Asian American, African American, Jewish American, white Protestant American, and Native American. Each essay testifies to the struggles of women within patriarchal cultures, and each explores how the different ethnic identities set the terms of these gender struggles. The essays also reveal the complications of other important social issues, such as class, sexual preference, and religion. Together, the essays indicate the complexity and significance of this cultural approach to women's fiction; they also demonstrate that neither ethnicity nor gender can legitimately be considered alone.

This collection is intended for those who wish to investigate the intersections of ethnicity and gender for personal and/or scholarly reasons. In particular, teachers and students interested in women writers, ethnic writers, American writers, and modern fiction in general may find that these essays enrich their readings of the short stories considered and also demonstrate the critical theories that are currently developing in the fields of gender and ethnic studies.

We would like to express special appreciation to our colleagues at the Centre d'Etudes et de Recherches sur la nouvelle en langue anglaise at the Université d'Angers and to the Presses de l'Université d'Angers, which publishes the *Journal of the Short Story in English*, where several of these essays first appeared. Our collaboration of some fifteen years with our colleagues in Angers continues to be a source of satisfaction and delight to us both. We also wish to express our gratitude to the School of Humanities and Education at Belmont University, which supported this endeavor with Faculty Development Grants.

Introduction

Corinne H. Dale and J.H.E. Paine

The essays in this collection seek in their various ways to chart the course of the feminine subject in the landscape of contemporary North American women writers. The stories that are discussed are tales of women in the United States who seek to define themselves as individuals within the contexts of ethnicity and gender. Often, they are literally stories of growing up. Many relate stories of individual empowerment as a writer articulating a personal voice that sometimes blurs the distinction between narrator and author. For the development of an individual voice is the expression of the individually created Self—not that of a socially constructed Other.

Ethnicity has always had a special resonance in the United States, a nation with a history of conflicts between native societies and immigrant groups, between colonists and slaves, and between established and new settlers. At present, the ongoing struggle with issues of diversity and multiculturalism is especially critical since we live at a time when the dominance of Northern European ethnicity is increasingly challenged by growing numbers of Hispanic, African, and Asian Americans, just to mention the largest groups of ethnic minorities.

These standard labels, not incidentally, illustrate the artificial nature of ethnic groupings, which collect people from different nations and vastly different cultures into seemingly homogeneous categories. Thus, Asian Americans include people from such diverse countries as China, Japan, India, and the Philippines. Similarly, first-generation Mexican Americans are grouped with people whose ancestors arrived in the Southwest from Spain centuries ago. Thus, the terms "Asian," "African," "Hispanic," "Native American," and "white" all suggest monolithic cultures, but have no corresponding national identities. Nevertheless, the exploration of multiculturalism and the affirmation of diversity relies on such uneasy groupings of "ethnic Americans."

As we celebrate multicultural diversity, we must paradoxically acknowledge these artificial constructions of ethnicity, the stereotypes that project a group as Other. Moreover, we must also acknowledge that the homogeneous identities of these Others have been constructed from the point of view, or gaze, of outsiders, especially those of the mainstream European-American culture. In fact, the construction of ethnic minority Others has developed in large part *in opposition to* the image of the European-American majority, as Toni Morrison has suggested in *Playing in the Dark: Whiteness and the Literary Imagination* (1992).

Recognizing the social constructions of Others empowers us to explore individuality within the artificial confines of homogeneous ethnicities. Such awareness alerts us to the ways in which our cultural identities are developed within and around us and the ways in which we are influenced by them even as we resist them. The essays in this collection undertake that probing of ethnic identity, especially as it intertwines with gender.

The acknowledgment of ethnicity as an artificial category has fueled a similar deconstruction of gender. Today we recognize that both gender and ethnicity are socially constructed: they do not define individuals but instead the cultural context in which we individually live. Ethnic identity describes a culture, both the ways that the culture defines itself and also the ways in which it is defined by other cultures. Women, too, have been constructed as a homogeneous Other. Women live in a patriarchal culture that has defined the feminine in opposition to the masculine, even though individual women experience that cultural context in a tremendous variety of ways, depending on many factors such as age, class, and sexual orientation—as well as ethnic identity.

The challenge to feminist studies by women of ethnic minorities presents a breakthrough in the understanding of gender: academic feminists are forced to acknowledge that "whiteness" is an artificial category, just as gender is. Yet this challenge is as old as the first woman who protested her individual truth in the face of the monolith of white, middle-class femininity, like Sojourner Truth when she claimed "Ain't I a woman?" and bared her breast to prove it in spite of her life of hard labor as a field slave. Women of ethnic minorities are doubly marginalized—dominated by the white patriarchal culture. Considering gender outside of ethnicity promotes a fragmentation of identity in which different parts of identity are pitted against once another. Gender cannot legitimately be claimed by white women; womanhood cannot be defined as white experience.

Equally important is the acknowledgment that whiteness is also a social construction of ethnicity. A white woman may not be doubly marginalized in the way that a Native-American woman is; still, being a white woman—even a middle-class, heterosexual white woman whose native language is English—means that attitudes about whiteness impinge on who she is and how others relate to her. Like all of us, white women live their lives in compliance with and in resistance to socially constructed definitions of homogeneous ethnicity and gender.

Gender, then, is more than just sex and more than the essential differences that biology entails, many of which are hotly debated: for example, whereas pregnancy, childbirth, and nursing are clearly biologically determined, how much of mothering is culturally influenced? Such questions lie on the vaguely defined boundary between essential and constructed differences between men and women. Although the boundaries are not clearly delineated, then, gender can be defined as the concepts of womanhood and manhood that are developed in a culture, providing a social context that individuals are immersed within even as their individual experiences are widely divergent.

Both gender and ethnicity are socially constructed identities attached to groups of individuals who share or are perceived to share common identities. As previously suggested, often such perceptions are clearly from the point of view, or gaze, of outsiders, especially the white patriarchal community. Thus, these ethnic and gender concepts reveal inventions, fantasies, that are real in the sense that they name and define groups in ways that reverberate in our culture and in our individual experiences.

Naming, or defining, is a powerful act, often aimed at controlling individuals. The desire to fix gender and ethnicity can and does lead to genocide by stereotype. But individuals are resilient, and the heterogeneity, or difference, of personal experience reasserts itself in literature as in life. For individuals can never be truly defined, or fixed, by social constructions. Gender and ethnicity are inventions that are constantly under revision, they are deconstructed and reconstructed by the tensions between individual differences and social commonalities.

The essays in this collection are organized according to ethnic groups: Hispanic American, Asian American, African American, white American, Jewish American, and Native American. The women in the stories must sort out their lives within the context of gender as well as within these specific ethnic groups. Their identities are also influenced by other social factors: they are heterosexual and homosexual and bisexual; they inhabit the world of a particular social class and religious faith; they are immigrant Americans and second-generation Americans and Native Americans whose ancestors go far back before recorded history. Importantly for the purposes of this volume, their lives are represented in the contexts of their social, historical, and linguistic worlds, worlds in which gender and ethnicity are constructed by the culture and are powerful shaping forces for individuals. The writers define their characters in opposition to the dominant European-American culture and to the dominant patriarchal cultures of their ethnic groups. Yet one finds again and again in their work the effort to surmount these oppositions and to establish themselves as autonomous subjects.

For essayist D. L. Madsen, Sandra Cisneros's *The House on Mango Street* articulates a Chicana feminist voice that interrupts the "false coherence of [both Anglo and Chicano] patriarchal language" through the use of discontinuous narrative form. The hybrid form of short stories that also may be read as one story allows Cisneros to depict the evolving identity of her adolescent Chicana narrator Esperanza, who establishes herself as the controlling subject of her stories against not only patriarchal but also Anglo-feminist narratives of women's lives. In the end, Esperanza has achieved adulthood and independence as an artist by developing a voice that can break the silence imposed upon her by the forces of sexual and racial oppression.

Similarly, for Nancy Chick, Judith Ortiz Cofer, in her story collection *Silent Dancing: A Partial Remembrance of a Puerto Rican Childhood*, "negotiates her own space within Puerto Rican and American literature" also by disrupting linear narrative form. She creates a hybrid form of narrative which she calls *ensayo* (including elements of the essay without its formal structure as well as elements of memoir and autobiography) as a vehicle for writing the oral *cuentos* told to her in her youth by her grandmother Mamá. This woman-centered series of stories by turns subverts and displaces the hegemonic power structures of the Roman Catholic Church, American imperialism, and the Puerto Rican pigmentocracy, all of which have sought to control gender, ethnic, and racial difference through strategies of containment. Chick's analysis of the stories that make up *Silent Dancing* demonstrates how Ortiz Cofer "opens up our conceptions of race, culture, and gender, each of which becomes a signifier for a multiplicity of ideologies and identities that renders a univocal articulation of idealized, sexualized, or racialized gender impossible." Ortiz Cofer's hybrid narrative form, in other words, enables her to negotiate reconstructions of gender identity in "spaces of cultural hybridity."

Marta Caminero-Santangelo reads Helena María Viramontes' short story "The Cariboo Cafe" as a different sort of challenge to Otherness. She finds an "identity-in-difference" figured in the losses of children suffered by both the Central American washer woman and the male cook (who seems white, but whose race and national origin are unspecified). Rather than articulating a specifically authentic Hispanic experience, Viramontes' story considers the possibility that a larger community might be founded on the common experience of suffering, which transcends gender and ethnic difference and demands ethical responsibility.

Lakshmi Holmström's discussion of Padma Hejmadi's "Weather Report" also suggests a new kind of community, but one grounded in ethnic identity as she explores the uneasy terrain between assimilation and separateness. The experience of displacement brought about by the South Asian diaspora leaves South Asian women in North America in the paradoxical dilemma of building a "home culture" in exile. Holmström argues that in Hejmadi's story this gendered experience of exile opens the possibility for the South Asian woman to negotiate a cultural space for herself where the differences between her "home culture" and her American cultural context can be mediated. Holmström compares this negotiation of gender and culture in "Weather Report" with Bharati Mukherjee's reinvention of self through the elision of class and ethnicity: Hejmadi seeks a reclamation of personal and collective history, which acknowledges sameness and difference throughout the South Asian diaspora.

In contrast to Hejmadi's "home culture," Hisaye Yamamoto exposes the enforced conformity of women within the Japanese-American community. In considering two of Yamamoto's "disobedient women," Veronica C. Wang explores how Yamamoto gives voice to Japanese-American women who have been doubly surrounded and silenced, by the repressive Japanese patriarchy as well as by the racist white American culture, which incarcerated them in relocation camps. Both Tome in "Seventeen Syllables," who dares to invade a traditionally male domain of artistic self-expression by writing (prize-winning) haiku, and the title character of "The Legend of Miss Sasagawara," who had been a ballet dancer before her internment and is unable to obey the repressive strictures of camp life, stubbornly insist on asserting themselves in ways that exceed traditional gender roles. Tome, having forsaken her loveless marriage and accepted her new-found voice as a poet, faces an uncertain future, while Miss Sasagawara's confinement deepens as she is declared "insane" and is institutionalized. Yamamoto subtly creates women who reject traditional Japanese gender roles and cling to individual difference at great personal sacrifice.

Mediating difference within and beyond gender is the focus of Charlene Ball's discussion of lesbian coming-out stories by Pat Suncircle and Audre Lorde. Ball demonstrates how these writers use both the Greek Demeter-Kore myth and the West African figure Esu-Elegbara to render African-American lesbian experience in fiction. This combining of two traditions enables Lorde to redefine European myth in ways that make it relevant to the experience of all women. She forges a re-visioning of Esu as Afrekete, which gives a feminine face to the androgynous Esu, "trickster, linguist, and mediator between gods and humans." Afrekete is empowered with the creative manipulation of language. The figure Afrekete enables negotiation of difference (male/female, black/white, African America and European America) and as a trickster dissembles and stirs up trouble as well as mediates and promotes alliances of mutual respect in spite of differences of race, gender, and ethnicity.

David Goldstein-Shirley examines Tony Morrison's remarkable strategy of setting issues of gender aside, in order to focus the reader's attention on race in her sole (and neglected) short story "Recitatif." This story can be seen as a "distillation of Morrison's grand project of deconstructing race and racism." Using an African-American oral storytelling style and employing ambiguous racial codes to disguise the racial identities of the story's important characters, she compels the reader to confront issues of racial difference within the story itself and, beyond this, to participate in the contemporary public dialogue in race relations. This strategy is effective, in good part, because Morrison's usual problematizing of gender is bracketed—males appear in only inconsequential roles in the story. Race, within and outside the story, is deconstructed through this process of participatory reading that Morrison demands of her audience. Goldstein-Shirley also reports on an exercise of reader-response analysis with undergraduate readers, the results of which confirm his claims for the story and Morrison's intent in writing it.

Elaine Orr's reading of Eudora Welty's "Moon Lake" takes as its point of departure Morrison's contention in *Playing in the Dark* that white American literature has relied on "the fabrication and then subjection of a buttressing Africanist presence." But Orr argues that Welty's story suggests "an incommensurate difference within whiteness," rather than the opposition of black/white. Instead of a systematic hiding of these points of difference attributed by Morrison to white American literature, the story presents an accompanying series of oppositions and a pattern of disclosure and illumination of power, color, and class. In a parallel move also originating in Morrison, Orr juxtaposes autobiographical moments of her own to the ironic illumination of the dark places within Welty's white middle-class girls' experience. Orr suggests that "Welty facilitates a reading of whiteness through the marginalization of blackness," but that it is not the Africanist presence which is betrayed: "[i]nstead, the white middle-class girl dreamer betrays herself."

In her essay on Cynthia Ozick's "The Pagan Rabbi," Kathy Rugoff also uses gender to probe ethnic values. Reviewing the thoughtful and nuanced feminism of Ozick's fiction and essays, Rugoff offers a revisionary reading of "The Pagan Rabbi," taking into account both Ozick's feminist views and her engagement with Judaism. Whereas previous readings of "The Pagan Rabbi" have tended to treat it as a moral tale of the dangers of giving in to the temptations of paganism and idolatry, Rugoff argues that it applies a major tenet of Judaism, which she understands as "the moral imperative of reciprocity and dialogic relation—the principle of maintaining a reciprocal relationship with the not I, the Other." The Other here is the wood nymph whose Otherness the rabbi fails to value, since he treats her solely as an object of sexual desire. This failure leads him to suicide. Other characters are similarly unable to tolerate the free agency of the nymph and suffer for their mistake. Ozick thus presents in "The Pagan Rabbi" an allegory of the dialogic relation between men and women which she finds embedded in Jewish tradition. The story illustrates the consequences of failure to respect this relationship.

In the last essay in this collection, Corinne H. Dale examines the complex interplay of ethnic and gender identities in Louise Erdrich's short story "Fleur." Pauline, the Chippewa narrator, relates the story of Fleur, a Chippewa woman ostracized by her tribe who comes to the white town settled by German Americans and refuses to conform to the white male conception of Squaw. When Fleur is gang-raped, Pauline retaliates by trapping the men and freezing them in a meat locker during a horrific storm. Subsequently, both women return to the tribe, where Pauline becomes a storyteller in her own right. Dale's analysis centers on Pauline's evolving perspective of Fleur, whom Pauline reads successively as Medicine Woman, Squaw, "avenging Mother," and at last as an "unknowable individual." Through this experience, which includes an alliance between the native women and the white women of the town against the men, "Pauline successfully negotiates both the Chippewa and the German-American constructions of women, making a place for herself as a storyteller within her tribe." For Dale, this story also foregrounds Erdrich's notion of "storytelling itself as a way of negotiating the postmodern dilemma of reconstructing history." The teller reminds us that all meaning is provisional, including the social constructions of ethnicity and gender—"we need to know that we do not know."

The writers discussed in these essays employ a variety of strategies as they inscribe their stories, or write their texts, upon different social contexts. Ultimately, these stories empower us all by revealing the commonality of human experience. Bearing witness to the common struggle to know ourselves as individuals, these stories break down categories of Otherness. When we develop an awareness of the social contexts that define us as part of a homogeneous group—when, in other words, we acknowledge ourselves as gendered and ethnic—we can then recognize our own efforts to negotiate individuality as the task of inventing the Self within homogeneous categories of Other. Paradoxically, in writing and reading personal stories, we come to experience a shared sense of ourselves as individuals who defy the definitions of society. In this way, the separation of Self and Other is bridged, and multiplicity can truly be celebrated.

WOMEN ON THE EDGE

CHAPTER 1

(Dis)Continuous Narrative

The Articulation of a Chicana Feminist Voice in Sandra
Cisneros's *The House on Mango Street*

Deborah L. Madsen

> We searched through
> our own voices
> and through
> our own minds
> We sought with our words . . .
>
> Tomás Rivera, "The Searchers"

Critical commentary on Sandra Cisneros's work has focused,
importantly, upon political, ideological, and cultural significances,
relating these contexts to her creation of complex individual subjects.
This is important and necessary work because the search for personal
and cultural identity is central to Mexican-American writing, a body of
work that expresses a hybrid cultural identity—neither American nor
Spanish/Mexican—which was brought into being by pure historical
contingency. This contingency, together with the socioeconomic
deprivation of the Chicano community, accounts for the importance of
historical context for the reception of Chicano literature. Dramatic
events brought about the simultaneous creation of and dispossession of
Mexican Americans—the secession of vast areas of the Southwest to
the United States, the transformation of the native inhabitants from
Mexicans to Americans, and the protection of their rights inscribed in
the Treaty of Guadalupe Hidalgo. The violation of these treaty rights,
especially, contributes to the profound distrust of Anglo-American
discourse and language expressed by Mexican-American writers. In a

lecture delivered as part of a 1976 Bicentennial symposium organized by Texas Tech, Edmundo García-Girón took this rather ironic opportunity to describe the highly problematical relationship that exists historically between Anglo and Chicano cultures and to relate this divisiveness to the writer's use of language: "... the speech of the Chicano is ... a new tongue, and as such is one of many forms of his protest.... The Chicano's speech, like his character and psyche, is hybrid—neither a complete fusion or [sic] replication of English and Spanish, but rather something new, an amalgamation of English and Spanish, but with a bonding agent which is neither: in short, an alloy, like bronze, the idiom of *la raza de bronce*" (100).

Anglo-American English articulates a voice of betrayal, duplicity: it is the master's voice. In a poem by Cherríe Moraga, the voice of Anglo literacy which she must resist threatens to transform hers into a monster's voice: "To gain the word / to describe the loss / I risk losing everything. / I may create a monster ... unintelligible illiterate" (166). The difficulty of negotiating the gaps and fissures of a hybrid culture and the *mestizo* self produced by that culture is focused most dramatically in the issue of language—the most authentic language to use in artistic production—and also the question of literary form, which is my interest in this essay.

Chicano literature is a literature of protest; like most Mexican-American cultural production, literature articulates Chicano opposition to the mainstream culture and embodies particular kinds of struggle against it. The narrative dialectics of this opposition have been analyzed extensively by Ramón Saldívar in *Chicano Narrative: The Dialectics of Difference* (1990). Dialectics is a very useful term to describe the condition of hybridity, which is not a simple opposition but a condition of profound interdependence. Chicanos write of not belonging in the place where they belong, of having a home that does not feel like home: the eponymous "House on Mango Street" is described by Cisneros's narrator as "the house I belong but do not belong to" (110). Contemporary Chicano writers, especially, describe the sense of violation that comes from a close proximity to Anglo culture and the pervasive, corrupting influence of Anglo-America upon Chicano communities. The title of Ana Castillo's recent novel, *So Far from God* (1993), alludes to the famous lament by Porfirio Diaz, dictator of Mexico during the Mexican civil war:

"So far from God—So near the United States."

The most common theme in Chicano literature is the experience of living in an occupied land (*Occupied America* is the title of Rudolfo Acuña's 1972 revisionist history of the Chicano). But for Mexican American women, the experience of living under conditions of occupation is most frequently represented as the condition of women's life under patriarchy. Herein lies the greatest difference between Chicana and Chicano writings. As Alvina Quintana has argued at length, much Chicana feminist writing of the 1970s and 1980s was deliberately opposed to the earlier discourse of the Chicano civil rights movement, which addressed racial and class differences while erasing gender differences (2916A). Chicana writers consciously re-place the female subject at the center of a deconstructed Chicano discourse, just as they insist upon the importance of ethnicity in its relation to dominant Anglo-feminist discourses. White feminists and Chicano men mark out the gap that Chicana writers negotiate through their writing.

Given an agenda such as this, Chicana writers confront the complex problem of creating a narrative or literary voice that will articulate an authentic experience of ethnicity, gender, and class, and simultaneously will speak against those cultural determinants of subjective expression: not just mainstream (popular) Anglo-American culture but white feminist and patriarchal Chicano cultures as well. It is therefore not surprising to find in Chicana writing a rich variety of formal and linguistic experimentation. This has been remarked upon by Renato Rosaldo who points particularly to the use of short-story sequences by Alberto Ríos, Denise Chávez, and Sandra Cisneros to argue that the formal marginality of the short-story cycle allows for a significant degree of free experimentation, "political innovation and cultural creativity" (Rosaldo 88). Sandra Cisneros has described her short-story cycle, *The House on Mango Street*, thus: "I wanted to write a collection which could be read at any random point without having any knowledge of what came before or after. Or that could be read in a series to tell one big story. I wanted stories like poems, compact and lyrical and ending with reverberation" (Cisneros, "Do You Know Me?" 78).

The book should then have unity without sacrificing the integrity of its parts. Cisneros wants the dramatic effect created by the short story but also the ability to unfold a complex story with all its sociocultural significances intact. This enormously ambitious narrative goal is achieved through the daring formal experimentation represented by this text.

The uncertain generic form of Cisneros's *The House on Mango Street* embodies above all the author's quest for a voice: a tentative and uncertain quest that is reenacted by the adolescent narrator, Esperanza. Only at the end of the sequence does the narrative resolve itself into the historical present, as the schoolgirl narrator is replaced with the mature voice of Esperanza the author, who promises to tell us "a story about a girl who didn't want to belong" (109)—which is, of course, the story we have just finished reading. This narrative voice, that acts as both goal and determinant of the text, is difficult to achieve because it must be adequate to articulate a kind of subjective experience that is so very different from the middle-class white experience commonly represented by continuous linear narrative that conventional means of narrative representation are rejected as inadequate.

Discontinuous narrative, the form that articulates Esperanza's experience, has the power to represent the experience of the self as marginal. This power is doubly significant for the Chicana writer, a writer made marginal both by her gender and her race. Cisneros is able to represent the experience of marginality by creating a narrative form that departs radically from patriarchal forms of representation. Essentially, this means a reliance upon imagistic and symbolic kinds of connectivity at the expense of a reasoned and discursive logical structure. Cisneros's hybrid narrative form, which hovers somewhere between poetry and prose, the novel and autonomous stories, embodies the experience of being Mexican American in an Anglo-dominated society and of being female in a patriarchal ethnic culture.

In what follows I want to explore Sandra Cisneros's use of discontinuous narrative in *The House on Mango Street*, paying particular attention to the ways in which narrative form is used to re-create the thrice-marginalized Chicana subject (who is oppressed by reason of gender, ethnicity, and class). First, I want to consider the issue of gendered discourse, to ask how language can be subverted and made to speak for rather than against those whom language so often betrays; then I turn to the concept of narrative itself, to consider in what ways narratives serve the patriarchy by defining female subjectivity and how Cisneros is able to subvert this oppressive function by creating discontinuous narratives that liberate instead.

I think an important reason why Chicana writing in general, but the work of Sandra Cisneros in particular, is so compelling is the interest of writers in representing not simply the material facts of deprivation and suffering but, more importantly, the cultural forms that determine the shape of reality for Mexican-American women. In books like *The House on Mango Street* and the collection *Woman Hollering Creek*, Cisneros does not shrink from the stark reality of Chicana life, but the brutal aspects of this reality are represented within the context of a feminist awareness of how the perpetuation of this stark reality can be transformed through imagination and politically motivated insight: in other words, by ideological analysis. Cisneros exposes, with great subtlety, the ways in which a racist, patriarchal culture lies to its children, particularly little girls. Esperanza repeatedly discovers that she has been deceived by (and about) the adult world; ironically, we can sometimes see where she cannot that those who mislead her are themselves misled by a society that promises much but delivers nothing.

The motif of the family house, repeated and elaborated throughout the sequence of stories, provides a shared point of reference for the characters' cultural aspirations and their own self-images. Esperanza believes the bedtime stories her mother tells about the house they will some day own: "Our house would be white with trees around it, a great big yard and grass growing without a fence" (4). But the only house they know that looks like this is the house where her father works as a gardener, the house the whole family visits on Sundays, his day off. But Esperanza stops believing in the promise, though her parents cling to the possibility that hard work will be rewarded, as America always assures its citizens: "I don't tell them I am ashamed—all of us staring out the window like the hungry. I am tired of looking at what we can't have. When we win the lottery . . . Mama begins, and then I stop listening" (86). At this stage in the story sequence, Esperanza has developed a painful awareness of the discrepancy between culturally determined expectations or assumptions and the reality of life for Mexican Americans. This painful gap between hope and fact begins to close only at the end of the narrative, when the witch woman's prediction that she shall have her own house, mysteriously described as "a home in the heart. . . . A new house, a house made of heart" (64), is realized as her new sense of belonging to her people, as part of the community, which is experienced as returning home, at last. It is the creative imagination of Esperanza the writer (which has allowed her to see clearly her true situation) that empowers her to bridge the gap between cultural expectation and social reality.

Awareness of the socioeconomic difference between poor Chicanos and affluent Anglos is painful for the young narrator, but far more brutal is her awakening to the difference between the discourse of romantic love and the reality of sexual oppression within Chicano culture. The adolescence of Cisneros's narrator is indicated early in the story sequence by her interest in the difference between boys and girls: "The boys and the girls live in separate worlds. . . . My brothers for example. They've got plenty to say to us inside the house. But outside they can't be seen talking to girls" (8). The house, the family, the domestic world, is increasingly identified as the primary site of women's oppression. Rosa Vargas is trapped by her many children and "the man who left without even leaving a dollar for bologna or a note explaining why" (29); Minerva is trapped by her children and the husband who comes and goes and beats her when he is around; to her daughter's amazement even Esperanza's mother is trapped in her domesticity: "She can speak two languages. She can sing an opera. She knows how to fix a T.V. But she doesn't know which subway train to take to get downtown" (90).

From the beginning, Esperanza has a suspicion of the misogyny that surrounds her; comparing herself with her great-grandmother with whom she shares her name and the coincidence of being born in the Chinese year of the horse "which is supposed to be bad luck if you're born female—but I think this is a Chinese lie because the Chinese, like the Mexicans, don't like their women strong" (10). This fiery ancestor, "a wild horse of a woman, so wild she wouldn't marry" (11) is forcibly taken by Esperanza's great-grandfather and lives out her days staring from her window. The narrator remarks, "I have inherited her name, but I don't want to inherit her place by the window" (11). However, this is precisely the place in which many of the women of Mango Street find themselves. Marin, the teenager brought from Puerto Rico to care for her young cousins is symbolically trapped in the doorway: "She can't come out - gotta baby-sit with Louie's sisters" (23); Mamacita across the street will not leave her apartment but "sits all day by the window and plays the Spanish radio show" (77); Rafaela is locked indoors "because her husband is afraid Rafaela will run away since she is too beautiful to look at" (79) and she too is left leaning from the window; Sally's father imprisons her in the house because she is too beautiful to be trusted, her father "remembers his sisters and is sad. Then she can't go out" (81); when Sally does marry, she exchanges one form of oppression for another, an abusive father for a husband of whom she is so afraid that she obeys when he forbids her to go out, to use the telephone, to have friends visit: he even forbids her to look out the window.

The reason for such widespread feminine submission to patriarchal oppression is not hard to find: poverty, illiteracy, inability to speak English, and, most fundamentally, violence against women, which is seen as inevitable. Sally is beaten and raped by her father; Minerva and other wives are beaten and abandoned. But violence against women is not just domestic; the outside world is also represented as threatening to women: when Esperanza begins her first job, she is sexually harassed by the only coworker who is friendly to her, "he grabs my face with both hands and kisses me hard on the mouth and doesn't let go" (55); when the girls dress up in women's shoes and parade up the street enjoying the attention they attract, the dangers of feminine sexuality become all too apparent in the frightening figure of the "bum man" who tries to buy a kiss for a dollar and yells after them when they refuse. The adult world is enticing and frightening; it is romantic and glamorous yet threatening. Esperanza both resists and wants to be part of the adult world: "Everything is holding its breath inside me. . . . I want to be all new and shiny. I want to sit out bad at night, a boy around my neck and the wind under my skirt. Not this way, every evening talking to the trees, leaning out my window, imagining what I can't see" (73). But her vision of the world is conditioned by her culture, and the romantic story of love and sex that is told in songs and magazines and on television and by her friends contrasts horrifyingly with Esperanza's reality.

In the story that has attracted much critical comment, "Red Clowns," Esperanza describes her violent sexual initiation. Though exactly what happens to her is not clear, in her monologue Esperanza impressionistically describes waiting for Sally to return from her liaison and her violent assault by a group of Anglos: "Sally Sally a hundred times. Why didn't you hear me when I called? Why didn't you tell them to leave me alone? The one who grabbed me by the arm, he wouldn't let me go. He said I love you Spanish girl, I love you, and pressed his sour mouth to mine" (100).

Here the rhetoric of love and sex is revealed in the harsh light of racial and gender oppression. As a "Spanish girl," Esperanza is most vulnerable to sexual attack; in the carnival grounds, she discovers why the world is such a threatening place for women, and colored women especially. Esperanza does not have the words to describe mimetically what has happened to her—the only words she has been taught are the romantic words of love, and these do not encompass the experience of sex as an expression of racial and gender hatred. Consequently, Esperanza directs her anger and shame not at Anglos and not at men but instead against women; not just Sally, who should have saved her, but all women, as María Hererra-Sobek explains: "The diatribe is directed not only at Sally the silent interlocutor but at the community of women who keep the truth from the younger generation of women in a conspiracy of silence. The protagonist discovers a conspiracy of two forms of silence: silence in not *denouncing* the "real" facts of life about sex and its negative aspects in violent sexual encounters, and *complicity* in embroidering a fairy-tale-like mist around sex, and romanticizing and idealizing unrealistic sexual relations" (Hererra-Sobek 178).

The dominant discourse of Esperanza's culture is gendered in such a way that it speaks for men and articulates only a patriarchal interpretation of the world. Most of the women of Mango Street are trapped inside the masculine constructs of Chicano culture; the possibility that women can subvert a masculine language and make it speak for feminine experience is enacted by Cisneros's use of a discontinuous narrative form that undermines the false coherence of patriarchal language. Patriarchal ideology is articulated by the meanings attached to things, including women and women's bodies. Alicia is told that "a woman's place is sleeping so she can wake up early with the tortilla star" to begin another day of cooking for and serving the family (31). Female functionality is also inscribed upon the feminine body, we discover, as the girls speculate about the real function of hips: "They're good for holding a baby when you're cooking, Rachel says . . . You need them to dance, says Lucy. . . . You gotta know how to walk with hips, [I say] practice you know—like if half of you wanted to go one way and the other half the other" (49). Within the terms of the patriarchy, women are defined by their relation to men and what meaning may be available to women is articulated by a language that carries this already-interpreted semantic freight.

The difficulty of self-definition is compounded in a hybrid culture where several discourses intersect. For Chicanas, the patriarchal dominance of Mexican-American culture is matched by the Anglo patriarchy; yet the subversions enacted by Anglo-American women may provide only a poor guide for women of color who set out to subvert and thus appropriate the master's language. Race and gender intersect here in a bewilderingly complex fashion. It is the coherence of racist patriarchal ideology that lends this ideology its power; therefore, Chicanas like Sandra Cisneros and Denise Chávez use *dis*continuous narrative to represent authentically the fragmented nature of the Chicana's world. This is the world of the marginal subject, where transient individuals (including husbands and fathers) appear and disappear, where glimpses of life are captured with no grand unifying structure to give them meaning—like scenes glimpsed from a window. There is no sense of belonging, no sense of living within a unified community. Cisneros's narratives, like the lives they describe, are fragmented into scenes and isolated images; within the narrative, selves are fragmented also so the women depicted do not constitute unified subjects. This fragmentation can be debilitating or alienating and it can also be liberating. The woman "Mamacita" who speaks no English and is paralyzed with homesickness for Mexico fails, as a result, as both wife and mother; she is reduced to a pathetic figure sitting alone at her window. But Alicia, who must rise before dawn to do her dead mother's work before going to school, resists the pressure of normalization (a patriarchally defined normality, articulated by her father) and spends her nights studying so that through education she might escape from Mango Street.

Esperanza encounters a number of women who are able to find some relief, if not escape, from the subjectivity imposed upon them by a patriarchal culture: Minerva and Aunt Lupe take refuge in poetry, and it is they who encourage Esperanza to seek freedom through her artistic intelligence. The fragmented narrative of *The House on Mango Street* embodies this quest for freedom, a true freedom that resolves rather than eludes the conflicts faced by the Chicana subject. Maria Elena de Valdes describes precisely how Cisneros's narrative technique relates to the twin themes of gender and racial identity: "The open-ended reflections are the narrator's search for an answer to the enigma: how can she be free of Mango Street and the house that is not hers and yet belong as she must to that house and that street. The open-ended entries come together only slowly as the tapestry takes shape, for each of the closed figures are also threads of the larger background figure which is the narrator herself." (de Valdes 293)

Cisneros uses poetic forms of expression, a highly metaphoric and allusive style that is subversive of rational patriarchal structures of thought. The threads that are the individual stories come together at the very end when the historical present gives way to the narrative present and the adult Esperanza takes over the narrative from her adolescent self. But the complex interweaving of those threads is continuous throughout the story sequence. Individual stories are not juxtaposed at random. Each story follows meaningfully from the previous, though the connection may not be a logical or explicit one. Often the link between stories is emotional or representative of subconscious promptings. For example, the story "And Some More" concludes with the girls chanting as they skip rope: "Jean, Geranium and Joe . . . / Cold *frijoles* / Mimi, Michael, Moe . . . / Your mama's *frijoles* / Your ugly mama's toes" (37-38). The next story picks up the reference to toes; in "The Family of Little Feet" Esperanza tells of dressing up in discarded women's shoes. The stories are linked by their shared concern with the concepts of beauty and ugliness; the girls play at insulting each other as they skip but in the following story they discover the dangerous potential of adult female beauty.

The juxtaposition of these vignettes dramatizes Esperanza's own intermediate condition: as an adolescent she is neither an adult nor still a child, and the juxtaposition of contrasting situations dramatizes her attempts to reconcile the realities of the adult world both with her childish imaginings and the things she has naively believed of adults. "The First Job" describes Esperanza's first experience of sexual harassment by a man old enough to be her father. In the following story, "Papa Who Wakes Up Tired in the Dark," Esperanza makes an important distinction between her own father (representing the personal) and other men (representing the political); upon hearing of her grandfather's death, she wonders how she would react to her father's death, "I hold my Papa in my arms. I hold and hold and hold him" (57). The next story, "Born Bad," continues the theme of death, this time the death of Esperanza's aunt, the aunt who listened to all her poems and who urged upon her the route to her freedom: "You must keep writing. It will keep you free" (61). Such subtle points of connection indicate the gradual maturing of the protagonist-narrator but at the same time these linkages do not disturb the realistic portrayal of the fractured Chicana subject. Esperanza is at once the same as the others around her and yet she is different, and this difference is finally revealed by the unity of her mature subjectivity.

Esperanza finds that, as an artist, her vision of the world is out of step with the patriarchal conditioning to which she is subject. Because she is an artist, a writer of imagination, she cannot become what others expect of her. Adrienne Rich explains this conflict and this peculiarly feminine failure: ". . . to be a female human being trying to fulfill traditional female functions in a traditional way *is* in direct conflict with the subversive function of the imagination. The word traditional is important here. There must be ways . . . in which the energy of creation and the energy of relation can be united" (43).

Failure to achieve such unity is often perceived by women as a personal failure or personal inadequacy and so becomes the cause for guilt and self-contempt—such as Esperanza experiences when she calls herself "an ugly daughter . . . the one nobody comes for" (88). It is only as an artist that Esperanza can transform herself into an actress in her own drama, rather than playing unsuccessfully at roles she knows to be false. The subversive imagination of the artist enables Esperanza to reach (though gropingly) an analysis of her situation that identifies her failures and inadequacies as political rather than personal failures. Blame for the failure to meet patriarchal expectations can then be shifted back to the racist, sexist society that created the expectations, and this process leaves Esperanza free to create herself. The ideological analysis of her life is written down as *The House on Mango Street,* and that narrative, in all its fragments, represents both what she must leave behind and that which she must embrace as part of herself: "I put it down on paper and then the ghost does not ache so much. I write it down and Mango says goodbye *sometimes*" (110, my emphasis).

The House on Mango Street is a modified version of the *Künstlerroman*: it is a portrait of the artist, modified to take account of the ethnic and gender differences involved when the developing artist is a young Chicana. It is typically a novel about young middle-class white men who realize their artistic ambitions by transcending the material (social and political) conditions of their early lives. James Joyce's *Portrait of the Artist as a Young Man* is the classic modern *Künstlerroman*. In very sharp contrast, Cisneros's heroine realizes herself as an artist by learning to speak, which for her means discovering what to speak. Even this is not, for her, a process of pure self-discovery: Esperanza is guided by the advice of her Aunt Lupe, by Minerva who writes poetry to maintain her sanity, and by the mysterious three sisters who identify Esperanza as special and who instruct her: "You must remember to come back for the others. A circle, understand? You will always be Esperanza. You will always be Mango Street. You can't erase what you know. You can't forget who you are. . . . You must remember to come back. For the ones who cannot leave as easily as you. You will remember? She asked as if she was telling me" (105).

It is counsel like this that brings Esperanza true freedom. Not the guilty denial that comes from complete rejection of one's origins, not the self-loathing that results from the denial of part of oneself. But acceptance within the context of reform and improvement. Juxtaposed with the story of the three sisters is the vignette, "Alicia & I Talking on Edna's Steps." Alicia repeats the sister's instruction in response to Esperanza's denial of Mango Street: "I don't belong. I don't ever want to come from here" (106). But Alicia replies forcefully, "Like it or not you are Mango Street, and one day you'll come back too"; Alicia also extends a challenge to Esperanza: if she will return only when things are made better on Mango Street, then who will make things better? "The mayor?" demands Alicia. "And the thought of the mayor coming to Mango Street makes me laugh out loud" (107).

Esperanza's analysis of the ideological roots of her oppression is complete only with the understanding that improvement will not come from the misogynistic Anglo mainstream; life will get better for Chicanas only if Chicanas work to make life better. It is then that she realizes in writing, in artistic creation, the potential not only for individual survival or endurance but also the possibility of real cultural change. In the story that follows, "A House of My Own," the dominating house motif undergoes a transformation. Instead of a physical space, or even "a house made of heart," the house of Esperanza's own is now identified with the occasion of creation. Belonging and creating are drawn together in this image: "Only a house quiet as snow, a space for myself to go, clean as paper before the poem" (108). So now, when she does leave Mango Street, it will be because Esperanza has "gone away to come back. For the ones I left behind. For the ones who cannot out" (110). The significance of Esperanza's freedom is defined by those she leaves behind; and the oppression suffered by those left behind is given meaning by Esperanza's escape. The two are locked in a dialectic that cannot be resolved but can be negotiated, as it is through discontinuous narrative.

The discontinuous narrative form permits the creation of a Chicana feminist *Künstlerroman*; it also allows the representation of a Chicana feminist protagonist. As I remarked above, the discontinuous narrative form embodies the fragmented subjectivity of the marginal subject. But, more than this, the looseness of the form means that the heroine-narrator is not constrained by the narrative structure as she might be by a more tightly unified linear narrative form. The discontinuous narrative allows us no foreknowledge of Esperanza's fate; we know of her only what she tells or what she betrays in the unconscious connections between adjacent stories. So the narrator has control over the sequential narrative representation of her own self and, consequently, agency in the unfolding of her life. This is a very important aspect of a narrative that is concerned with subverting the manifold ways in which patriarchal structures of thought and belief determine feminine subjectivity and female lives.   Cisneros is able to substitute a feminist analysis of Esperanza's life for the patriarchal view that usually bestows meaning and unity upon Chicana lives. The feminist *Künstlerroman* claims the authority to represent change, growth, and development in an individual woman's life, but this is inevitably played off against pervasive racial and gender oppression: the conditions that limit female potential for all women and that only the exceptional woman is able to overcome. But even this functions only to make more urgent Esperanza's mission as a Chicana artist. Again, Adrienne Rich describes the mission of the feminist writer or artist: "Our struggles can have meaning and our privileges—however precarious under patriarchy—can be justified only if they can help to change the lives of women whose gifts—and whose very being—continue to be thwarted and silenced" (38).

The kind of change that the Chicana writer can most effectively bring about is change in the external gaze that is fixed upon, and which fixes, the marginal subject in a position of oppression. For instance, in *The House on Mango Street* racial oppression is not represented directly but is linked to poverty and marginality in the child's experience. In the first story, Esperanza describes a nun who meets her outside her house one day: "You live *there*?" asks the nun. "The way she said it made me feel like nothing. *There*. I lived *there*" (5). Later, when Esperanza asks permission to eat lunch in the school canteen rather than go home, the Sister Superior makes her point out her house from the window: "That one? she said pointing to a row of ugly three-flats, the ones even the raggedy men are ashamed to go into. Yes I nodded even though I knew that wasn't my house and started to cry" (45). What the nuns are telling Esperanza is what the mainstream culture expects of Chicanos; the child is made to feel humiliated by this expectation and ashamed by the personal failure of which these expectations are symbolic. Esperanza feels herself to be nothing even while she feels guilty for being nothing in the eyes of the nuns. What the Chicana writer achieves in such a text as *The House on Mango Street* is a political analysis of this marginality, this position of nothingness, which is where Chicanas are situated by the white patriarchal gaze.

This feminist narrative of her life provides meaning in Esperanza's life. The narrative explores her inability to derive any meaning from the sources that satisfy many of her contemporaries: romantic love, religion, popular culture. Esperanza is influenced by all of these expressions of patriarchal culture but all of these media are transformed under the influence of her own desire for self-expression, for a genuine experience of belonging within her own ethnic and gender group. But within Chicano culture, the place of communal history is taken by the capitalist/racist/patriarchal value structure derived from Anglo-America, and the women, especially, who accept those values find themselves imprisoned by them. The character Marin epitomizes the female victim of patriarchal popular culture. She continually sings popular songs of romantic love; she tells the girls "how Davey the baby's sister got pregnant and what cream is best for taking off mustache hair and if you count the white flecks on your fingernails you can know how many boys are thinking of you and lots of other things I can't remember now" (27). Marin's ambition is to work in a department store where she can look beautiful and wear nice clothes and where you might meet someone to marry. Her entire worldview is determined by the ideologies of romantic love and personal beauty. Responsibility for her life, for her self, she thinks of as belonging to someone else, and so she remains "waiting for a car to stop, a star to fall, someone to change her life" (27). If Esperanza's parents fall victims to the capitalist ideology of the American Dream, which says that hard work and individual effort will be materially rewarded, so Marin is a victim of the patriarchal ideologies that make similarly empty promises of individual fulfillment. Esperanza's mother tells of her own life as a warning to her daughter; how she left school because she had no nice clothes to wear, because she was poor and failed to see that education perhaps could offer a means of escape from a life of continued poverty. Her mother was a victim of the ideology of personal beauty but only when it is too late to change the course of her life does she see how she was deceived.

Patriarchy employs specific narrative modes that are used to write the female experience, to deceive women and cheat them out of their potential. These are cultural narratives that embody how women should live: like the Mexican soap operas or *telenovelas* described in the title story of the collection *Woman Hollering Creek*: "Cleofilas thought her life would have to be like that, like a *telenovela*, only now the episodes got sadder and sadder. And there were no commercials in between for comic relief. And no happy ending in sight" (Cisneros, *Woman Hollering Creek* 52-53). When individuals make their lives conform to their stories, when words succeed in keeping women in their places, patriarchal culture consolidates its power and influence over women and men alike. Only by challenging the narrative basis of patriarchal ideology, by undermining the claim to linear coherence and narrative unity, by subverting these claims and appropriating the means to articulate a marginal, Chicana subject from a feminist perspective, only then can we believe that promise that one day, in places like Mango Street, things might get better.

WORKS CITED

Bardeleben, Renate von, ed. *Gender, Self and Society: Proceedings of the IV International Conference on the Hispanic Cultures of the United States.* Frankfurt am Main: Peter Lang, 19s93.

Calderón, Hector, and Jose David Saldívar, eds. *Criticism in the Borderlands: Studies in Chicano Literature, Culture and Ideology.* Durham, N.C.: Duke University Press, 1991.

Castillo, Ana. *So Far from God.* 1993. London: The Woman's Press, 1994.

Cisneros, Sandra. "Do You Know Me? I Wrote *The House on Mango Street.*" *The Americas Review* 15. 1 (1987): 77-79.

————. *The House on Mango Street.* 1989. London: Bloomsbury, 1992.

————. *Woman Hollering Creek and Other Stories.* 1991. London: Bloomsbury, 1993.

García-Girón, Edmundo. "The Chicanos: An Overview." *Ethnic Literatures Since 1776: The Many Voices of America.* Ed. Wolodymyr T. Zyla and Wendell M. Aycock. Lubbock: Texas Tech Press, 1978. 87-119.

Hererra-Sobek, María. "The Politics of Rape: Sexual Transgression in Chicana Fiction." *Chicana Creativity and Criticism: Charting New Frontiers in American Literature.* Ed. Hererra-Sobek, María, and Helena María Viramontes. *The Americas Review* 15. 3-4 (1987). 171-181.

Horno-Delgado, Asunción, et al., eds. *Breaking Boundaries: Latina Writings and Critical Readings.* Amherst: University of Massachusetts Press, 1989.

Moraga, Cherríe. "It's the Poverty." *This Bridge Called My Back: Writings by Radical Women of Color.* Ed. Cherríe Moraga and Gloria Anzaldúa. New York: Kitchen Table, Women of Color Press, 1983. 166.

Quintana, Alvina. "Chicana Discourse: Negations and Mediations." *Dissertations Abstracts International* 50. 9 (1990): 2916A. University of California, Santa Cruz.

Rich, Adrienne. "When We Dead Awaken: Writing as Re-Vision." *On Lies, Secrets and Silence: Selected Prose 1966-1978.* New York: W.W.Norton, 1979. 33-49.

Rocard, Marcienne. "The Remembering Voice in Chicana Literature." *The Americas Review* 14 (1986): 150-159.

Rosaldo, Renato. "Fables of the Fallen Guy." *Criticism in the Borderlands: Studies in Chicano Literature, Culture and Ideology.* Ed. Héctor Calderón and José David Saldívar. Durham, N.C.: Duke University Press, 1991. 84-93.

Saldívar, Ramón. *Chicano Narrative: The Dialectics of Difference.* Madison: University of Wisconsin Press, 1990.

Thomson, Jeff. "'What Is Called Heaven': Identity in Sandra Cisneros's *Woman Hollering Creek." Studies in Short Fiction* 31,3 (1994): 415-424.

Valdes, María Elena de. "The Critical Reception of Sandra Cisneros' *The House on Mango Street.*" Bardeleben, *Gender, Self and Society.* 287-300.

CHAPTER 2

Beyond Otherness
Negotiated Identities and Viramontes' "The Cariboo Cafe"
Marta Caminero-Santangelo

While the stance of regarding Otherness and difference as that which cannot be comprehended seems to have some currency within academic circles, postcolonial critics such as Sara Suleri warn of the dangers of such an approach: "... the subordinated subject 'as other' frequently serves as a site for the breakdown of interpretation: otherness as an intransigence thus ... serves as an excuse for the failure of reading.... Much like the category of the exotic in the colonial narratives of the prior century, contemporary critical theory names the other in order that it need not be further known" (12-13). Suleri is concerned with the problem of using difference from the so-called Other to justify continued exclusion of that Other from subject matter for study. Her fear might be restated as a simple question: if we acknowledge that our differences from another group are so great that we will never fully understand its experiences or perspective, then why try? Linda Martín Alcoff gives a concrete example of this perspective in action: she tells of

> a recent symposium ... [at which] a prestigious theorist was invited to lecture on the political problems of postmodernism. The audience, which includes many white women and people of oppressed nationalities and races, waits in eager anticipation for his contribution to this important discussion. To the audience's disappointment, he introduces his lecture by explaining that he cannot cover the assigned topic because as a white male he does

not feel that he can speak for the feminist and postcolonial
perspectives that have launched the critical interrogation of
postmodernism's politics. Instead he lectures on architecture. (97)

Suleri and Alcoff are both critical of the cop-out in understanding
that occurs when self-identified representatives of the dominant culture
or mainstream, acting out of supposedly ethical considerations of
cultural sensitivity, retreat from discussion about the Other. But as
theorists and critics become increasingly attuned to the differences
among groups previously homogenized under some label designating
Otherness (such as women or Latinos), the danger of retreat from
understanding carries over as well. In other words, I am concerned with
what happens when, in the crucial process of recognizing the differences
among people who have been regarded as Other, we treat those
differences as though they render more and more groups of people
absolutely alien and inncomprehensible—in this way we create a variety
of Others. As Alcoff asks of the process by which "groups. . . [are]
delimited. . . . [H]ow narrowly should we draw the categories? The
complexity and multiplicity of group identifications could result in
'communities' of single individuals" (99).

This problem was vividly illustrated for me by an example from
my own teaching, involving an experience mentoring a Chicana
undergraduate who was writing a research paper on Chicana/o literature.
Although the student described her own interests as marking an
intersection between ethnic studies and feminism, the way this
intersection seemed to work for her was to drastically narrow the texts
in which she could find any value or with which she could identify.
Asked by her faculty advisor to read Hélène Cixous' "The Laugh of the
Medusa," this student criticized Cixous for her Eurocentrism, without
recognizing any value for the project of feminism. Of course, many
feminists have critiqued Cixous precisely on the grounds that she
presents a potentially essentialist view of womanhood, that obscures
material differences in the conditions of actual women, and thus ignores
the necessarily context-specific nature of effective forms of resistance.
The student was making an insightful and pertinent criticism of a
theorist to whom she had just been exposed for the first time. The
problem for me, as a teacher, was that the student was not really
interested in discussing Cixous. She felt that her advisor's insistence
that she read Cixous and other (non-Chicana) feminist theorists was
simply an attempt to place her interests within the institutional

framework of an oppressive, white European tradition. In other words, she not only felt Cixous did not speak to her, she also did not want to speak to Cixous. And while I understood and agreed with her insistence that she not have to legitimate her own writing by reference to canonical white feminist writers, I was troubled by her unwillingness to engage with Cixous' text at all.

Alternatively, this student read *Bless Me, Ultima* by Rudolfo Anaya, considered one of the classic Chicano novels, only for its sexism—because it included a representation of "*La Llorona*" that seemed, on the face of it, to be traditional and uncomplicated by critique. "*La Llorona*" refers to the Mexican and Central American folk legend of a woman who eternally wanders, weeping, through the night in search of her lost children—and in at least one version of the story, she killed her children herself. This image has been read by Chicana feminist critics as heavily mysogynistic in its traditional form, on several levels: the woman as a murdering mother figure is meant to evoke fear in children, who are taught that if they are in the streets after dark she might take them to replace her own lost children; she is, as well, a signifier of the dangers for women of straying from their own, traditional, maternal roles. (See, for example, Anzaldúa, *Borderlands* 36.) My student claimed that in Anaya's novel *La Llorona* was simply a sinister image of womankind, to be feared and avoided.

A feminist reading critical of Anaya's novel is certainly legitimate; for example, Anaya portrays women in his novel, including Ultima herself, the spiritual mentor of the narrator, as taking on importance only insofar as they shape, affect, and impinge upon the destiny of men (247)—the destinies of the women are apparently irrelevant. But given this student's particular interests and commitments, such an approach strikes me as extrememly limited. It fails to consider, for example, what the novel says about a collision of cultures. *Bless Me, Ultima* offers a constellation of myths and folklore—potentially if not explicitly including *La Llorona*—which are excluded by and in conflict with the narrator's Spanish-Catholic upbringing but which nevertheless end up holding more power for him. Ultima, who is a *curandera*—a healer—is the representative of this excluded religious tradition—and significantly, she is read by much of the community as a dangerous and threatening *bruja*, or witch, who herself needs to be expelled. Further, significantly, the narrator does not wish to completely abandon the Catholic religion imported by Spanish conquerors—he wishes to forge a new religion out of all the mythical materials that he finds at hand. Thus Anaya presents us with a model potentially useful to feminists, in which the materials of the oppressors are appropriated by the oppressed in order to forge a new identity. I engage in this quick sketch of a potential reading of Anaya's novel in order to suggest that despite its male focus, it holds rich material for a Latina feminist criticism and need not simply be rejected by it on the grounds that it is written by a man.

To return briefly to the issue of multiplying Otherness, postmodern notions of fragmented identity, as well as a growing awareness of differences within groups that have historically been marginalized by dominant culture, have produced the concept of "positionality" or "negotiated identity" within feminist and multicultural studies. Thus Cynthia J. Davis writes that "positionality allows for an identity politics that is constantly questioning what identity (gender, race, class, sexual preference, etc.) means at any given moment in any given context" (414). Chela Sandoval calls for "a self-conscious flexibility of identity" that "allows us no single conceptualization of our position in society" (67). And John Higham describes the process by which, "[i]n changing circumstances, individuals continually . . . renegotiate the loyalties they must choose among, or alter the dimensions of a predominant identity that begins to pinch" (203). It seems to me that my student was engaged in the task of negotiating identity, identifying herself as Chicana when discussing Cixous and as feminist when discussing Anaya—but her negotiation constructed feminism and ethnicity as a dichotomy in which she felt forced, in any given context, to choose one or the other. (Note that there is nothing inherent in the concept of "negotiated identities" that opposes this possibility.) As a result, in a field of all possible subject positions, only those who were also Chicana feminists could speak to her. Surely such a narrowing of the playing field, and such a cutting off of all conversations, is antithetical to the aims of both multiculturalism and women's studies—rather than dismantling categories of Otherness, it only multiplies them.

An alternative model for the negotiation of identities is offered by Gloria Anzaldúa, a Chicana feminist who, like my student, is constantly renegotiating her loyalties; she is "an Indian in Mexican culture, . . . Mexican from an Anglo point of view," as well as a woman facing patriarchal society and a lesbian confronting heterosexism. But for Anzaldúa, it is precisely the Chicana's "plural personality" that allows the conversation to expand. Indeed, Anzaldúa warns that "it is not enough to stand on the opposite river bank. . . . A counterstance locks one into a duel of oppressor and oppressed. . . . At some point, on our way to a new consciousness, we will have to leave the opposite bank . . . so that we are on both shores at once." Instead of rejecting out of hand the opposite bank, Anzaldúa advocates a perspective in which "nothing [in one's own multiple subjectivity] is thrust out, the good, the bad and the ugly, nothing rejected, nothing abandoned" (*Borderlands* 78-79). Anzaldúa's multiple identities become not a limitation of the playing field but an expansion of it.

I would like to read growing awareness of differences among Others, not as a means by which more and more people are seen as Other (incomprehensible, utterly alien) to an already marginalized self, but as a way in which the reification of the category of the Other is being broken down. This process necessitates that we recognize and account for difference without allowing it to overwhelm our vision to the point that we cannot also locate what Norma Alarcón calls "points of . . . identities in the present [that is, in any given context, which enable us] to forge the needed solidarities against repression and oppression" (102). To be able to locate points of "identity-in-difference" (a term Alarcón adopts from Lorde and Spivak) entails moving beyond Otherness as an absolute difference-from-oneself that cannot be bridged.

This is particularly important for the study of Latina/o literature, since it includes a body of writers who, in many cases, have little in common besides the Spanish language and a history of Spanish colonization. Racial, cultural, and class differences among Latino groups in the United States vary so widely that we must wonder why we should group these disparate identities under one heading at all. Nevertheless, the critical project of finding "identity-in-difference" in a group of texts labeled "Latino" goes hand-in-hand with the institutional project of giving more attention to these texts. "Identity-in-difference" is also important in another sense for Latina/o writers, many of whom are engaged in the project of trying to understand and make sense of the process by which they were separated from their countries of origin— Julia Alvarez's *In the Time of the Butterflies* and Cristina Garcia's *Dreaming in Cuban* are two such works.

In this paper, however, I wish to focus on a shorter and less mainstream text than those two novels: Helena María Viramontes' short story, "The Cariboo Cafe," which I find remarkable precisely because of its insistence on problematizing the category of Otherness and on the dangers in a perspective which cannot locate "identity-in-difference." Told in shifting perspectives and parallel narrative lines, the story centers on the trope of the broken family. The first part tells of two young illegal (probably Mexican) immigrant children who find themselves locked out of their house one day while both parents are at work. Instilled with an omnipresent fear of the immigration officers, the children wander the city trying to find a safe hiding place.

The narrative now shifts to that of a working-class man, probably white, who operates a rundown cafe frequented by "illegals." Between bits of flashback that reveal the death of his son JoJo in Vietnam and the breakup of his marriage to his wife Nell, he relates watching the two young children come into the cafe with another illegal, a woman (at this point, we don't know who she is). The cook later discovers from a news report that the children are missing and begins to suspect something; his narrative ends when, having just turned a group of illegals in to the immigration officers, he sees the children entering his cafe once again, with the woman. The narrative shifts again, to that of the mysterious woman; she is, we learn, a washerwoman who has lost her five-year-old son Geraldo to a repressive Central-American government; the government claimed the five-year-old child was a spy working for rebel forces. The woman has immigrated to the United States; when she sees the two Mexican children, she mistakes Macky, the boy, for her son Geraldo, and descends into madness. The story ends as the washerwoman, betrayed by the cook, engages in a violent struggle with the immigration officers for the children—a struggle that, the conclusion strongly hints, ends very badly.

I should simply note here that within each narrative line lies an ambiguity regarding the markers of identity. Yvonne Yarbro-Bejarano, who has written the introduction to Viramontes' short-story collection, which includes "The Cariboo Cafe," identifies the washerwoman's country of origin quite firmly as El Salvador, while Nicolás Kanellos, the editor of *Hispanic American Literature*, a collection in which the story is anthologized, identifies the country as Nicaragua based on a mention of "contras"—but *contra* just means "against" in Spanish and could potentially refer to any rebel forces. I believe that this confusion underscores the fact that the Central-American country is not specifically identified, either directly or indirectly, within the story itself. Likewise, the children are probably from Mexico, because they fear being deported to Tijuana, but the story never definitively tells us so. (Among Latinos, *La Migra* is not known for being scrupulous about returning illegal immigrants to their "correct" countries of origin.) The cook is probably white, given that he seems to feel a marked distance between himself and the dark-skinned immigrants. He looks at the washerwoman and sees only Otherness, foreignness, in the woman's physical differences: "Round face, burnt toast color, black hair that hangs like straight ropes. Weirdo, I've had enough to last me a lifetime" (69). Once again, however, the story never says for sure. This indeterminacy of race and of national origins is, I believe, thematically crucial, and I will return to it later.

Given the intimate historical connection between Chicano art and literature and Chicano movements of political resistance, the question of resistance is not only pertinent but perhaps crucial to any study of Chicano literature. This story's gesture of "resistance" seems superficially to reside in the acts of the woman who attempts to rescue and protect her son in Central America and then, madly, duplicates her efforts in the United States. The strongest language of resistance is to be found in the context of the washerwoman's delusion that Macky is her son Geraldo: "I will fight you for my son until I have no hands left to hold a knife. I will fight you all . . . " (79). But such resistance is problematic, since it in no way affects what is obviously a situation of complete powerlessness. Furthermore, madness as a social signifier marks the space of absolute Otherness, so this resolution seems to rigidify the boundaries marking "central" and "Other," rather than to work to dismantle them. And finally, the washerwoman's resistance is entirely consistent with an ideology of gender that historically has constituted women as "mothers" and limited our range of actions to those in keeping with that position. As madwoman/mother, the washerwoman not only fails to achieve any real political subversion, she also reinforces the construct of irrational femininity, the function of which is to legitimate women's banishment from the political sphere.

It is precisely through this troubled representation of subversion, however, that the story undermines conceptions of absolute Otherness—its true resistance, as I wish to sketch out. I will begin by pointing out the highly ambiguous role that family plays in the narrative. As Barrie Thorne has noted, "During the 1970s [white, middle-class] feminists were so intent on criticizing the prevalent ideology of The Family that they paid insufficient attention to other meanings and experiences of 'family'" (8). We often find that women of color are less willing than their white, middle-class counterparts (at least in theory) to completely jettison the category of the family; the authors of an article entitled "The Costs of Exclusionary Practices in Women's Studies" suggest that for marginalized cultural or racial groups it is essential "to create spheres where men, women, and children are relatively protected from racist cultural and physical assaults. . . . [I]t was and is critical for Black people and other people of color to nurture each other. This is a primary fact about the communities of racially oppressed peoples" (Zinn et al. 33).

The family, that is, may operate both as ideologically conservative and as a locus of resistance. Indeed, Viramontes has suggested in an autobiographical essay that family can function as a building block for communities of people oppressed racially and otherwise; she describes how her own "family always extended its couch or floor to whomever stopped at our house with nowhere else to go. As a result, a variety of people came to live with us" ("Nopalitos" 291). In "The Cariboo Cafe," the concept of family suggests for the washerwoman a potential point of identification between herself and her oppressors that ideally would regulate their behavior; she asks, "Don't these men have mothers, lovers, babies, sisters?" (75). The ruptured nuclear families in the story work metaphorically as the point of "identity-in-difference" for the three perspectives, to open a space for the possibility of realignments, new (if provisional and shifting) affiliations. The "power of imagination," Viramontes has written, lies in "peeking beyond the fence of your personal reality and seeing the possibilities thereafter" ("Nopalitos" 292); the "personal reality" of each family represented in the story has the potential to expand into some larger vision than a narrowly personal one.

Family rupture in the story is linked to political oppression—the cook and the washerwoman share the experience of having children who became the casualties of government policies undertaken in the name of national security, but which in fact destroy their own citizens. It is also linked to economic oppression: both parents of the two young Mexican children must work, leaving the children alone to face potential capture by immigration officers after school. Analogously, the arrest and murder of the woman's son is precipitated, the story suggests, by their poverty. As she explains to the government official who accuses her son of working for rebels by selling subversive pamphlets: "'Señor. I am a washer woman. You yourself see I cannot read or write. There is my X. Do you think my son can read?' How can I explain to this man that we are poor, that we live as best we can? 'If such a thing has happened, perhaps he wanted to make a few centavos for his mamá. He's just a baby'" (73-74). And in fact, like the parents of the two Mexican illegal immigrants, this woman has been separated from her child by economic necessity: "I am a washer woman, Lord. . . . When my son wanted to hold my hand, I held soap instead. When he wanted to play, my feet were in pools of water" (74).

The parallel causes of the three ruptured families open the space for new alliances based on categories of experience other than nationality, ethnicity, or race—and here lies the significance, I believe, of why concrete national or racial identities are not insisted upon in the story. This not to say that such identities are not important—each character's political and social subject-position is a crucial part of his or her story—but simply that they are not all-determining. The washerwoman rejects nationalism ("Without Geraldo, this is not my home, the earth beneath it, not my country" [75])for an imagined community with those who share her experience: "It is the night of *La Llorona*. The women come up from the depths of sorrow to search for their children. I join them, frantic, desperate. . . . I hear the wailing of the women and know it to be my own" (72-73). Viramontes obviously is rewriting the myth of *La Llorona* here into a symbol of resistant political coalition and collective action based on women's roles as mothers of lost children, reminiscent of the protest of the mothers of "disappeared" children in front of Argentina's Plaza de Mayo. (I will return to the significance of the *La Llorona* figure later.)

Although the washerwoman identifies the community of those who suffer through being robbed of their children as a community of women, in fact the cook—at least potentially—belongs to this community as well. This man strikes a defensive posture in which he claims to be motivated sheerly by economic interests—"Like I gotta pay my bills too, I gotta eat. So like I serve anybody whose got the greens" (69). Yet what filters through his aggressive-sounding discourse is a suppressed empathy based on his identity as father of a dead son. He explains why he does not "refuse service to anyone": "The streets are full of scum, but scum gotta eat too is the way I see it"; the particular "scum" he is referring to here is Paulie, who is "JoJo's age if he were still alive. . . . Maybe why I let him hang out 'cause he's JoJo's age" (68). Similarly, when the washerwoman enters the cafe with the boy and his sister, the cook thinks, "he's a real sweetheart like JoJo. You

know, my boy" (70); it is perhaps this connection that motivates him
to serve them burgers, even though he is later "surprised" that the
woman has money to pay for the food (suggesting that he did not
necessarily expect payment). The connection drawn beween the cook's
charitable impulses and his identification of others with his son
suggests the possibility that family ties could serve as the basis for a
larger community, based not on generalized, monolithic categories of
identity ("white," "American," "illegal") but on an "identity-in-
difference" that calls for ethical responsibility.

Given this possibility, why does the story end so badly? Debra
Castillo suggests that for the cook, "All stories become one story, the
story of JoJo and Nell," and that the cook's story "turns, thus, on
misreading and misinterpretation, on the error of inserting another face,
another body, into the absences left by the doubled zeros. . . . [T]he
cook's story turns on the impossibility of storytelling" (84). If
storytelling assumes a distance that must be bridged, then the cook's
misidentification of others with his son—so Castillo's argument
goes—"ends" the possibility of storytelling because there is no *need* to
tell the story—every story is the same. But I would argue that it is
important to make a distinction between the cook's recognition of
certain points of identity between Macky and JoJo, or Paulie and JoJo,
and a collapsing of difference into identity. (The distinction is all the
more apparent because, as I shall discuss, the washerwoman does
literally collapse differences into identity.)

The story insists upon the quite different implications of simile
(Macky is like JoJo) and metaphor (Macky is JoJo). The moments
when the cook compares someone else to his son are marked by an
optimistic empathy and stand in sharp contrast to those jarring
situations in which empathy breaks down. So, for example, despite the
fact that the cook himself has been subjected to prejudice and
intimidation on the part of the police, he betrays to the immigration
officers a group of illegals who run into his cafe's bathroom for hiding.
Although he "swore I wouldn't give the fuckin' pigs the time of day"
(71), he finally chooses to side with, as it were, the oppressors rather
than the oppressed. On one level, of course, this move gives him a
degree of relative power over those with even less power. The
determining factor in his action is not his points of identity with the
illegals—who not only are his "regulars" (and to whom he is thus
linked by economic interest) but more importantly share with him an
analogous experience of harrassment and intimidation. What finally

motivates him is instead the points of difference between them. As he says of the washerwoman, "she's illegal, which explains why she looks like a weirdo" (70). Furthermore, the cook sees his act as one of self-protection from his own oppressors—it is his attempt to convince them that he runs "an honest business" (71), so that he will not continue to be harassed by the police. Being "honest," that is, seems ultimately to be linked in his mind with being "law-abiding," rather than with any ethical imperative that might transcend the laws of his own country.

But the most interesting part of the explanation the cook provides for his actions has to do with his own family situation. When he turns in the group of illegals he says, "I haven't seen Nell for years, and I guess that's why I pointed to the bathroom" (72). Whereas, elsewhere, the cook's recollections of his family seem to suggest the basis for other connections, in this moment he translates the loss of his family—that is, of his "identity-in-difference" with others—into an unmooring from any sort of connection or ethical obligation. He now identifies the illegals as "roaches," an image of absolute Otherness (recently used in advertisements for the anti-immigration policies of certain political candidates), rather than as somehow connected to himself. He can turn in the family of illegals because he is indifferent to their outcome in the face of his own personal tragedy; the family has collapsed into the individual.

In this moment, it is the cook's inability to make the connection between his story and those of others that threatens the possibility of narrative. It is not that others' stories collapse into and become identical with his own, but that others' stories become irrelevant in the face of his own. And although the cook's narrative begins with a refusal of responsibility ("Don't look at me"[68]), the close of his narrative challenges his rejection of the accusing gaze through the language of violated familial ties: "The older one, the one that looked silly in the handcuffs on account of she's old enough to be my grandma's grandma, *looks straight in my face*" (72; emphasis mine). The cook later tries to rectify his betrayal by turning in the washerwoman on the grounds that "Children gotta be with their parents, family gotta be together" (77); but even this act is represented in the story as morally suspect, given that the cook really just "hopes they have disappeared" (77).

Disappearance is of obvious importance in a story that is named for a cafe referred to as "the zero zero place" (68) because all the letters of the sign reading "Cariboo" have worn off except for the two "O's." The most obvious twin absences gestured toward in the story are the two dead children; and the story seems to be contrasting how the Central-American washerwoman and the cook attempt to cope with those absences. I would like to suggest that the distinction seems to reside in the possibilities of imagining; since the moment and method of death in both cases is unknown and indefinite, both parents must imagine how their children have died. Vietnam has been represented again and again in our popular culture as a war against the anonymous Other; the Central-American woman, in contrast, knows what her enemies look like—indeed, they might look much like herself. The cook's mode for dealing with JoJo's absence finally appears to be driven by imagining Otherness; as he says when discussing the unevenly sized breasts of Paulie's girlfriend Delia—breasts that mimic the double-zero image—"you could see the difference" (69).

It is intriguing to consider the possibility that it is precisely because Geraldo's mother need not resort to obvious physical differences to imagine her son's murderers that she does not operate on the defensive principle of Othering. Yet her desire to identify Macky literally with her own son, rather than analogously or metaphorically, blinds her to the reality that her kidnapping tears Sonya and Macky away from their own parents—who must then become the parents of lost children, like herself and the cook—and subjects all to the immigration officers. That is to say, the washer-woman sees only identity without recognizing crucial differences; and *her* story (not the cook's) revolves around the "error of inserting another face, another body, into the absences left by the doubled zeros . . ." (Castillo 84). Thus when she sees Macky, and is reminded of her son Geraldo, she thinks to herself, "Why would God play such a cruel joke, if he isn't my son?" (76). The only meaning Macky's appearance can have for the washerwoman is strictly personal; she, like the cook, is ultimately unable to use her personal family experiences to build a larger sense of community based on ethical responsibility.

Caring for and protecting Macky can only be done if he is hers, and according to the context in which her own son disappeared. Her fierce protective instinct is thus badly misguided—just when she thinks she is protecting Macky the most, she is actually exposing him to the most violence. When the cook betrays the washerwoman to the immigration officers—resulting in a deadly confrontation—we, as readers, are privy to the woman's thoughts: "I will fight you for my son until I have no hands left to hold a knife. . . . I am laughing, howling at their stupidity. Because they should know by now that I will never let my son go and then I hear something crunching like broken glass against my forehead and I am blinded by the liquid darkness. But I hold onto his hand. That I can feel, you see, I'll never let go. Because we are going home. My son and I" (79). The final passage of the story brings us back full circle to the myth of *La Llorona*. Like *La Llorona*, the washerwoman replaces her child with another, and it is this act of replacement (of identity without difference) that causes tragedy and dissipates the metaphorical potential for a larger collective resistance. Further, the washerwoman, crying for her lost son, fails to see how she might herself be contributing to a devastating outcome for the child she mistakes for her own; thus she becomes a figure of the murdering mother.

I'd like to close by discussing some implications of this paper for what is loosely termed "multicultural education." Trinh T. Minh-ha has critiqued the "automatic and arbitrary endowment of an insider with legitimized knowledge about her culture heritage" (374) as well as the implied lack of legitimacy involved in speaking of any culture other than one's own. Both of these positions reinforce what she calls "the narrow conclusion that it is impossible to understand anything about other peoples, since [these positions assume] the difference is one of essence" (375). That is, both positions reinforce Otherness. Trinh's alternative to this position involves the stance of what she calls an "inappropriate other or same" who, "undercutting the inside/outside opposition . . . moves about with always at least two gestures: that of affirming 'I am like you' while persisting in her difference[,] and that of reminding 'I am different' while unsettling every definition of otherness arrived at" (375). In "The Cariboo Cafe," the final tragedy evolves because the cook can see only "not you" and the washerwoman only "like you," but not both simultaneously.

The figure of the "inappropriate other or same" is not, I would argue, to be found within "The Cariboo Cafe," but is rather enacted by Viramontes herself. As an American-born Chicana, Viramontes is "not like" any of the characters in her short story (that is, she is neither a Mexican illegal immigrant, nor a victim of an oppressive Central-American regime, nor yet a working-class white man) and yet her gesture is precisely the affirming one of "not you"/"like you." This is also the gesture, I believe, represented by the designation "women of color"—aiming to locate a point of identity while simultaneously reminding us of the differences among the women it names.

Given that the particular perspective from which one writes is always important and always conditions the writing, I would like to end this paper with a note on my own position. As a Latina, I often seem to be included under the designation "women of color"; yet as a woman who looks white, I am different from "women of color": I have never faced the particular forms of prejudice (personal and institutional) attached to color of skin. To me this is more than just a trivial distinction; I may consciously reject the privileges that attach to whiteness, but in everyday life I continue to benefit from them, in ways it is impossible to escape. I like to see my own position as one of "identity-in-difference" with a group that is itself constituted by that principle. While the difference means that I must be self-conscious and self-critical in approaching Viramontes' writing, I would nevertheless like to believe that it does not render Viramontes' writing incomprehensible to me; to believe otherwise, I am convinced, would be to believe that Otherness is an insurmountable category.

WORKS CITED

Alarcón, Norma. "Chicana Feminism: In the Tracks of 'the' Native Woman." Trimmer and Warnock 96-106.

Alcoff, Linda Martín. "The Problem of Speaking for Others." *Who Can Speak? Authority and Critical Identity.* Ed. Judith Roof and Robyn Wiegman. Chicago: University of Illinois Press, 1995. 97-119.

Alvarez, Julia. *In the Time of the Butterflies.* New York: Plume/Penguin, 1995.

Anaya, Rudolfo A. *Bless Me, Ultima.* Berkeley: Tonatiuh International, Inc., 1972.

Anzaldúa, Gloria. *Borderlands/"La Frontera."* San Francisco: Spinsters/Aunt Lute, 1987.

———, ed. *Making Face, Making Soul/Haciendo Caras: Creative and Critical Perspectives by Women of Color.* San Francisco: Aunt Lute Foundation Books, 1990.

Burton, Robert S. "Talking Across Cultures." Trimmer and Warnock, 115-136.

Castillo, Debra A. *Talking Back: Toward a Latin American Feminist Literary Criticism.* Ithaca, NY: Cornell University Press, 1992.

Davis, Cynthia J. "Identity Politics." *The Oxford Companion to Women's Writing in the United States*. Ed. Cathy N. Davidson and Linda Wagner-Martin. New York: Oxford University Press, 1995. 413-415.

Garcia, Cristina. *Dreaming in Cuban*. New York: Ballantine, 1992.

Higham, John. "Multiculturalism and Universalism: A History and Critique." *American Quarterly* 45.2 (1993): 195-219.

Kanellos, Nicolás. *Hispanic American Literature: A Brief Introduction and Anthology*. New York: HarperCollins, 1995.

Sandoval, Chela. *Feminism and Racism: A Report on the 1981 National Women's Studies Association Conference*. Oakland, CA: The Center for Third World Organizing, 1982. Anzaldúa, *Making Face*. 55-71.

Suleri, Sara. *The Rhetoric of English India*. Chicago: The University of Chicago Press, 1992.

Thorne, Barrie. "Feminism and the Family: Two Decades of Thought." *Rethinking the Family: Some Feminist Questions*. Ed. Barrie Thorne with Marilyn Yalom. 2nd ed. Boston: Northeastern University Press, 1992.

Trimmer, Joseph, and Tilly Warnock, eds. *Understanding Others: Cultural and Cross-Cultural Studies and the Teaching of Literature*. Urbana, IL: National Council of Teachers of English, 1992.

Trinh T. Minh-ha. "Not You/Like You: Post-Colonial Women and the Interlocking Questions of Identity and Difference." *Inscriptions* 3/4 (1988): 71-77. Anzaldúa, *Making Face*. 371-75.

Viramontes, Helena María. "The Cariboo Cafe." *The Moths and Other Stories*. Houston: Arte Publico Press, 1985.

———. " 'Nopalitos': The Making of Fiction." Anzaldúa, *Making Face*. 291-94.

Yarbro-Bejarano, Yvonne. "Introduction." *The Moths and Other Stories*. Helena María Viramontes. Houston: Arte Público Press, 1995. 9-21.

Zinn, Maxine Baca, et al. "The Costs of Exclusionary Practices in Women's Studies." *Signs* 11.2 (1986). Anzaldúa, *Making Face*. 21-41.

CHAPTER 3

Judith Ortiz Cofer's *Silent Dancing*

Making More Room for Puerto Rican Womanhood

Nancy L. Chick

Puerto Rico has produced a complex literature that defies simplified, reductionist discussions. Originally a free island inhabited by Arawak (renamed "Taino") Indians, Borinquen became San Juan Bautista and then Puerto Rico, a Spanish colony for four centuries and one of the many outposts of African slavery (Novas 145). The Spaniards brought Catholicism, perhaps their most powerful and lasting import, to missionize the Taino Indians and the Africans. Rather than being completely erased, however, the distinct Taino and African cultures mixed with the Spanish culture through constant interaction and marriage to form what is now an ethnically syncretic Puerto Rican heritage. At the end of the Spanish-American War in 1898, the island became a U.S. protectorate and then a U.S. territory, allowing Puerto Ricans to travel freely to the mainland and back as U.S. citizens, marking the island's recent history as one of constant migration, immigration, and U.S. commercial and industrial imperialism. In 1952 it became a commonwealth, an ambiguous political designation as a U.S. territory that allows Puerto Ricans to elect their own local political officials. So while Puerto Rico has maintained a distinct culture, the island has also been situated within American politics and culture for the last century. Because of this complex history, the literature of Puerto Rico has been ignored in discussions of American literature. When it is included, its cultural specificity is in danger of being erased within the broader context of American literature.

Because categories of genre and aesthetics are constructed out of social and cultural ideologies, we must "be willing to bend, reshape, and even create new ones" in order to accommodate the writings produced by other cultures, as demonstrated by Charles Tatum's analysis of nineteenth-century Hispanic literature (203). The most frequently cited example of this literary reshaping is found in Latin American writers Juan Rulfo, Carlos Fuentes, and Gabriel García Márquez, who hybridized the traditionally realistic novel with their works of magical realism. Similarly, Judith Ortiz Cofer negotiates her own space within Puerto Rican and American literature. While she has written in practically every conventional genre, the prose pieces in her 1990 collection *Silent Dancing: A Partial Remembrance of a Puerto Rican Childhood* defy easy categorization. Often called "essays," Ortiz Cofer clarifies in her preface that they are "creative explorations of known territory," which she calls "*ensayos*," a Spanish term with the literary meaning of an essay, but also a theatrical "dress rehearsal" and the general meaning of "trying" or "testing" (12). She notes that at the time of the writing, publishing, and marketing of the book, she called them "*ensayos*" because she did not want them called "essays" and the term "creative nonfiction" was then nonexistent (personal interview).

She sought to distinguish these pieces from the genre of the essay, a "formal structure with supporting material leading to what we hope is an interesting, informative conclusion" (personal interview). Inspired by Virginia Woolf's *Moments of Being*, Ortiz Cofer claims that an *ensayo* is faithful to the "'truth' of art rather than the factual, historical truth" (12). Her memory is just "the 'jumping off' point," so she uses the "techniques of fiction—dialogue, setting, a little bit of plot—to dramatize these incidents that could be told in three minutes" (12; personal interview). As in the titular *ensayo*, her "partial remembrances" are like dancers in the silent movies of her distant childhood: she adds the colors, the details, and the music to give them meaning to her now. In most of her *ensayos*, the author's narrative, autobiographical voice frames the memory of a *cuento*, a morality tale told to her as a child by her maternal grandmother, embedding her family's traditional, oral tales within the new genre. These layers of stories, oral and written, become one of many narrative negotiations of Ortiz Cofer's literary space as a Puerto Rican woman.

These *ensayos* blur the boundaries between nonfiction and fiction, essay and short story, residing somewhere in the middle. Her definition is active, in motion, moving back and forth between the spheres of memory and storytelling, prose and narrative. They reflect the migratory Puerto Rican history as a "nation of movement" between the island and the mainland that produces a "literature of straddling" (Acosta-Belen 180; Flores 66). The nonfiction English essay becomes the partially fictionalized Spanish *ensayo*. Specifically, the motion and hybridity of this genre resemble Ortiz Cofer's own migratory and bicultural life. A self-proclaimed navy brat, she spent her childhood moving back and forth from the island to Paterson, New Jersey, and later to Augusta, Georgia.

Within this genre, Ortiz Cofer creates a "catachrestic space" in which traditional meanings and contexts are stripped away from words, images, or ideologies in the act of "reversing, displacing and seizing the apparatus of value-coding" (Bhabha 449; Spivak 225). An *ensayo* dismantles the value-coding of the conventional essay with Ortiz Cofer's own cultural and personal associations of movement and border-crossing so that it is no longer formed only by a Euro-American ideology, but a Puerto Rican ideology as well. This historical, cultural, and personal sense of movement across borders and residing in catachrestic spaces not only influences her genre, but emerges also in the characterization, content, and themes of her *ensayos*. Ultimately, the *cuentos* told by her grandmother establish this subversion as a proud tradition of her female ancestors. Within this cultural space of her *ensayos* and their embedded *cuentos*, Ortiz Cofer catachrestically deconstructs the feminine archetype of the flower, negotiating traditional female definitions and the spaces they inscribe.

Popularized during the English Renaissance, the floral symbol constructs an idealized femininity. For instance, in Sonnet 64 of Edmund Spenser's sonnet sequence *Amoretti and Epithalamion* (1595), the speaker "smelt a gardin of sweet flowres" when he kisses Elizabeth, whose "lips did smell lyke unto Gillyflowers, [carnations] / Her ruddy cheekes, lyke unto Roses red; / Her snowy browes, lyke budded Bellamoures, [bellflowers] / Her lovely eyes, lyke Pincks but newly spred. . . ." (2, 5-8) And Thomas Campion's seventh song in *The Fourth Booke of Ayres* (1617) canonizes a woman with "a Garden in her face, / Where Roses and white Lillies grow" (1-2). The pristinely lily-white skin, the innocently blushing rosy cheeks, and the soft rose-red lips encode a very specific portrait of womanhood that has been canonized to denote the "universal" woman: fragile, domesticated, pedestalled, pure, virginal, and white. By inscribing a homogenous monolith of the sexual and cultural identity of Woman, this archetype masks ethnocentric blindspots and erases heterogeneous groups of women.

In four of the thirteen *ensayos* in her collection of creative nonfiction and poetry entitled *Silent Dancing: A Partial Remembrance of Puerto Rican Childhood*, the geographical, ethnic, and cultural context for this reconstruction is appropriately Puerto Rico. This island is a place of indistinguishable boundaries through the syncretic mixtures of Spanish, Indian, and African cultures. Removing the flower image from its traditional setting of white Britain or North America, Ortiz Cofer unpacks this monocultural icon and excavates the multiplicity of womanhood by displacing the Eurocentric archetypal image with a multivalent, multiracial, multiethnic context.

Despite the proliferation of American culture, commercialism, and industry on the island over the last century, the influence of the Catholic church is stronger. In 1986, the narrative present of the *ensayos*, Hormigueros is built up with shopping malls, Burger Kings, and condominiums, yet the "church bells drown the noise of traffic" (152). In this town, the reign of the church has a specific history: within a century after Spain colonized the island, the Virgin Mary appeared to a local peasant. A shrine was built on the site, which became a great church and the center of the town that grew around the church. Significantly, the Virgin of Hormigueros is known as "the Black Virgin" and the "lovely dark Lady" (43, 151). Although brought by Spaniards in their attempt to missionize and pacify the Taino Indians and the Africans, she was racially redefined by the local populations to reflect their own creolization. Nonetheless, while she now mirrors the hybridized ethnicity of Puerto Rico, the layout of the town reflects the centrality of the Virgin Mary as she became the arbiter of women's roles, values, and aesthetics, teaching "chastity and modesty as the prime virtues for the town's daughters" (154).

For the Spanish patriarchy, this figure of the Virgin represents a dual colonial paradigm: she is not only a symbol of cultural colonization in the name of Catholicism, but also a powerful instrument of gendered colonization. As Marina Warner proposes in *Alone of All Her Sex: The Myth and the Cult of the Virgin Mary*, "it is this very cult of the Virgin's 'femininity,' expressed by her sweetness, submissiveness, and passivity that permits her to survive, a goddess in a patriarchal society. For her cult flourishes in countries where women rarely participate in public life and are relegated to the domestic domain . . . in which women are expected to be, and are, men's devoted mothers and wives" (191). She defines the role of women within the spheres of virginity, marriage, and motherhood. She is the ultimate figure of perfection, unmarked by human faults or desires. In "Stabat Mater," Julia Kristeva deconstructs her as "one of the most powerful imaginary constructs known in the history of civilizations," emphasizing that she is *mater* without material: though she gave birth, she is fleshless, uncorrupted by sin and sex, as well as death (237).

In this translation of a spiritual ideal to a code of behavior, the Virgin poses an impossible ideal for real women, like her secular counterparts in the chivalrous woman on the pedestal, the Victorian angel in the house, and even the models in contemporary fashion magazines. By valorizing virginity above all other characteristics, she becomes a symbol of containment, enabling the Church to control female sexuality by enforcing the virtue of self-denial and renunciation of the flesh. Therein lies the paradox of the ideal that cannot be resolved by real women, for the Virgin Mary is also the Virgin Mother. As Warner explains, "Mary establishes the child as the destiny of woman, but escapes the sexual intercourse necessary for all other women to fulfil [sic] this destiny. Thus, the very purpose of women established by the myth with one hand is slighted by the other. The Catholic religion therefore binds its female followers in particular on a double wheel, to be pulled one way and then the other" (336). Since real women cannot perform this sleight of hand of motherhood without sex, they can never reach the ideal to which they are taught to aspire. They cannot have sex, nor should they even want to; however, they must in order to fulfill their destinies. Yet intercourse—the only natural path to motherhood—must be accommodated, so the Church sanctions female sexuality only in marriage, thereby carefully containing it.

This ideology is embedded in the rose, the traditional Catholic symbol for the Virgin. Rosaries, the necklaces originally made of dried rose petals and worn in devotion to the Blessed Mother, were popularized in the 1400s through the Church's commissioned artwork that represented her enclosed in rose gardens or surrounded by garlands of roses (Classen 20; Warner 306). Afterwards, the scent of the rose became one of the detectable "proofs of holiness" that verified miracles and visions (Warner 99; Classen 28). In the legend of the Virgin of Guadalupe in Mexico, her sign to Juan Diego is the miraculous appearance of Castillian roses on a hilltop in the cold of December. So the rose bears not only the gendered definitions of womanhood associated with the ladies of English lyric poetry but also the cultural icon of the Virgin Mary.

In *Silent Dancing*, there are two figures who embody this icon: Maria La Loca, the eternal virgin, and Flora, the eternal mother. Maria La Loca is the main character of Mamá's *cuento* in "Casa," the first *ensayo* in the book. She is a local woman, middle-aged, unmarried and crazy. Years earlier, she was left at the altar with a "bouquet of fresh flowers in her hands" (16). These wedding flowers, representing a woman's progression from virgin to wife as sanctioned by the Church, are prematurely cut: she remains unmarried and a virgin. The effects are physical and psychological: she has the "thick body and wrinkled face of an old woman," but she "walk[s] and move[s] like a little girl," "hopping and skipping" like a "grotesque Little Red Riding Hood" (17). Her extended virginity is unnatural. She is the Virgin who cannot become Mother, *la loca*, crazy Mary. With no place in the Hormigueros social order, she lives with her mother at the town's outskirts, a marginalized other to the norm of the young virgin who becomes a wife with the wedding bouquet.

Flora, as her name suggests, embodies the wedding flowers of the Blessed Mother who has lost her virginity. Yet her flowers, rather than being prematurely cut, are fading: she is a toothless, "chronically ill woman" with asthma in the story "More Room" (27). In "bed more than on her feet," Flora is wasting away from the physical exhaustion accompanying the twelve pregnancies that result from sex under the Catholic prohibition of birth control. Like Spanish women colonized by the Crown and the Cross, Flora deteriorates under the pressures of being a mother. Ortiz Cofer's wedding flowers encode the oppression of the Roman Catholic ideology on women's minds and bodies. As the rosary encircles the virtues of the Virgin, the icon of the Virgin becomes a carefully contained, gendered enclosure defined by the biological conditions of virginity and motherhood.

Ortiz Cofer does suggest that some women disrupt these gendered spaces of womanhood. They are women who cross the rigid borders of these prescribed gender roles and make room for themselves by rejecting these biological definitions and subverting this system from within. The model for this woman is Mamá, the narrator's maternal grandmother. In the first paragraph of the first *ensayo*, we learn that she has a "beautiful garden where prize-winning orchids grew" (14). These orchids are coveted gifts from her, rooted from the "original plants from the plant festival in Aibonito" a town in the mountains of central Puerto Rico where an annual Fiesta de las Flores is held to show and sell the island's most prized flowers (Ortiz Laureano personal e-mail). She also has rosebushes in that garden, underneath which she allegedly buried money. This legend links her flower garden with the enormous chifforobe in her room, another hiding place for her money, as well as other symbols of both her femininity and her power, such as "jewels, satin slippers, and elegant sequined, silk gowns of heartbreaking fineness" or the "legendary gun salvaged from the Spanish-American conflict over the island" (24-25). These orchids and rosebushes thus represent not Mamá's containment but her pride, her authority, and her autonomy, all inscribed within her private flower garden and her own bedroom.

However, she once resembled Flora as the wife and mother who suffers under the "burdens" of giving birth to eight children, three of whom died at birth or shortly thereafter (27). Contrary to the model of motherhood embodied by the Blessed Mother, the *mater* without the material, Flora and Mamá reconstruct the flesh, the blood, and the risks of maternity. While Mamá's husband—"the benevolent dictator of her body and her life"—had celebrated each birth with his friends, singing the praises of "his fecund wife," Mamá "lost in heart and energy" and realized that "if she had anymore children, her dreams and her plans would have to be permanently forgotten," like Flora (26-27).

With this self-awareness, Mamá decided to seize control of her societal role rather than be oppressed by it. She reversed her destiny of becoming a "chronically ill woman" by using "the only means of birth control available to a Catholic woman of her time: sacrifice" (28). She gave up her sexuality for autonomy, self-determination, and a longer life. She let Papa think she was pregnant so that he would build another room, but when it was finished, she told him that it was his new room. Mamá literally negotiated her own space: she took over the "queen's chamber" at the heart of the house, thus claiming a room of her own within the house, within the prescribed gender roles, and within the spaces that define womanhood (23-24).

Some readers might cry foul at Mamá's negotiation at the high cost of an active sex life, but within her own culture, within her own subversive standards of female empowerment, Mamá becomes a figure of great matriarchal power as a result of this "bloodless coup for her personal freedom" (26). She inherits the sexual autonomy of the matriarchal Taino women of pre-Columbian Puerto Rico, who "made a choice to take control of their lives, including their reproductive function" by living apart from their husbands, summoning them when "they wanted to 'lie with them'" ("Taking the Macho" 64). Like these "*unnatural* females," as Columbus's son called them, identified by Ortiz Cofer as women who "take the macho," Mamá is a "macho woman," claiming catachresis with the "semantic controversy" of appropriating a "masculine modifier" that signifies courage, bravado, and power and transgressing gender boundaries of Spanish colonialism (64, 66).

It is no surprise, then, that Mamá is first identified in *Silent Dancing* by her orchids, a species of flowers particularly associated with the feminine because of their "strongly developed 'labiae,'" yet also rooted in a masculine element for the etymology of "orchid" goes back to the Greek noun *orkhis*, or "testicle" (de Vries 352). Mamá cultivates these beautiful, ornamental flowers, a seemingly feminine enterprise, yet the orchids also represent her subversion of the Spanish cultural influence on indigenous Puerto Rican gender roles. According to Ortiz Cofer, the Spanish conquerors came from a society "dominated by *pelotas*-equipped machos"—*pelotas* are "playing balls" used here as a pun on "testicles"—which "determined a woman's value by how well she fitted her predetermined role" (63-65). Like the orchid, Mamá's negotiation of her gender role to attain control over her own body signals her cultural inheritance from the Taino women who exhibited "macho" power, thus uniting the binaries of male-female and demonstrating that gender roles are socially constructed. Through such intercultural negotiations, Mamá unmasks the Spanish conflation of sex and gender and reconstructs gender identity in spaces of cultural hybridity.

In "Tales Told Under the Mango Tree," Mamá claims more room for herself and subverts power structures again—this time American imperialism, rather than Spanish Catholicism and colonialism. Her house is adjacent to the property of "'The American'" and his sugar refinery, called *La Central*, which is marked by a barbed-wire fence (76). In the wake of the 1947 Industrial Incentives Act and Operation Bootstrap, which encouraged mainland investors to relocate industry onto the island and to take advantage of the cheap labor market, *La Central* looms large. When the narrator as a child swings high into the air, she sees the "big house" and the "church tower," while "far in the distance, below me, my family . . . [was] receding, growing smaller," suggesting that American industry and commercialism and the Catholic church are now equally powerful colonizers on the island (80).

She sees the laborers swinging machetes to harvest the sugar cane for *La Central*, not realizing until much later that their graceful choreography is not for aesthetic purposes but for survival. These laborers or *jíbaros* hired for this dangerous work in the cane fields were the "backbone" of the Puerto Rican agricultural system (Novas 154). When the United States took control of Puerto Rico, the island's history of a varied crop economy was streamlined to produce only sugar to give America a monopoly over the world's sugar market. Mamá refers to this American's white house, enclosed by the contemporary moats of a barbed-wire fence and a screen porch to keep the mosquitoes out, as for a place of "kings and queens and castles," suggesting the former, semi-feudal colonial economy under a succession of laisser-faire Spanish kings (78). The American's white house resembles both a master's Big House overlooking the African and Taino field slaves as well as the White House metaphorically overseeing its imperial expansion that culminated in the 1898 takeover of the island after the Spanish-American War.

The barbed-wire fence that enclosed the American's land, however, proves useless in Mamá's hands. She puts a stick under the wire to create an entrance for herself, her daughters, and their children to pass freely back and forth across this imperial boundary, asserting that their Puerto Rican heritage, which dates back before the American presence on the island, gives them more authority than the American. Mamá treats the barbed-wire fence like the national border between Puerto Rico and the United States, theoretically rendered invisible in 1917 with the Jones Act's inclusion of Puerto Ricans as U.S. citizens with the right to enter the mainland without a passport. However, also like the Puerto Rico-United States border, the fence remains a symbol of American exclusion based on racism and ethnocentrism.

Thus, Mamá's tendency to "relish" sneaking onto the American's property is significant. Within this American cultural space, she sits on her natural "throne" of a great mango tree and embroiders "trailing vines and flowers" into linens as she spins great tales of other trespassers for her daughters and their daughters (74, 76). Whereas Mamá tells *cuentos* about being a Puerto Rican woman in her own privately redefined space of a garden of orchids and rosebushes, the tale of the "'prevailing woman'" is told on the American's land, under his mango tree, beyond a barbed-wire fence, and while sewing flowers that spill out of their containers (14). The cultivated, domestic flowers and the wedding flowers become trespassive and uncontained as Mamá's tales of what it means to be a Puerto Rican woman become more liberating, negotiating the confining spaces of Puerto Rican femininity.

Significantly, Mamá tells this *cuento* of a woman who cannot be contained several years before she told the *cuento* of Maria La Loca, establishing early in the narrator's mind the subversive possibilities of being a woman. Mamá's stories balance what the young narrator learns about expectations of women, opening up her own understanding of self as Puerto Rican and female. Maria Sabida is the "'smartest woman on the whole island'" who "'slept with one eye open'" (Ortiz Cofer "The Woman Who Slept" 80). As her name suggests, Maria Sabida is the wise, brave, and cunning alternative to the defeated Virgin Mary figure, Maria La Loca, the "poor girl who gave it all up for love, becoming a victim of her own foolish heart" (76). In Mamá's tale, set when Puerto Rico was still a Spanish colony and the King of Spain "had forgotten to send law and justice," murderous thieves or *ladrones* rule the island (69). At fifteen, Maria Sabida set out to "either conquer or to kill" the *ladron* who terrorizes her pueblo (70). Like Mamá with her orchids that unite the male-female binary, Maria Sabida is "a beautiful girl with the courage of a man." The original trespasser, she surreptitiously enters the *ladron's* house, a "'man-place' . . . built for violence." To avenge her pueblo, she puts sleeping powder into his food, waits for him in his bedroom, and beats him. When he later comes for her, bringing musical instruments and a marriage proposal instead of weapons, the townspeople "cross themselves at the miracle she had wrought," connecting her with her namesake, the Virgin Mary (72).

Maria Sabida's wedding night—like Maria La Loca's bouquet and Flora—signifies the devastation of a woman's body that comes with marriage and motherhood under Catholicism. The loss of virginity in this *cuento*, however, is represented more violently and directly than the fading flowers that symbolize the slow deterioration of a woman's strength and sanity: the fading flowers become a female body made of honey, the by-product of flowers, symbolic of blood as the body is ravaged on the wedding night. The *ladron* intends to kill her with a dagger "concealed beneath his clothes," but Maria Sabida anticipates the danger (73). She places a decoy full of honey in the bed so that when he attacks her, he "stabbed the doll's body over and over with his dagger." When he punctures the doll and covers himself with honey, he licks his lips and says, "'How sweet is my wife's blood,'" finally submitting to her. Like Mamá in "More Room," Maria Sabida inverts the sexually oppressed position of women and takes control of her own body.

While the women sew and Mamá tells her *cuentos*, the narrator and her "girl-cousins" do "some imaginative stitch work of our own" by imitating these women (79). The girls substitute "the tightly wrapped buds of the hibiscus flowers" for the women's cigarettes and glue "wild flower petals to our fingernails" to resemble the painted nails of the women "pushing needle and thread through white linen" as they sew trailing flower-vines for the girls. The "womanly" activity of needlework, historically associated with the highest rate of exploitation on the island according to the U. S. Department of Labor, becomes a medium for passing on new roles for women, like storytelling (Rivera Quintero 13). These moments under the American's mango tree, listening to the oral stories while mimicking the storytellers with hibiscus buds and other flowers indigenous to the island, thus symbolic of Taino women, represent the girls' initiation into the trespassing women's culture. This culture of border-crossing lived by Mamá and Maria Sabida also invokes the trickster figures of both African and native ideologies, a figure that dances across borders, implodes boundaries, and playfully disrupts the prevailing power structures. It is also a figure traditionally transmitted orally, passed on in stories and songs, just as Mamá passes on the tale of Maria Sabida, which the narrator soon makes her own.

The narrator emulates the grown women first with hibiscus buds and wildflowers and later with her own *cuentos*, uniting the flowers and the stories as "imaginative stitch work." She begins to make up her own stories of Maria Sabida at six years old, roughly the narrator's age at the time of the action. Maria Sabida must enter a dragon's lair to pick "enchanted" guavas for her dying brother, so she discovers the way to trick the dragon, using her grandmother's lore of mixing coconut oil with rainwater, which is full of starshine (84). By putting this mixture on a mule's hooves, she leaves a lighted trail on a dark night and safely enters the dragon's lair and gathers three guavas, curing her brother and all other sick children. As in Mamá's tales, Maria Sabida successfully trespasses onto dangerous territory to protect her social and familial community.

This first narrative expression by Judith Ortiz Cofer, then, is a *cuento* about the legendary trespasser-trickster who defines her own spaces and maintains her autonomy. As the original teller of these tales, Mamá is Ortiz Cofer's literary mentor before the author ever discovered Virginia Woolf, to whom Ortiz Cofer pays tribute in her preface to *Silent Dancing*. Her literature evolved out of the oral storytelling of her grandmother, transcribing and translating *cuentos* to *ensayos*, a woman-centered, communal form of an oral genre to a written genre, Spanish to English. Both Mamá's *cuentos* and Ortiz Cofer's framing *ensayos* negotiate the societal standard of "what it was like to be a woman, more specifically, a Puerto Rican woman." Maria La Loca and Flora are defeated by the Roman Catholic paradigm of the Virgin Mary, which proscribes virginity and then marriage. However, Ortiz Cofer cites the two options for women that have been orally passed down to her: "You can either be devastated by what you love, or you can vanquish the assassin by marrying him" (personal interview). Maria Sabida and Mamá win their autonomy by subversively making room for themselves as trespassers onto forbidden territories, expanding the spaces that constitute traditional gender roles and giving them new meanings in acts of catachresis.

The penultimate *ensayo*, "Marina," is framed with the narrator—now an adult—and her mother as they struggle with the translation of "key words for both of us," "'woman' and 'mother'" (152). The narrator's mother raised her children in New Jersey and Puerto Rico, moving to the island when her husband went on his tours of duty in the navy. During all the years in New Jersey, she maintained a traditional Puerto Rican household, never learned to speak English, and led a "life of isolation and total devotion to her duties as a mother" and as a "Penelope-like wife . . . always waiting, waiting, waiting, for the return of her sailor, for the return to her native land" (152). When she did return after the death of her husband, she went "totally `native,' regressing into the comfortable traditions of her extended family and questioning all of my decisions" (151). Those decisions include marriage and having a daughter, but the narrator redefines traditional gender roles to "experience life as an individual" (153). She begins a writing and teaching career while her American husband becomes "as good a parent as I am, and a much better cook." Like Mamá and Maria Sabida, the narrator negotiates her own spaces to include her independence and escape from the traditional role of wife and mother.

These clashing gender definitions are resolved through the memory of Mamá's *cuento* about Marina. While walking around the church, the narrator and her mother see an old man with a little girl, reminding them of Mamá's story. This man had grown up with Mamá before the island had been "touched by progress," when it was ruled solely by the Church (154). Girls were enclosed within a narrow social sphere under this reign: the only place they were allowed to go unchaperoned was the Rio Rojo, the river circumscribing the mountain where the Virgin Mary appeared. It is bordered by the island's "most fragrant flowers" and royal poinciana trees covered with blooms. These native flowers mark this sacred space devoted to the Virgin Mother and the maintenance of her power in defining roles for the island's "maidens." This "female place" was set apart by the Church for local virgins to experience their narrowly defined freedoms, where they could "bathe nude" and "luxuriate in their bodies" but were still "forbidden" to discuss sex (154-55). They were kept ignorant of sex until their *quinceañera*, their fifteenth birthday, when they were "given to strangers" before discovering sex on their own. So before female sexuality is contained by marriage, it is guarded within the Rio Rojo and its flowered borders.

Marina is the shyest of the girls who spend their summers within the river. She never joins the other girls in their nude bathing, leading them to believe that she is preparing for the convent; however, Marina's modesty masks the fact that she is a boy. His father had drowned shortly before his birth, so his mother in her grief named him after the element that made her a widow and raised him as a girl. Marina crosses the flowered borders of the Rio Rojo, an invasion that disrupts this "female place," the sacred territory of the Virgin, and the cultural definition of womanhood. In this trespassing, Marina dismantles the construction of an archetypal essence of womanhood, such as the Virgin surrounded by the flowered borders, or the icon of the Blessed Mother. Like Mamá, he proves that gender is defined beyond sex, separating the socially constructed roles of such "female places" from virginity and reproductive capacity, a separation that Flora did not recognize. Gender is also defined beyond mere sexual difference, a definition that would distort differences among women as they are set apart solely by their difference from a universalized man. Significantly, Mamá spends her final days of virginity at the Rio Rojo with Marina. Years later, Mamá would cross the American's barbed-wire fence and tell tales of legendary women who trespassed into a "male-place," applying this gender-bending to the ways the community of women around her can translate gender roles from containment to empowerment.

While subverting the rigid gender boundaries, Marina also challenges the ethnic hierarchy that characterized the Puerto Rican "pigmentocracy" (Gutiérrez and Padilla 19). Some Puerto Ricans claim a pure Spanish ancestry with "no mixture of [African and Taino] blood, but that's a myth," according to Ortiz Cofer, for "we're *mestizos* all" (personal interview). Contrary to the divisions of African, Taino, and Spanish ancestry suggested by a pigmentocracy, a *mestizo* cuture is syncretic, irreducibly mixed. At the Rio Rojo, Marina meets Kiki, the mayor's daughter who had been sheltered by the "cool shade of mansions and convent schools" before she was finally and reluctantly allowed to join the girls from the pueblo at Rio Rojo, solely as her father's political appeal to the local farmers (156). Among the "brown nyads" at the river, Kiki is a "pale fish" with "freckles on her shoulders, her little pink nipples, like rosebuds, her golden hair" (157). She represents the white elite of the island who claim pure Spanish bloodlines, untainted by Taino or African ancestry. She is the Puerto Rican embodiment of Spenser's Elizabeth and Campion's woman with a garden in her face: the pure, untouched, virginal, white girl, the essence of the Virgin Mary originally brought to the island by the Spaniards and fully contained within a flowered boundary.

Kiki, though, is neither conventional nor fully contained for long. She befriends Marina, not only a disguised boy trespassing into the "female place" but also more ethnically representative of Puerto Rico's mixed heritage with "cafe-con-leche skin and green eyes" and "thick black Indian hair" (156). One day, while gathering flowers at the edge of the river, Kiki and Marina elope, escaping under the guise of a safe and natural activity for virginal girls, yet also suggesting their future marriage and loss of virginity through their symbolic deflowering. As Mamá exhibits Taino-like power over her own sexuality by choosing to withhold it, Kiki and Marina choose to have sex outside of marriage and inside the Catholic borders of virginal space. To pay for their passage to New York, Kiki sells her pearl necklace, "the family heirloom given to her by her parents to wear at her *quinceañera*," thus symbolically exchanging the idealization of her virginity and her whiteness for sexuality on her own terms and entry into the true Puerto Rican ethnicity (159). Ortiz Cofer uncovers both the cultural fiction of pure whiteness in a multiethnic nation and the culturally inscribed standard of female identity.

At the end of the *ensayo*, the narrator and her mother continue to stand near the church and watch Marina, now an old man, with his granddaughter, the ultimate embodiment of Marina's simultaneous dismantling of the Puerto Rican pigmentocracy and the rigid definition of womanhood. He lifts the little girl "to smell a white rose that grew from a vine entangled on a tree branch. The child brought the flower carefully to her nose and smelled it. Then the old man placed the child gently back on the ground and they continued their promenade, stopping to examine anything that caught the child's eye" (160). Marina is introducing his granddaughter to the femininity represented by the tangled white rose high in the air, suggesting both the whiteness atop the Puerto Rican racial hierarchy and the constrictive gender role of the Catholic, pedestalled women imprisoned in mansions, convents, and gendered spaces. But as Marina allows the girl to continue in her exploration, it is clear that this white rose does not symbolize a unitary category of Woman. As in his deconstructive border-crossing years earlier, Marina demonstrates that womanhood is not a monolithic ideal: it is fluid like his name, sexually uncontained, ethnically syncretic, and ultimately heterogeneous. Just like Mamá with the American's barbed-wire fence and Maria Sabida in the *ladron's* castle and the dragon's lair, Marina renders the flowered boundaries surrounding gender permeable as the "womanly" spaces of gardens, needlework, and storytelling are wrenched from their traditional meanings and given subversive and liberating possibilities.

As the narrator and her mother witness this scene after struggling with their opposing definitions of their gender, they recognize that "we now had a new place to begin our search for the meaning of the word *woman*" (160). Earlier surrounded by quotation marks, *woman* is now italicized, an English word written as Spanish words are marked, suggesting a blurring of borders in the deconstruction and reconstruction of definitions. The oppositional translations of womanhood have been resolved by bridging their differences and acknowledging multiplicity.

By exploring the spaces in between fiction and nonfiction, male and female, "macho" and "maiden," American and Puerto Rican, oppressor and oppressed, Ortiz Cofer blurs boundaries and envisions a world beyond these binary restrictions. She opens up our conceptions of race, culture, and gender, each of which becomes a signifier for a multiplicity of ideologies and identities that renders a univocal articulation of idealized, sexualized, or racialized gender impossible. A writer with the new consciousness of Gloria Anzaldúa's new *mestiza*, Ortiz Cofer reveals multiple modes of existence, like the flowers beyond the archetype: the wedding flowers, the fading roses, the tangled white rose, the wildflowers, the orchids, the rosebushes, the poinciana blooms, the hibiscus flowers. Like Maria Sabida, Marina, and Mamá, the narrator and author claims more room for genre, gender, and ethnicity to resemble Mamá's casa: a "chambered nautilus . . . that has grown organically, according to the needs of its inhabitants," full of stories about all kinds of women and men (23).

WORKS CITED

Acosta-Belén, Edna. "The Building of a Community: Puerto Rican Writers and Activists in New York, 1890s-1960s." *Recovering the U.S. Hispanic Literary Heritage.* Ed. Ramón Gutiérrez and Genaro Padilla. Houston: Arte Público Press, 1993. 179-195.

Bhabha, Homi K. "Postcolonial Criticism." *Redrawing the Boundaries: The Transformation of English and American Literary Studies.* Ed. Stephen Greenblatt and Giles Gunn. New York: Modern Language Association of America, 1992. 437-465.

Campion, Thomas. *The Fourth Booke of Ayres.* 1617. *Campion's Works.* Ed. Percival Vivian. Oxford: Clarendon Press, 1909. 178.

Classen, Constance. *Worlds of Sense: Exploring the Senses in History and Across Cultures.* New York: Routledge, 1993.

de Vries, Ad. *Dictionary of Symbols and Imagery.* London: North-Holland Publishing Company, 1974.

Flores, Juan. "Puerto Rican Literature in the United States: Stages and Perspectives." *Recovering the U.S. Hispanic Literary Heritage.* Ed. Ramón Gutiérrez and Genaro Padilla. Houston: Arte Público Press, 1993. 53-68.

Gutiérrez, Ramón, and Genaro Padilla, eds. *Recovering the U.S. Hispanic Literary Heritage.* Houston: Arte Público Press, 1993.

Kristeva, Julia. "Stabat Mater." *Tales of Love.* Trans. Leon S. Roudiez. New York: Columbia University Press, 1987. 160-186, 234-63.

Novas, Himilce. *Everything You Need To Know About Latino History.* New York: Penguin, 1994.

Ortiz Cofer, Judith. Personal e-mail. 13 June 1996.

———. Personal interview. 4 June 1996.

———. *Silent Dancing: A Partial Remembrance of a Puerto Rican Childhood.* Houston: Arte Público Press, 1990.

———. "Taking the Macho." *Prairie Schooner* 68. 4 (1994): 63-67.

————. "The Woman Who Slept with One Eye Open: Notes on Being a Writer." *The American Voice* 32 (Fall 1993): 80-91.

Ortiz Laureano, Zeydy, and Jose Pietri. "Puerto Rico's Culture, Politics, and Society." Soc.Culture.Puerto-Rico (11 July 1996).

Rivera Quintero, Marcia. "The Development of Capitalism in Puerto Rico and the Incorporation of Women into the Labor Force." *The Puerto Rican Woman.* Ed. Edna Acosta-Belén. New York: Praeger, 1979. 8-24.

Spenser, Edmund. *Amoretti and Epithalamion.* 1595. *The Works of Edmund Spenser.* Ed. R. Morris. London: Macmillan, 1909. 582.

Spivak, Gayatri Chakravorty. *In Other Worlds: Essays in Cultural Politics.* New York: Methuen, 1987.

Tatum, Charles. "Some Considerations on Genres and Chronology for Nineteenth-Century Hispanic Literature." *Recovering the U.S. Hispanic Literary Heritage.* Ed. Ramón Gutiérrez and Genaro Padilla. Houston: Arte Público Press, 1993. 199-208.

Warner, Marina. *Alone of All Her Sex: The Myth and the Cult of the Virgin Mary.* New York: Knopf, 1976.

CHAPTER 4

Flight and Arrival
A Study of Padma Hejmadi's Short Story, "Weather Report"

Lakshmi Holmström

The increasing self-awareness of the new South Asian diasporas in the First World is reflected in the stories that they tell about the experience of displacement. In the following essay I would like to demonstrate how Padma Hejmadi, in her story "Weather Report," reflects this experience as an ongoing one: one which negotiates a changing relationship with a host country, and equally a changing relationship with one's country of origin. In doing so, I believe Hejmadi tells a more credible story than the stories of assimilation as a one-way process, told by Bharati Mukherjee.

Padma Hejmadi was born in Madras and grew up in India. She studied at the University of Michigan, Ann Arbor, and has lived in the United States since then. Her collection of short stories *Birthday, Deathday* was published under the name Padma Perera and was first published by The Women's Press, London, England in 1985. It contains twelve stories altogether, written over a period of some ten years. All except the story under consideration here, "Weather Report," were published earlier, from 1974 onward, several of them in *The New Yorker*.

It is important to note that most of the stories are placed in India. Eight of them are written as memories and vignettes that tell of characters belonging to an extended family: upper class, highly educated Saraswat Brahmans, originally from Mangalore, but seen in different settings in different parts of India. The narrative perspective is often that of a child or of a young woman growing up in a secure environment

with loving and loved parents: " ... the parental heritage: no
vehement claims on virtue, merely this willingness to take each
moment wholly and then leave it wholly behind: receive and relinquish
with both hands" (15, from the title story). These stories constantly
refer to a core of orthodoxy—or rather of established ritual and
tradition—that is represented by the narrator's grandparents' generation,
and that is not at all seen as threatening or restricting. For, on the other
hand, the passage of time and history makes available a modern—and
indeed internationalist—lifestyle for the younger generation, should
they decide to choose it.

It is against the buttress of this somewhat idealized picture of
modern Indian life that four stories are pitched, whose central themes are
exile in North America and the experience of marginalization there.
"Birthday, Deathday" and "Letter" deal specifically with the possibility
of cultural displacement and exile that a cross-cultural marriage could
entail: in the first, the protagonist accepts such a marriage and makes it
work; in the second she decides against it. The other two stories,
"Monologue for Foreigners" and "Weather Report," are concerned more
generally with the experience of foreignness and of finding an identity
in exile. They are the only two that are actually placed in North
America. The first, "Monologue for Foreigners," is an almost abstract
study of anonymous "wanderers" forgathered in an all-night cafe, "when
this world's clamour only makes silence clearer. Its prejudices strip
away our skin, its labels and advertisements cancel our names entirely
and allow us to come together unclaimed like pieces of stranded
luggage—*world people matching difference to sameness: nothing else*"
(55, my emphasis). "Weather Report" is a more specific story of the
gendered experience of exile, of a young Indian woman entrapped by the
patriarchal tyranny of a newly formed—and forming—"Asian" diaspora
and her eventual flight from that tyranny and in search of a centered self.
As such, in this story, Padma Hejmadi parallels to a remarkable degree
the themes that we recognize in the stories and novels of better known
writers such as Bharati Mukherjee. Yet her treatment is more complex,
and her resolution is more open-ended; the point of the story lies in its
problematizing of the uneasy terrain between assimilation and
separateness.

The shape or form of the story is significant for several reasons: it
follows a bus journey that the protagonist takes, from Rockville in
Colorado to Albuquerque. During the first part of the journey, events
leading up to the young woman's flight from her husband are recalled.

Halfway along the story (or the journey) the flashbacks catch up with the present, and with the lives of the passengers on the bus, as they all move into the unknown future. The journey as literary device enables both the recapitulation of the past with its theme of escape and a speculation about the future with its theme of quest.

Before we look more closely at Hejmadi's treatment of the theme of escape, it might be useful to examine the notion of an Asian diaspora, and the political difference between an Asian diaspora in England and in the United States. The South Asian diaspora in England can never be unaware of its postcolonial position, not least because the term "Asian" first began to be used widely in the 1970s and 1980s to describe a migrant group from East Africa who were originally from the Indian subcontinent. This was so, despite the fact that an earlier wave of migration had happened in the 1950s, consisting of peasant groups, mainly men, coming into England directly from the Panjab, Gujarat, and what is now known as Bangladesh. These people came to England in response to the postwar demand for cheap labor, and they were joined a decade or so later by the women of their respective communities. "Asian" is quite clearly a diasporic term, not one that describes either nationality or even (strictly) geographic origin. It has been claimed in England particularly by second- and third-generation settlers conscious of common (or at any rate overlapping) politics, and sometimes, of shared cultural suppositions.

Diaspora means dispersion or scattering; it has come to mean a community that is displaced, but has very strong ties with a "notional" or even imagined cultural home. The British Asian diaspora is made up, of course, of individuals with very particular personal histories and who have therefore come to England (or to Britain) by many different routes. Yet now it is impossible to be indifferent to a history of Asian migration, not only of the recent past, ever since the partition of India in 1947, but of yet other migrations, going back to the indentures that occurred in colonial times, in the late nineteenth century. So, more and more, in Britain, at least, there is an awareness of a "layered" colonial history that impinges on the present; thus "Asian" in Britain takes on cross-class, political overtones.

The Asian diaspora that Hejmadi sketches in "Weather Report" is set against the very different politics of (im)migration. It is more overtly caricatured in such stories as Bharati Mukherjee's *Wife* (1987). This diaspora is made up of middle-class professionals, extremely conscious of their privileged position. Ramesh, whom the protagonist of "Weather Report" joins as a young bride, is a "rising electronic engineer," finishing his Ph.D. thesis; later he heads a research project at the university, and is at the same time a consultant to a firm. He states his requirements very clearly, "I'm traditional . . . I don't want Western ways in our house" (150). The cultural space he occupies in North America is a carefully negotiated one: "Television was all right; international by now, Ramesh said, and no longer merely Western . . . he likes television, including those greed shows where frenzied contestants slaver over prizes, and Hindi songs; he doesn't care for the theatre or for Western music; he enjoys group outings with other Indians, and having dinner with American friends who are not what I would call friends ('You are too critical': he's right): they are contacts" (151).

Ramesh's position is that of the middle-class professional safeguarding his place of privilege, but it is also that of the migrant setting up certain patriarchal parameters for a new Asian diaspora in North America. This raises immediately the question of exile as a gendered experience.

Archetypically, women of the Indian subcontinent have married and left home. And in the new Asian diasporas women often find themselves in other countries than that of their birth, not because of their own choice, but by virtue of being a daughter, a sister, a wife. In this case, the young woman who is the narrator of the story becomes a bride who leaves home, because her father and her oldest uncle answer an advertisement in the matrimonial columns of *India Abroad*, placed there by Ramesh's parents. According to their views, they are doing their best for her, buying into success. The operative conditions put forward by the prospective parents-in-law are significant: "Pretty, fair, convent-educated virgin under 23 . . . caste no bar. . . ." (148). Ramesh is not interested in the negotiations; it is the prospective parents-in-law who accept the girl by proxy, and all the arrangements are made through letters and family connections.

"Our culture told us what to do and we listened, but we were in another country" (150). The gendered experience of exile has a neat ironic twist. Women find themselves in exile, not by their own choice, yet paradoxically, it is they who are looked upon to build a home that replicates home, to anchor the family and to become the icons validating a cultural group in exile: thus, Ramesh's choice of a bride from "home," his warnings to his young wife not to get too friendly with "these people," and his forbidding her to wear Western clothes, whatever discomfort this should mean to her in snowy and inclement weather. At the same time, Ramesh is very much aware of being part of a professional diaspora—a socially aspiring one where "contacts" are more significant than "friends"—and requires his decorative Indian wife to display a variety of culinary skills and social graces, to curb her vehemences and enthusiasms, and above all never to express political or critical opinions.

The point that Hejmadi is moving toward is the moment of awareness in the young wife when the tyranny of this new cultural construct is no longer supportable. Now, Ramesh is not to be seen by the reader as crudely representative of the patriarchal aspects of the Asian diasporic culture. Hejmadi even suggests the loneliness and reserve into which he as an individual character is trapped. All the same, it is he who sets down the terms and conditions for his wife's life in America. If she cannot live in the way that he asks her to, then he can withdraw his support for her status as wife and "send her back." And she knows that in failing by the standards of the diaspora, she would fall short of the family's aspirations and, therefore, have no place "back home" either: "To be sent back by your husband: used goods, useless goods. Not because I was barren, too soon for that. Worse. It would mean I had failed, been found wanting beyond physiology. My family, my entire clan, would never be able to hold up their collective and metaphoric heads again" (156).

The "escape" narrative, which is made up of the flashbacks, is bracketed within two realizations that make possible that escape: "I didn't know I was divided so irrevocably, or that I was so exiled from myself . . . " (150) and "I was finished with building my comfort out of other people's anguish" (163)—the comfort, that is, that so many people have it so much worse.

But does the rejection of the (patriarchal) tyranny of the diasporic culture—which the female narrator achieves at last, walking out into the inclement weather wearing Western clothes, and armed with bus timetables and plane connections—necessarily mean rejection of the whole culture and its sources? It is worth noting that the narrator's real name is never revealed; the only name she allows herself in the long-distance bus is Latin American, Conchita Perez. Staying within the diaspora afforded a social status; outside it, becoming Conchita, she can only seek a *"personal* birthright": the short story that has thus far been one of escape slides into a different theme, one of quest.

Let us look again at the form of the story. It starts with a young woman at a bus terminus in Denver, Colorado, who gets a ticket to Albuquerque by mistake—all she had wanted to do was to find her way to the international airport. The flashbacks are built into the description of the journey through the snow, taking us through the events of the past three years: the marriage advertisement, the first year of marriage, the narrator's growing feeling of despair and anger, the moment when she leaves. It is in a sense both an actual and a metaphysical journey. (The very notion of a diaspora, scattering, generates a number of repeated images, metaphors, myths: of journeys, maps, new boundaries; Derek Walcott's endless beckoning islands, Salman Rushdie's "imaginary homelands.") It becomes another sort of migration, from past to future life, as described by Grewal et al. in *Charting the Journey*: "that other form of migration—movement across the frontiers of life into new, unchartered territories of the self" (2).

Halfway through, the story changes in its focus and indeed method, from intense self-reflection to an observation of others: from the parameters of the self within the diaspora, to the kind of community within the bus of which "Conchita" has inadvertently become part. The "escape from" becomes "journey toward"; the theme is less exclusively diasporic and more mainstream American; the bus journeys across the continent (it has crossed Wyoming and Colorado, is passing through New Mexico, and will end in San Diego) and signals toward American themes and narrative formats of "on the road."

Now, implicit in the early part of the story are the cultural differences between "them" (mainstream American) and "us" (Asian diaspora). And these are seen both through the perspective of Ramesh and through that of the narrator. He has no difficulty in buying into the enterprise culture and its competitiveness, but he looks upon the intimacies and friendships about him with suspicion. He must safeguard his reserve and his difference. It is she who reflects with the greater irony upon sameness and difference, who finds "mirror-images" from the beginning, between herself and what she sees about her. She (unlike Ramesh) rejects—or is suspicious of—the picture that is propagated of "homogenised milk-white America," and is appalled by the relentless optimism and self-congratulation she sees often. This is typified for her by the university student with the snazzy sports car whom she once saw, who had just bought himself an even snazzier pair of skis, "how he stood on the sidewalk surveying his possessions as he ate a quart carton of yoghurt, shovelling it into his mouth with a plastic spoon, and saying, 'I'm gonna live forever'" (154).

The fragility of that optimism, however, is well understood by the narrator, because of the ambiguous position of at least two groups of marginalized people with whom she (but not Ramesh, safe in his diaspora position) identifies. Understanding the complexities of skin-color and prejudice, she says always she has "seethed at the tan of privilege as opposed to the dark of prejudice"; but she admits that her own comparatively light-colored skin has been "ignominious passport" both to her marriage three years ago and now to acceptance as "Conchita." Linked by color (and the language she learns and comes to love) to the Latin American, she finds herself linked also to the American Indian because of the mistakes of language and history: 'I gripe about the old and perpetuated misnomer via Columbus, 'Indian'." In this way, the optimism of the all-American dream and the superficial advertisement-world picture in which "Everyone [is] tall and blond and strapping, with lots of orthodontia" is undermined by her awareness that all those who are not those things are marginalized or made invisible.

There is a more profound division, though, of which she begins to be aware, as the community of travelers within the bus begins to take shape—and that is between the "winners" and the "losers." As the bus travels further and further south, not only do the small American towns and the landscape become more concrete and vivid, so do the people. So far the narrator has only registered the anonymity of the passengers through the graffiti they have (significantly) left behind: "I was not here"; "Kevin was here but now he's gone. He's left his name to carry on. . . ." But now names and faces begin to register, facilitated through the woman, Judy, who gets on at Pueblo.

This is the other important narrative device that Hejmadi builds into the second (quest) half of the story. She brings another viewpoint, an American perspective. The protagonist perceives the other passengers in relation to Judy: the man from Casper, Wyoming who sits in front of her; the Hispanic couple behind her, Dick from Walsenberg across the aisle. Judy becomes the secondary narrator, enabling the telling of other and others' stories.

These stories make possible a devastating understanding: "Conchita" who is running away from her life, Judy who is smoking her life away, Dick who has been traveling ever since his wife died in an accident and has traveled three thousand miles already, carrying his photographic album that he shows to utter strangers—these form a community of lost souls. "Then I realize which section of the bus I'm in, and how those up front, like the kid eating yoghurt, will live forever" (166).

The theme of marginalization, that is, is explored throughout the story, within the Asian diaspora and outside it, and given a context in a wider geography and within the movements and aspirations of mainstream culture. The easy optimism of a melting-pot culture making possible a reinvention of the self is not offered; instead we are made aware of a microcosm of the world outside, deeply riven.

About midway in the journey, the narrator also realizes that going home (to India?) is no longer even an option. This is the epiphany that precedes the other realization: the awareness of the community of losers and lost souls. It is the moment when she understands that her destination is not going to be another international airport in place of Denver's Stapleton. But the moment is also not one of absolute despair; seeing the destination "San Diego" spelled out on the bus, she thinks, "Maybe that's the answer. Keep traveling until I reach the warm amniotic fluid of an ocean and regain some sense of personal birthright" (164). To "*regain* some sense of personal birthright." The phrase is echoed right at the end, when Conchita aligns herself with Dick and the others: "All the alphabets of living to be *re-learned* so painfully in the weather of subsequence" (167, my emphasis).

The "quest" half of the story is bracketed within these multiple images: the "warm, amniotic fluid of an ocean" suggests both the comfort and safety of the womb as well as the largeness/largesse of a shared heritage; while "alphabets of living" points to what is not "given" so easily, what must be learned singly and alone in the inclement "weather of subsequence." A remaking of the self by a single flight, is demonstrably not possible in the world of this story. The quest then is to regain a personal birthright: the rights and privileges to which one is born as a human being and as a person with a particular culture and a particular sex. The emphasis is on regaining and relearning, painfully and slowly, from the logic of personal history or "subsequence."

Something needs to be said about the framework of linked images, the "weather" against which the narrative device of the journey is plotted. The story begins with a reference to snow: the land of snow is seen as exotic and alienating; the falling of snow is almost a metaphor for alienating silence. "I wish there had been some definite and explosive denouement to split us apart. None. The snow kept coming down, that was all; doors opened only to close" (162). The weather reports, watched obsessively by everyone in America, in order to "measure their movements of the following day," also gives room for errors. Thus, the Thanksgiving blizzard, which, by holding up Ramesh at his conference gives the protagonist her opportunity to escape, is also the reason for her "snowblindness" and taking the wrong bus. The snowy landscape is a constant referent, obliterating distance and boundaries between states, and providing a "white uncharted space" that insistently asks, why? where to? It makes possible the central question of the story, "Do I know my own space? . . . If I can't go home, where *can* I go?" The weather, in this way, is both enabling and disabling in the story; predictable and unpredictable; like personal history, "subsequence," the narrative of what has happened, and must happen following that, it simply provides the conditions for relearning.

The openness of the ending of the story includes an appropriation of that agenda for relearning and a partial hope that there will be enough time—and buses to catch—to accomplish that. Hence losers can also be gainers in one sense. But it also includes an admission of loss in another sense, "Ramesh and me reckoning hereafter with the end of each undone day" (167). "Undone" suggests here both unfinished and destroyed. The admission of loss is also one of compassion.

I return now to the comparison I suggested earlier, between the ways Padma Hejmadi and Bharati Mukherjee chart an Indian woman's quest for selfhood in North America. Mukherjee has written extensively about Asian and other immigrants coming to North America, both Canada and the United States. The introduction to *Darkness* (1985), her first collection of short stories, makes plain her own literary trajectory and aesthetic manifesto. Until 1984, when she was doing a residency in Atlanta, Georgia, she says she had thought of herself as an "expatriate." "In my fiction, and in my Canadian experience, 'immigrants' were lost souls, put upon and pathetic. Expatriates, on the other hand, knew all too well who and what they were" (*Darkness* 1). Her earlier writing, *Tiger's Daughter* (1971) and *Wife* (1987) come out of this stance. "I used a mordant and self protecting irony in describing my characters' pain. Irony promised both detachment from, and superiority over, those well-bred post-colonials much like myself, adrift in the new world, wondering if they would ever belong." (*Darkness* 2).

Bharati Mukherjee writes in bitter terms of the mosaic model of multiculturalism officially espoused by Canada, and which she says, masked the actual hostility toward incoming Asians. She compares this position to the melting-pot model of assimilation in the United States, where, she claims, she finds herself as "just another immigrant." In a much quoted passage, she writes, "I see my 'immigrant' story replicated in a dozen American cities, and instead of seeing my Indianness as a fragile identity to be preserved against obliteration (or worse, a 'visible' disfigurement to be hidden), I see it now as a set of fluid identities to be celebrated" (*Darkness* 3). It is from this latter literary and political position that she has written her two sets of short stories, *Darkness* and *The Middleman and Other Stories*, and her next novel, *Jasmine* (1991).

The clear division that Mukherjee sees between the expatriate and immigrant position and perspective is worth noting. In *Wife,* first published in 1975, she gives us a portrait of an expatriate young woman, Dimple Dasgupta, who arrives in New York through an arranged marriage. Krishna Baldev Vaid, reviewing the novel, describes the movement from "the mildewed middle-class life in Calcutta in Part One to the morbidly materialistic Indian ghetto of New York City in Parts Two and Three" (155). The cultural confusions manifest in the displaced community into which she is transported eventually lead to Dimples's psychic breakdown. The point, however, is that, compared to the protagonist of "Weather Report," there never were any subtleties or cultural certainties about Dimple; she is portrayed as being bred only to marriage and servicing her husband. (Mukherjee's cool contempt for her protagonist is revealed in the letters Dimple writes to Miss Problem-walla c/o Eve's Beauty Basket, Bombay.)

The description of another diasporic community, Panjabi, this time, rather than Bengali, in *Jasmine*, is shown to be even more stifling and restricting: the apartment in Flushing, of "professorji" who gives a home to the protagonist for five months, when she is completely alone, is described by Jasmine as being a place of "artificially maintained Indianness," "I was spiralling into depression behind the fortress of Panjabiness," she says. "I felt immured. An imaginary brick wall topped with barbed wire cut me off from the past and kept me from breaking into the future. I was a prisoner doing unreal time" (*Jasmine* 145).

Thus, group and communal affiliations are seen by Mukherjee as impediments to the growth of the single individual self. The diasporic communities in her narratives represent the overload of the past that must be jettisoned; and always a violent process is involved. In *Jasmine*, there is a rape, a murder, and a burning of the symbols of the past before the birthing of the new is made possible. A crucial statement by the protagonist is made, early on in the novel: "There are no harmless, compassionate ways to remake oneself. We murder who we were, so we can rebirth ourselves in the images of dreams." (29). Again we can contrast this to Hejmadi's protagonist, whose journey, rather, is toward "regaining a personal birthright," which involves a reclaiming of the past in new ways, and whose last reference to her husband is one of compassion.

The violence in Mukherjee's short stories, particularly in the collection *The Middleman and Other Stories*, many of which are first-person narratives of non-European immigrants, exists also because private and individual destiny is often seen as a direct reflection of a current, violent political scene: it could be Vietnam or Bangladesh or anywhere else. Jyoti/Jasmine's life reflects almost stereotypically, the recent politics of a violent and terrorist-torn Panjab. The immigrant world is also one of violence: of dismemberment and scattering of individuals from communities. And it is those individuals in flight who will be the survivors and winners, unlike Dimple Dasgupta and the professorji's wife, lost forever in their communal ghettos. More and more, it is the winners like Jasmine who interest Bharati Mukherjee; those who can choose to "re-position the stars" so easily, "greedy with wants and reckless with hope" (241).

The romantic epic, that is, the success story of the immigrant, in Mukherjee's fiction, all the same, is dubious in a variety of ways. It is to some extent constructed by homogenizing all immigrant experience from nontraditional emigrant countries: the "we" in Jasmine's statement when she says "[w]e murder who we were so we can rebirth ourselves" is inclusive of her and her adopted Vietnamese son. And it is significant that the Jasmine of the novel, a Panjabi peasant girl from Jullundhur, by the author's own admission, grew out of an earlier Jasmine, a Trinidadian Indian, whose story is included in *The Middleman and Other Stories*. It seems even more significant that the author positions herself as an immigrant American, "in the tradition of other American writers whose parents and grandparents had passed through Ellis Island. My Indianness is now a metaphor . . . "(*Darkness* 3). There is a dubious elision here, pointed out by Anindyo Roy: "By subsuming her post coloniality in the Eurocentred aesthetic rite of passage, Mukherjee seeks to legitimize her own romantic 'epic' imagination, seamlessly weaving it into the archetypical European immigrant experience in the New World" (130).

And there is also another dubious elision that makes possible the success story of the immigrant, and that is the elision of the class issue. An outstanding example is the manner in which the Panjabi peasant woman, Jyoti, so seamlessly acquires the middle-class American voice of Jane Ripplemeyer. Does the melting-pot make possible with such ease the erasure of these distinctions of class and ethnicity?

In a working paper entitled "The Disembodiment of Culture: Postmodernism and Postcolonialism in Bharati Mukherjee's *The Middleman and Other Stories* and *Wife*," Gail Low aptly sums up the world of Mukherjee's fiction as "an amoral one of dog eat dog where the survivor is one that cuts his/her losses (including his/her ethnic group identity) and freewheels into the future" (12-13). It is underpinned by a worldview that does not unpack or problematize "the uneasy overlap between a flight from identity and a negation of identity in the immigration process." Low ends her paper, "My difficulty with Mukherjee's work turns on the question of how to preserve the complexities and contradictions of the migrant position, and yet preserve an awareness of the politics of cultural differences within the metropolitan centre" (13).

I suggest that "Weather Report" takes on board some of the paradoxes that Gail Low sees as fundamental to the migrant position, particularly from the perspective of a woman. The overlap between escape or flight from diasporic identity and quest for new personhood is neatly encapsulated in the very form of the story. The bus itself becomes a microcosm—"Our lives are bounded by the edge of the bus" (164)—of the world outside and reflects its margins and marginalizations, the fissures beneath its homogenizing surface. The quest is not for total reinvention, but a reclamation with due regard to personal (and national) histories. The immigration process, therefore, is seen not as "murder[ing] who we were so we can rebirth ourselves in the images of dreams," but to "regain a sense of personal birthright." But "Weather Report" is also contextualized within a collection of stories whose intertextual references allow the articulation of the strengths and restrictions of a "home culture," and hence also the tracking of sameness and difference elsewhere, in the diaspora.

WORKS CITED

Grewal. S, J. et al. "Preface." *Charting the Journey: Writings by Black and Third World Women*. London: Sheba Feminist Publishers, 1988.

Low, Gail Ching-Liang. "The Disembodiment of Culture: Postmodernism and Postcolonialism in Bharati Mukherjee's *The Middle Man and Other Stories* and *Wife*." Unpublished working paper, 1993.

Mukherjee, Bharati. *Darkness*. Harmondsworth: Penguin Books, 1985.

———. *Jasmine*. London: Virago, 1991.

———. *The Middleman and Other Stories*. London: Virago, 1989.

———. *Tiger's Daughter*. Boston: Houghton Mifflin, 1971.

———. *Wife*. Harmondsworth: Penguin Books, 1987.

Perera, Padma. *Birthday, Deathday, and Other Stories*. London: Women's Press, 1985.

Roy, Anindyo. "The Aesthetics of an (Un)willing Immigrant: Bharati Mukherjee's *Days and Nights in Calcutta* and *Jasmine*." In *Bharati Mukherjee: Critical Perspectives*. Ed. Emmanuel S. Nelson. New York and London: Garland. 127-41.

Rushdie, Salman. "Imaginary Homelands." *London Review of Books* 7 Oct. 1982: 18-9.

Vaid, Krishna Baldev. Review of *Wife*. *Fiction International* 415, (1975): 155-7.

Walcott, Derek. *Collected Poems 1948-1984*. London: Faber & Faber, 1992.

CHAPTER 5

Subversive Extravagance

Women in Hisaye Yamamoto's "Seventeen Syllables" and "The Legend of Miss Sasagawara"

Veronica C. Wang

As one of the earliest Japanese-American women writers emerging from World War II to be published in mainstream journals, Hisaye Yamamoto must have felt her share of anxiety of authorship both as a woman author and as a member of a recently condemned racial minority. Presenting a Japanese-American woman's perspective in her short stories, she writes with indirection, humor, and gentle irony about those of her compatriots whose strife and plight she explores with tolerance and compassion. Though seldom would she come out directly to condemn racial injustice inflicted on minorities or denounce unspoken oppression suffered by women within Japanese patriarchy, Yamamoto invariably gives voice to characters who have thus far been violated and silenced. In her often coded utterances, she exposes racial prejudice against minorities, sexual and artistic repression of Japanese-American women, and the intolerable conditions of relocation camps borne by Japanese Americans during World War II.

A California-born Japanese American of immigrant parents, Yamamoto can hardly be oblivious to the constrictions experienced by Japanese-American women nor the increasing hostility against people of Japanese descent during the period of World War II, when more than 110,000 people of Japanese ancestry were incarcerated. She and her family, among thousands, were interned for three years in Poston, Arizona, where she worked as a reporter and columnist for the *Poston Chronicle*, the camp newspaper, and at the same time published a serialized mystery entitled "Death Rides the Rails to Poston" (1943-44).

As her stories appeared in various journals, she began to receive national recognition in spite of continued anti-Japanese sentiment after the war. Though the incarceration of Japanese and Japanese Americans had ended with the conclusion of the war, as King-Kok Cheung observes, "political and social constrictions imposed by the dominant culture necessitated textual constraints beyond the duration of the physical confinement" (130); and furthermore, Cheung reiterates that "as a woman writing at a time when feminist sensibilities were scarcely publishable, the *nisei* author couches her sympathy in a disarming style that keeps alarming subtexts below the surface" (29-30). Perhaps as a measure of self-censorship, Yamamoto would often use young, naive narrators whose innocence and naivete could serve as a disguise to deflect attention from the writer's self-revelation or some key issues of authorial concern.

Several recurring issues dominate Yamamoto's early stories, one of which focuses on the sexual repression of Japanese-American women trapped in unhappy marriages, as brilliantly depicted in the haunting story of Mrs. Hayashi as she struggles to free herself from a stifling marital predicament by articulating her emotions in classical Japanese haiku in "Seventeen Syllables" or in the tragic tale of Miss Sasagawara, whose relentless struggle to assert her individuality against sexual and social repression of women is further explored and intensified in a dislocated setting of a relocation camp. In "that unlikely place of wind, sand, and heat" (20), a desert place of numbing imprisonment, the difficulty of communication sharpens even more between the *issei* (first-generation) father, a consummate Buddhist priest, "whose lifelong aim had been to achieve Nirvana," (32) and a *nisei* (second-generation) daughter, a sensitive and passionate ballet dancer, whose emotional development is not only incarcerated by her father's spiritual oblivion but by the actual relocation camp experience itself during World War II. Her meager effort at artistic expression leads only to eventual confinement in a mental institution, as she becomes increasingly isolated not only from her alienated father but from the community at large.

The repression of women in its various disguises becomes a key concern in several of Yamamoto's major stories, and her compassionate treatment of the plight of these women—molded by cultural constraint, victimized by marital violence, maddened by frustrated desires, and traumatized by hostile environment—provides a rare insight into the continuous struggles of women across ethnic and cultural boundaries.

"Seventeen Syllables," which originally appeared in *Partisan Review* in 1949, is the title story in a collection of fifteen stories in a volume entitled *Seventeen Syllables and Other Stories* published in 1988. The story of a Japanese immigrant farming family in southern California is told from the point of view of the American-born adolescent daughter, Rosie Hayashi, whose absorption in her own emerging sexuality renders her a little less attentive to her observation of her parents' conflicts. Through a double-voiced account joining the struggles of both mother and daughter in their journey of self-discovery against a backdrop of Japanese patriarchy and the persistent hardship of daily toil for survival on American soil, Yamamoto explores the explosive collision between individual desires and traditional roles of women.

As an *issei* woman, Rosie's mother, Tome, labors alongside her husband and fulfills her daily obligations faithfully as a hard-working farmer's wife for at least fifteen years since her arrival in the United States as a "picture bride," in spite of the fact that she married her simple-minded husband out of desperation as "an alternative to suicide" (18) after a failed love affair in Japan. Under her taciturn husband's supervision, Tome has cooked, washed, and managed the household as well as toiled in the tomato field under the hot sun in harvest time. As busy and accommodating as she appears in her daily occupations, Tome could find self-fulfillment only in her newly discovered aspiration as a poet of haiku. In fact, she has become such an "extravagant contributor" (9) to a San Francisco newspaper, the *Mainichi Shimbun,* which devotes a section to haiku each week, that Tome even takes for herself a flowery pen name, Ume Hanazono; but her self-gratifying endeavor is not without some sting felt by both husband and daughter:

> So Rosie and her father lived for awhile with two women, her mother and Ume Hanazono. Her mother(Tome Hayashi by name) kept house, cooked, washed, and, along with her husband and the Carrascos, the Mexican family hired for the harvest, did her ample share of picking tomatoes out in the sweltering fields and boxing them in tidy strata in the cool packing shed. Ume Hanazono, who came to life after the dinner dishes were done, was an earnest, muttering stranger who often neglected speaking when spoken to and stayed busy at the parlor table as late as midnight scribbling

with pencil on scratch paper or carefully copying characters on
good paper with her fat, pale green Parker. (9)

As Tome continues her self-expressive endeavor in writing—a
privilege usually reserved for males—in isolation from her family, she
is perceived as being extravagant or even subversive, undermining the
harmony of the family. As observed by the narrator, ". . . if a group of
friends came over, it was bound to contain someone who was also
writing haiku and the small assemblage would be split into two, her
father entertaining the non-literary members and her mother comparing
ecstatic notes with the visiting poet" (9). This transgression of gender
roles is amply illustrated on two occasions: first, when the Hayashis
visit a neighboring family, the Hayanos, Tome devotes the entire visit
to discussing haiku with the "handsome, tall, and strong" (10) Mr.
Hayano while her husband is relegated to sitting alone and talking
occasionally to the shivering and semivegetative Mrs. Hayano; second,
when the elegant and "good-looking" (16) haiku editor of the *Mainichi
Shimbun* stops by the Hayashi farm to deliver Tome's first prize won
in a haiku competition sponsored by the newspaper, it is Tome who
defies her traditional role of a submissive wife by inviting him to have
tea with her and expound haiku theories while she knows that her
husband wants her to be out in the hot sun packing tomatoes. Tome's
crossover into the male realm of self-assertion not only causes spousal
jealousy, since both men with whom she discusses haiku are handsome
and strong, but also undermines patriarchal control, a stance not to be
tolerated for too long. In fact, Tome's poetic venture has lasted only
three months, exactly the lifespan of the flower signified by her pen
name.

In traversing the gender boundary, Tome is seen as involving
herself in some illicit activity, an activity possessing a validity
independent of the woman's prescribed social roles. As Stan Yogi
notes, "An *Issei* woman's primary concern was to provide for the well-
being of her family. In this context, *Issei* women's efforts at self-
fulfillment outside the boundaries of family and community necessarily
become rebellions against cultural standards" (131). Women's natural
desires and yearnings, if they are not in compliance with accepted social
norms, are viewed as subversive and must be suppressed at all cost.
Even the *nisei* daughter in her own awakening sexuality must hide her
desires under cover of some necessary bodily needs. Twice in
expectation of meeting her lover, Jesus Carrasco, Rosie has to use the

pretense of going to the *benjo*, or the privy, an activity regarded as necessary rather than extravagant. Meeting one's lover without the sanction of marriage, just like writing poetry, which infringes upon the male mode of articulation, would be considered extravagant and therefore forbidden. As Sau-ling Cynthia Wong observes, "An underlying relationship—a Freudian influence, conscious or unconscious, is detectable here—has been posited between artistic creativity and erotic desire: both are presented as manifestations of an extravagant spirit, flouting the counsel of a socially defined, rational calculus" (169).

In her refusal to be totally subsumed in the confines of her life as wife, mother, and laborer, Tome asserts her individual identity by continuing her haiku-writing and discussing poetic theories whenever possible with men who also share her creative passion. Inevitably her persistent pursuit of an identity other than the culturally prescribed one incurs her husband's anger, although he suppresses his feelings, as expected of the male in Japanese culture. However, in the climactic scene when the elegant Mr. Kuroda, the haiku editor, appears in the midst of a pressing tomato harvest to present Tome with her first prize award, a *Hirosege* print, Tome defies her expected wifely role of subservience by boldly inviting the haiku expert inside the house alone for tea and rapt poetry discussion. Evidently stunned by jealousy and humiliated by his wife's ignoring his command to return immediately to the tomato field, Mr. Hayashi emits an angry cry to Rosie: "Ha, your mother's crazy!" (17). And furthermore, when Tome continues to disobey her husband's command, the patriarchal voice reverberates with explosive rage, "exactly like the cork of a bottle popping" (17). With the force of a whirlwind, he stalks angrily into the house, chases the haiku editor out, smashes the picture, and burns the wreckage, making "sure that his act of cremation was irrevocable" (18). While Mr. Hayashi is enforcing his patriarchal authority over a disobedient subject, the act of his violence, however, traumatizes mother and daughter so much that it ironically joins them together in a moment of epiphany: "Rosie ran . . . toward the house. What had become of her mother? She burst into the parlor and found her mother at the back window watching the dying fire. They watched together until there remained only a feeble smoke under the blazing sun. Her mother was very calm" (18).

Tome's uncanny calmness reveals the depth of her desolation as she silently watches the last ember of her creativity smoldering before her eyes. The frightening violence inflicted on her psyche, in spite of an apparent calmness, serves to catapult her to break the silence that has hitherto separated mother and daughter emotionally. In a torrent of confession, Tome pours out her frustrated desires and tragic loss. Instead of confining her intense emotions in seventeen-syllabled haikus, she is set free to articulate her feelings openly by telling her daughter the painful events in her young life when she suffered desertion by a socially superior lover, still-birth of an illegitimate son, exile and rejection from home and family, not to mention the suffocation that she has endured in a loveless marriage. In a dramatic moment of self-revelation,

> suddenly, her mother knelt on the floor and took her by the wrists. "Rosie," she said urgently, "Promise me you will never marry!" Shocked more by the request than the revelation, Rosie stared at her mother's face, Jesus, Jesus, she called silently, not certain whether she was invoking the help of the son of the Carrascos or of God, until there returned sweetly the memory of Jesus' hand, how it had touched her and where. Still her mother waited for an answer, holding her wrists so tightly that her hands were going numb. She tried to pull free. Promise, her mother whispered fiercely, promise. Yes, yes, I promise, Rosie said. . . . Rosie, covering her face, began at last to cry, and the embrace and consoling hand came much later than she expected. (19)

In this powerful concluding paragraph, Yamamoto conjoins mother and daughter with such a force that neither can ever be as insulated, complacent, and indifferent as before; for better or worse, both lives have gone through a transformation from silence and passivity to articulation and self-discovery. In response to her mother's bitter insistence "Promise me you will never marry!" Rosie couches her affirmative answer in an invocation to her lover, Jesus, and feels poignantly the sweet memory of his hand, "how it had touched her and where." With the mother's newfound voice and the daughter's awakening sexuality, both are embarking on a path where they can share the pain and joy of a life, though still full of continued ambiguity and strife, that promises unchartered possibilities.

The possibilities may not necessarily lead to complete individual freedom, for Rosie's response to her mother's desperate plea still sounds as feigned and as glib as her earlier reaction to her mother's haiku. The two women are, however, joined together in that epiphanic moment through suffering and love to combat their uncertain future. The patriarchy, which has thus far shackled Tome's struggle for self-fulfillment, may dominate her yet in the guise of another patriarchal culture represented by Jesus's Mexican heritage, if Rosie proceeds in her sexual dalliance with Jesus. Furthermore, Rosie's continued relationship with Jesus, whose family works as seasonal field hands for the Hayashis, may also strike a class issue like that which ended Tome's pursuit of happiness with her socially superior Japanese lover. Will Rosie share a similar fate or will she rise above culture and class to determine her own destiny? With the changing circumstances, particularly her newfound knowledge of her mother's tragic past, a painful knowledge that could free her from the innocence of childhood, and her own emerging vision of the multiplicity of human reactions, Rosie may indeed take an alternative path contrary to her mother's despite the tyranny of class and culture.

Yamamoto further explores the repression of women in "The Legend of Miss Sasagawara," a story originally published in *Kenyon Review* in 1950, just one year after the publication of "Seventeen Syllables." Like Tome Hayashi, who must struggle to break out of the silence of the prisonhouse of her passionless marriage, Mari Sasagawara also has the personal need to assert her individuality in an environment that seeks to deny it. The story is told from the point of view of a twenty-year-old narrator, Kiku, a fellow inmate at Poston internment camp. To this vast bleak prisonhouse of "wind, sand, and heat" where individuality is an anathema and conformity a virtue for 15,000 inmates, Mari Sasagawara, a strikingly beautiful ballet dancer, has lately arrived with her Buddhist priest father from another internment camp after the death there of her mother. Her finely decorative and flamboyant appearance, a sharp contrast to the drabness of the camp environment, arouses suspicion and perhaps even undue jealousy:

> Her daily costume, brief and fitting closely to her trifling waist, generously billowing below, and bringing together arrestingly rich colors like mustard yellow and forest green, appeared to have been cut from a coarse-textured homespun; her shining hair was so long it wound twice about her head to form a coronet; her face was delicate and pale, with a fine nose, pouting bright mouth, and glittering eyes; and her measured walk said, "Look, I'm walking!"

as though walking were not a common but a rather special thing to be doing. (20)

Being perceived as aloof and eccentric—in brief, as an "Other"—Mari responds accordingly by withdrawing herself further from family and community. Her self-imposed isolation and unconventional behavior, in turn, cause the spread of gossip, which in time drives her "insane" and finally confines her to an asylum. After the war, the narrator Kiku, while doing research for her studies at college, discovers a published poem by Mari Sasagawara, which exposes the poet's own voice describing the agony of her struggle at the internment camp where she had to live so closely with a spiritual man who was completely devoid of human emotions. Kiku makes it quite clear that the man described in the poem resembles the Reverend Sasagawara:

> This man was certainly noble, the poet wrote, this man was beyond censure. The world was doubtless enriched by his presence. But say that someone else, someone sensitive, someone admiring, someone who had not achieved this sublime condition and who did not wish to, were somehow called to companion such a man. Was it not likely that the saint, blissfully bent on cleansing from his already radiant soul the last imperceptible blemishes . . . would be deaf and blind to the human passions rising, subsiding, and again rising perhaps in anguished silence, within the selfsame room? The poet could not speak for others, of course; she could only speak for herself. But she would describe this man's devotion as a sort of madness, the monstrous sort which, pure of itself, might possibly bring troublous, scented scenes to recur in the other's sleep. (33)

Mari's revelation of her daily claustrophobic existence in the camp cubicle with her father, whose devotional fanaticism stifles her passionate yearnings for self-expression, uncovers the root of her sexual and artistic frustration. In spite of his love for his daughter, Reverend Sasagawara is apparently blind to both the physical and psychological suffering of his daughter. As if human affairs were beneath his concern, he is described as wearing "perpetually an air of bemusement, never talking directly to a person, as though, being what he was, he could not stop for an instant his meditation on the higher life" (22). During several of Mari's admissions to the local hospital, the other-worldly father was noticeably absent leaving her totally alone under the intense gaze of strangers. The more she insists on her privacy, the more eccentric the internees seem to regard her. Though both father and daughter maintain a certain distance from the Japanese-American community, their aloofness would be judged differently on account of gender. As Cheung aptly observes, "It is not surprising . . . that the Reverend's blankness is deemed lofty and religious, while the daughter's similar expression is considered unfriendly and unhealthy. His attitude is respected, hers suspected" (57).

From the very moment Mari arrives in the camp environment, she refuses to regard it as just normal communal living by choosing not to eat with the rest of the internees in the mess hall but to take her meals in the privacy of her own cubicle. Not only eating alone, she also chooses to take her shower in privacy in the middle of the night when nobody else is using the public showers. When she first moves into the barracks with her father, Mr. Sasaki, a coinhabitant of the same barracks, offers to clean up the dust-ridden place with a hose. Instead of accepting the offer with gratitude as expected, Mari looks upon it as an unwanted intrusion of her privacy and therefore screams at him: "What are you trying to do? Spy on me?" (21). Her insistence on personal privacy is viewed as antisocial and earns her the name "madwoman" from Mr. Sasaki, whose opinion of her mental aberration is thus spread far and wide beyond their crowded barracks.

In her effort to protect her privacy, Mari runs afoul of the gender expectations of her community and is consequently encircled by its critical gaze. The fact that she is an unmarried thirty-nine-year-old woman, still strikingly beautiful, is enough to set her apart from a society that views a woman as a daughter, a wife, and a mother. Aside from her single status, that she has spent the prime of her life in a highly adventurous and globe-trotting career as a ballerina also sets her further apart from the rest of the internees, who are likely to see her as an outsider, an object of idle gossip: "If Miss Sasagawara was not one to speak to, she was certainly one to speak of, and she came up quite often as topic for the endless conversations which helped along the monotonous days" (22). The more they whisper about her, the closer she appears to them to be the stereotypical spinster with notorious idiosyncracies. One rumor is told by Mrs. Sasaki, who happens to catch Mari watching several teenage boys, the Yoshinagas, play basketball. Mrs. Sasaki claims that the dancer was so transfixed by the boys' playfulness that she scolded Mari by announcing "What's the matter with you, watching boys like that? You're old enough to be their mother!" (31).

The sequel to this episode is then told by one of the boys, Joe Yoshinaga, who claims that he was awakened one night to find Mari sitting silently by his bedside, "her long hair all undone and flowing about her. She was dressed in a white nightgown and her hands were clasped on her lap. And all she was doing was sitting there watching him" (31).

These oral accounts, however reliable or unreliable, reveal a woman desperately struggling against an overwhelming oppression of mind and spirit in an atmosphere of mass conformity. As a dancer, Mari may derive a special pleasure in observing the rhythmic motions of boys playing basketball or marveling at the mysterious stillness when someone is asleep. Who is to say that she is wrong when she is just expressing her artistic yearnings in watching the Yoshinaga boys at play or at rest? Kiku, "who had so newly had some contact with the recorded explorations into the virgin territory of the human mind," offers her analysis: "Miss Sasagawara had no doubt looked upon Joe Yoshinaga as the image of either the lost lover or the lost son" (32). Even Kiku's newfound psychological probe, however superficial, reflects the prevailing patriarchal attitude that women are somewhat incomplete without the presence of men—sons and lovers—in their lives. Yet much due to her youth and flexibility, unlike the other internees who all seem to know what is wrong with the dancer, Kiku at least admits that she could be mistaken by qualifying her previous observation: "My words made me uneasy by their glibness" (32). Whether she is mistaken or not, the community's unsolicited intrusions inevitably cause Mari to feel hypersensitive in her reaction and even more withdrawn from the community. With tragic consequences, her apparently disturbing behavior leads to her permanent confinement in an asylum.

We are thus confronted with the question of insanity: Is Mari insane or are those who accept the life of the camps insane? As Shoshana Felman has pointed out, female defiance of gender roles is often interpreted as mental deviance (6-7). We cannot help but wonder whether the dancer—judged deviant by the community for not behaving "normally" under custody—is any more peculiar than Kiku and her friend Elsie, who cherish their "good old days" in camp; or than her father, who upon his imprisonment "felt free for the first time in his long life" because since "circumstances made it unnecessary for him to earn a competitive living," he could then "concentrate on that serene, eight-fold path of highest understanding, highest mindedness, highest speech, highest action, highest livelihood, highest recollectedness, highest endeavor, and highest meditation" (32-33).

In an interview with Charles L. Crow, Yamamoto reiterated that "she didn't really consider her [Mari Sasagawara] insane . . . I tried to say that if it weren't for being put in the camp, she might have gone on" (81). As Fredric Jameson has commented, Third World texts "necessarily project a political dimension in the form of a national allegory" (69). Cheung also points out that "The politics of the time not only contributes directly to Miss Sasagawara's distress but also figures indirectly at the allegorical level of the story. The congestion at camp intensifies the gaze on Miss Sasagawara and accelerates the spread of gossip. As an allegory, the scandal-loving and finger-pointing community has a counterpart in the white majority, who allowed themselves to be swayed by prejudice and hearsay into endorsing the imprisonment of an entire people" (65). Moreover, the mainstream press, politicians of all stripes, patriotic organizations, and "voices from farming interests" have all clamored for the removal of the Japanese (Takaki 389). The isolation and ultimate internment of Japanese Americans clearly have their parallels in the exclusion and final institutionalization of Mari Sasagawara.

As transparent as the political allegory appears to the reader, Yamamoto, however, does not directly criticize the Japanese-American community nor openly condemn the existing racist hysteria; she simply dramatizes the title character in her personal reactions to the external circumstances, some of which include an utterly passionless and obsessively spiritual father, a relentlessly rumor-mongering community, and a claustrophobic surrounding that stifles individual difference. As a strong-willed, independent woman and artist, Mari perhaps exhibits the only appropriate response to the oppressive circumstances; her insistence on individual selfhood, which, in the community's view, reeks of "madness," is no more than a gesture of refusal to accept blind conformity and massive tyranny. By writing her poem, signed by "an evacuee from the West Coast making her home in a War Relocation center in Arizona" (32), which Yamamoto aptly places at the conclusion of the story, Mari unleashes her own voice, challenges our earlier perceptions of madness and saintliness and makes us wonder who really was the guilty party during those "years of infamy" when Japanese Americans became "the victims of gossip, their own and the nation's" (Chan et al. 29). In refusing to go along with the status quo and in asserting her own voice in the haunting poem, Mari provides a platform for a critique of conventional gender expectations in a patriarchal culture. Despite her double incarceration, first in a War Relocation center and then in a state mental institution, the voice of Mari Sasagawara continues to reverberate with an "erratically brilliant" (32) tone that unlocks human passion and negates society's intolerance of individual differences.

Both Tome Hayashi and Mari Sasagawara are passionate women who refuse to adhere to the traditional roles for women and remain submissive. Although their disobedience fails to bring them the self-fulfillment they seek, their efforts are not totally futile. In taking a course of action that is directly contrary to the prescribed female roles, they articulate through newly released voices and bear witness to the primacy of individual feelings and the complexity of human desires and dreams.

WORKS CITED

Chan, Jeffery Paul, et al. "Resources of Chinese and Japanese American Literary Traditions." *Amerasia Journal* 8.1 (1981): 19-31.

Cheung, King-Kok. *Articulate Silences: Hisaye Yamamoto, Maxine Hong Kingston, Joy Kogawa.* Ithaca and London: Cornell University Press, 1993.

Crow, Charles L. "A *MELUS* Interview: Hisaye Yamamoto." *MELUS* 14.1 (1987): 73-84.

Felman, Shoshana. "Women and Madness: The Critical Phallacy." *Feminisms: An Anthology of Literary Theory and Criticism.* Ed. Robyn R. Warhol and Diane P. Herndl. New Brunswick, N.J.: Rutgers University Press, 1997. 7-20.

Jameson, Fredric. "Third-World Literature in the Era of Multinational Capitalism." *Social Text* 15 (1986): 65-88.

Takaki, Ronald. *Strangers from a Different Shore: A History of Asian Americans.* Boston: Little, Brown, 1989.

Wong, Sau-ling Cynthia. *Reading Asian American Literature: From Necessity to Extravagance.* Princeton, N.J.: Princeton Univ. Press, 1993.

Yamamoto, Hisaye. *Seventeen Syllables and Other Stories.* New York: Kitchen Table Press, 1988.

Yogi, Stan. "Rebels and Heroines: Subversive Narratives in the Stories of Wakako Yamauchi and Hisaye Yamamoto." *Reading the Literature of Asian America.* Ed. Shirley Geok-lin Lim and Amy Ling. Philadelphia: Temple University Press, 1992. 131-150.

CHAPTER 6

Afrekete Rising

Two Coming-out Stories by African-American Lesbians: Pat Suncircle's "A Day's Growth" and Audre Lorde's "The Beginning"

M. Charlene Ball

Audre Lorde and other lesbian authors of color, by drawing on and re-visioning both non-Western and Eurocentric mythic material, are creating new patterns for women's narratives. Both European and African mythic patterns structure two coming-out stories by African-American lesbian authors: "A Day's Growth" (1977) by Pat Suncircle and "The Beginning" (1981) by Audre Lorde (the Lorde story, slightly altered, forms Chapters 18 and 19 of *Zami: A New Spelling of My Name* [1982]). The Greek myth of Demeter and Kore (Persephone) informs both stories; in addition, the West African trickster Esu-Elegbara figures in each. Yet neither European nor African content adequately accounts for these stories' renderings of African-American lesbian experience nor for their mythic power. Another figure is needed to complete the pattern. This figure is Afrekete, Audre Lorde's creation in *Zami*.

The coming-out story has been dismissed by some anthologists with the implication that such narratives are of little literary interest. Margaret Reynolds, in her introduction to *The Penguin Book of Lesbian Short Stories* (1997), says that coming-out stories "always cover the same ground" (xxvi). It might be pointed out that men's coming-of-age stories (regardless of sexual orientation) frequently cover the same ground; yet this family resemblance does not discredit them but makes them "universal." Women's writing, as Joanna Russ points out—especially writing that rejects patriarchal structures and images—

gets marginalized and dismissed again and again on the basis of what Russ calls "the double standard of content"; critics judge "one set of experiences [men's]" as being "more valuable and important than the other [women's]" (40).

The coming-out story, as Bonnie Zimmerman has shown, is a branch of the quest narrative, in particular the *Bildungsroman* or coming-of-age story (34-35). Zimmerman says that the lesbian hero, like the male hero of quest narrative, "is marked as special from birth, undergoes journeys and adventures, sometimes conquers" (60). She may have to descend to an underworld and suffer real or metaphoric imprisonment or death. She does, however, usually succeed in escaping and growing up rather than "growing down," in Annis Pratt's words— the usual fate for heterosexual female heroes (14).

While a number of lesbian narratives do follow the pattern of the male hero's quest narrative, the pattern of the male hero's journey often fails to account for crucial elements in women's coming-of-age narratives. Meredith A. Powers suggests a different pattern for women's heroism, seeing interdependency and connections among women as characterizing the quest of a female hero (36-37). The myth of Demeter and Kore (Persephone) is interesting to feminists since it describes a woman-centered quest. Annis Pratt has noted that this myth occurs frequently in fiction by women (170). Powers sees the Demeter-Persephone myth as an alternative to the more usual (male) quest in that the women heroes are assisted by a network of other women. This myth, which appears in its earliest written form in the seventh-century B.C.E. Homeric *Hymn to Demeter*, partially conceals earlier pre-Hellenic (matriarchal or matrilineal) mythic material under a patriarchal surface. Jung observes that the Demeter-Kore myth "bears all the features of a matriarchal order of society" (203). Helene P. Foley notes that the *Hymn to Demeter* places "special emphasis on female experience" (103) and "represent[s] a genuine challenge to . . . patriarchal politics" (114).

The *Hymn to Demeter* recounts the myth of Demeter, the Great Goddess, and her search for her daughter Kore. It is the story of the death and resurrection of a young girl, abducted and raped on the brink of adulthood. That she can return to earth at all is due to the persistence of her mother, disenfranchised but still powerful. Demeter is assisted in her search by other female figures who are also aspects of the pre-Hellenic Goddess: Gaia or Earth; Rhea, mother of Demeter; and Hecate (in some myths called a daughter of Demeter). Demeter,

Kore/Persephone, and Hecate also form the triad of Mother, Maiden, and Crone, three aspects of every woman (36-37). Powers notes that although the patriarch Zeus remains in control, "a complex power is still associated with the goddess, a power related to the mother-child dyad" (35).

Coming-out narratives bear a special relationship to the Demeter/Kore myth since coming out is often symbolized in lesbian narrative as a return to the mother. Zimmerman says that lesbians of color and Jewish lesbians in particular use maternal images as "sources of personal and collective identity. . . . [They] connect the protagonist to her racial and sexual heritage" (191). Although coming out in lesbian narratives may be symbolically represented as a return to the mother, the mother-daughter relationship described is likely to be problematic. The mother is frequently absent, dead, or estranged from her daughter. "My mother had turned into a demon intent on destroying me," Audre Lorde writes ("The Beginning" 267). Pat Suncircle's young hero Leslie lives with an aunt, her mother being dead. With the mother estranged or absent, a young woman is, like Kore, vulnerable and threatened.

Young women are frequently in danger in patriarchal culture. C. G. Jung observes that "[t]he maiden's helplessness exposes her to all sorts of *dangers*" (184; Jung's emphasis). In *Death and the Maiden* (1989), Ken Dowden shows that in ancient Greek culture, the initiation of young girls into adulthood was linked with images of death and sacrifice (2-4). A recent sociological study of adolescent girls, *Reviving Ophelia* (1994), has documented how young women are still threatened psychically and physically, despite changes brought by the women's movement (Pipher passim). Young lesbians are threatened as much or more than other young women; and young African-American lesbians are three times at risk: as young women, as lesbians, and as blacks.

In coming-out narratives, the lesbian hero of color is not rescued by her mother. She typically leaves her family of origin and her mother to find a lover or lovers and a community of women who become her spiritual mothers. This interdependency among women is crucial to her survival. Audre Lorde writes: "Interdependency between women is the only way to the freedom which allows the 'I' to 'be,' not in order to be used, but in order to be creative" ("The Master's Tools" 111). The lover, the lesbian friend, or the lesbian community help the lesbian hero as Demeter and Kore are helped by Hecate, Rhea, and Gaia.

Yet how can this European myth suffice as a framework for the narrative of a lesbian of color? While white feminist critics must avoid the racist and ethnocentric assumption that black and white women share the same experience, we must also not fall into the reverse error of assuming that the two have nothing in common. Lorde has challenged white women to look beyond Eurocentric archetypal experience and to "re-member what is dark and ancient and divine within yourself that aids your speaking," reminding us that "[t]he oppression of women knows no ethnic nor racial boundaries . . . [n]or do the reservoirs of our ancient power know differences" ("An Open Letter to Mary Daly" 70). By drawing from and revising both European and African mythic material, Lorde clears a space not only to bring in African myth but to begin to redefine European myth in ways more consonant with all women's experience. She is deliberately inclusive; as AnaLouise Keating says, "[Lorde's] revisionist mythmaking offers women of all races an image of ancient female wisdom and strength which empowers them to put their differences into words and create networks connecting them to other women" ("Making 'our shattered faces whole'" 31).

Images of women in European narrative are often incomplete, broken—mirroring the brokenness of women's experience and women's selves under patriarchy. Keating says that Lorde and other nonwhite women authors decentralize and deprivilege European myths and "reject the false images of women embodied in phallocentric (white) narratives" (Myth Smashers" 76). I would argue, however, that these European myths are not so much false as truncated, partial. The images of women in the Demeter/Kore myth describe parts of women's experience under patriarchy. These parts are separation from the mother, separation from other women, and separation from oneself. As Kore is separated from her mother, so is Demeter separated from her own youthful, innocent aspect. The European myths tell what is and what has been in some women's experience, but not necessarily what will be or what has to be.

So although the Demeter-Kore myth partially structures both stories, it is not adequate to account for them. Another figure needs to enter the narrative; another story must intersect with this one to bring the myth back to its beginnings and to bring the African-American lesbian hero back to her origins. Esu-Elegbara, the West African trickster god, appears in African-American literature in a number of guises, as Henry Louis Gates, Jr. has shown (8-88). Esu, who appears in the oral narrative traditions of the Yoruba of Nigeria, the Fon of Benin, and other black cultures, is the messenger and translator of the gods. Esu represents "individuality, satire, parody, irony, magic, indeterminacy, openendedness, ambiguity, sexuality . . . disruption and reconciliation, betrayal and loyalty, closure and disclosure, encasement and rupture" (6). Ayodele Ogundipe calls Esu "the Yoruba god of chance and uncertainty" and compares him to the Greek Hermes; each is a "wayfarer, god of the countryside and god of the roads. . . . Like Hermes . . . Esu lives outdoors, at the crossroads, and at entrances to houses and cities" (229-30). He also stands at the crux between genders, being both male and female (172-78).

A female figure who appears in *Zami* is Afrekete. Afrekete represents, as Keating and Kara Provost have pointed out, Lorde's re-visioning of Esu-Elegbara (Keating, "Making 'our shattered faces whole'" 27; Provost 46). In a powerful act of imaginative theological re-creation, Lorde has renamed Esu—who is androgynous to begin with—as Afrekete. The name *Afrekete* appears to come from a nickname given to Legba (Esu's trickster counterpart in Fon mythology)—*Aflakete*, meaning I have tricked you" (Pelton 72). By this name, Lorde gives a feminine face to the trickster, linguist, and mediator between gods and humans. Thus she envisions as her guide a goddess as powerful as Demeter but not limited to maternity nor to earth and grain, possessing youth and freshness like Kore but not vulnerable and prone to sacrifice. This goddess, like Esu-Elegbara, embodies the power of language and its creative manipulation. Joanne Braxton points out that a female trickster figure often appears in African-American women's writing and notes how this character's "sass and impertinence . . . [and] use of disguise and concealment, and of trickery and wit" help her to keep her self-esteem and to overcome adversaries (30). Lorde's Afrekete stands in this tradition of African-American female tricksters. She is the "youngest daughter" of MawuLisa: youngest since latest-named; she is the "mischievous linguist, trickster, best-beloved, whom we must all become" (*Zami* 255).

In both "A Day's Growth" and "The Beginning," Afrekete stands at the crux of a young lesbian's rite of passage into adulthood. The hero in each story descends into an "underworld" of threats, violation, and danger. She is spiritually mothered by several women. The nurturance they provide is partial yet significant. Lorde notes that an "either/or model of nurturing" is patriarchal and alien to black lesbian experience ("The Master's Tools" 111). Yet despite their limitations, these women provide self-sufficient, women-loving images that help the heroes make their spiritual escapes and find means of survival. Their survival is related to learning to signify, name, and dissemble. Afrekete stands at the threshold as their guide, helping them to cross over by teaching them to manipulate the power of language. Claiming this power—one that belongs particularly to Afrekete—enables the African-American lesbian hero to survive, name herself, and join forces with other black lesbians.

In Pat Suncircle's "A Day's Growth," a young girl grows from Kore to Afrekete, from vulnerable girl-child to trickster, in the course of a day. I define this story as a coming-out story although no sexual experience occurs, since coming out can mean acknowledging one's lesbianism, naming oneself as a woman-identified woman, or choosing to identify with a community of women-identified women. In "A Day's Growth," Leslie undergoes a symbolic descent to an "underworld" and comes out by asserting her identity and naming herself. Like the Kore archetype described by Jung, fifteen-year-old Leslie appears as an "unknown young girl," rebellious and isolated (184). She feels insubstantial, invisible, ghostlike: "I pulled off my shoes and socks and walked like a ghost down the stairs . . . through the darkness" (8). In her isolation, Leslie searches for mother-figures to assist her in her passage to adulthood. Miss Katheryn and Miss Renita, two women who live together down the street, fascinate her; she suspects she and they have some secret in common. The women have "quiet-appearing expressions" and wear "tailored suits"; they are "the only women on the block whose voices I didn't hear straining out the names of children." Leslie soaks up their "cool breeze presence," chanting over and over: "I am fifteen and I want to be like Miss Katheryn. I'm fifteen and I want to be like Miss Renita" (3).

Leslie's Aunt Cynthia, with whom she lives, gives her no help in her maturation process. Aunt Cynthia is unmarried; her name reflects the virgin goddess of the moon. But she is no Artemis; she is virgin but devoted to the male, white, Christian god. Aunt Cynthia prays for Leslie and pressures the girl about attending a revival and making a profession of faith—"it's time to make your choice for the Lord"—adding, "You know I love you and I don't want to see you lost" (9). Ironically, Leslie is "lost" and searching for what neither Aunt Cynthia nor the church can give her. Leslie has gotten into trouble with Aunt

Cynthia by bringing home a white girl she has met at a school dance and dancing with her to loud music in her room: "I danced with her like the whole world was watching and I was fifteen and bad and yeah! dancing with a girl . . . danced when we got to my room and couldn't think of anything to say danced through the silence between the records as fast as hard as we could high as platforms and adidas could take us stomping down kicking around around around" (4).

Jung describes the Kore figure as a dancer (184). Whenever Leslie is bored and restless, she turns on her record player and dances: "If I could I would . . . turn it up as high as James [Brown] could scream and go crazy . . . dance flinging my body . . . sling the shit against my walls for everybody to see . . . shadow boxing with the spirit . . . slinging away opponents so ugly they can't be seen and they sure can't be described in the English language dance and look good dance and chunk it away feel good dance" (8). Leslie can dance, but she has not yet found her voice. The English language is insufficient for her experience since at this point in her life it is the language of school and of the prayers her aunt prays over her.

On the evening of the dreaded revival, Leslie puts on her church dress and walks barefoot out to "where the country [creeps] in" (6). Leaning on a fence, she fantasizes about dancing on a beach with Miss Renita: "We're out on a beach and the portable radio sets in the sand. . . . Miss Renita . . . holds me against her with the look I sometimes notice in her smokey grey eyes, mischievous and a bit sad" (6).

Miss Renita is "grey-eyed" like Athena, the virgin goddess of wisdom and crafts who wears armor and protects her city. Although reduced in classical literature to a sexless, obedient daughter of the patriarchal Zeus, Athena still retains her identity as an image of female competence and protection. Leslie falls into a fantasy that combines erotic feeling with a child's yearning to be held by her mother: "sweet and warm and rock me . . . quiet and warm as I'm held between sleep and daylight all night long baby . . ." (6). As Leslie daydreams, instead of Hades rising out of the earth to abduct her, an unpleasant memory rises up. She has witnessed an intoxicated man accost Miss Katheryn and Miss Renita at the bus stop. He calls out to the women, "Ain't you got time for no man?" He refers to them as "men," and addresses them by male forms, calling them "Mr. Katheryn" and "Mr. Renita" (6).

The man's homophobic attack can be understood as taking place within the African-American tradition of signifying. This term covers a variety of linguistic rituals, games, and strategies: "marking, loud-talking, testifying, calling out (of one's name), sounding, rapping, playing the dozens, and so on" (Gates 52). It can range from highly structured verbal games to speaking in a veiled, indirect way (Mitchell-Kernan 311). Roger D. Abrahams emphasizes its element of ridicule; it is "the trickster's ability to talk with great innuendo, to carp, cajole, needle, and lie. . . . making fun of a person or situation (51-52). One may signify in order to cause "feelings of embarrassment, shame, frustration, or futility, [or] to diminish someone's status" as Thomas Kochman notes; in such cases, "the tactic employed is direct in the form of a taunt" (Kochman 32; qtd. in Mitchell-Kernan 312). The man's signifying certainly causes embarrassment and shame while diminishing the women's status. His taunting is like a verbal form of rape. He has "called them out of their names"—giving them wrong names ("Mr.") that are honorific when used to address men but degrading and humiliating when applied to women.

He escalates his attack by pointing to Leslie and saying, "You want that delicate youngblood over there, don't you?" (7). The descriptor for Leslie ("delicate") is both accurate and demeaning, since its use implies a level of intimacy between the speaker and the addressee that does not and cannot exist in these circumstances. Also, the man has "loud-talked" Leslie, referred to her in an indirect way that makes it impossible for her to respond directly and defend herself (Gates 77). He has used a word that is innocuous—"delicate" is no insult—yet in this context the word implies and mocks Leslie's vulnerability. "Youngblood," an African-American term for a young black person, ordinarily positive, becomes in this context an attack upon Leslie since it stresses her youth and is more often used to refer to males (Major 519). The man has perceived Leslie's youthful lesbian passion by naming her as a young man and is exposing it to humiliate her. Leslie is delicate and young, vulnerable, not able to defend herself. "Blood" suggests her lifeblood and her passion. The man's using the word "blood" in this context suggests mockery, and also sacrifice and vulnerability. Leslie's blood has been metaphorically spilled like the Kore's.

The man continues to taunt the women, combining masculine and feminine terms of address: "Mr. Renita with the lipstick," referring to the small size of their breasts: "Hey, Mr. Katheryn with the 32 triple

A" (7). He refers to their "mannish" clothes: "Hey, Mr. Renita in the tailored suit" (7). A tailored suit is a masculine uniform, appropriate for men but not for women. Miss Renita has stepped out of her place by wearing it. Finally the women get away, and Leslie goes home, in her mind "conjur[ing] up tortures too heinous for words" like a budding queen of the underworld (7).

Negative though it be, the man's signifying has a significant effect. By loud-talking Leslie, the man has linked her with Miss Katheryn and Miss Renita. And although he has made public Leslie's secret longings, he has also by naming them revealed them to her. So his function is double-edged, double-tongued. He persecutes Leslie, yet gives her the gift of naming her longing and herself. Signifying bears a special relationship to Esu. In this story, the man plays the role of Esu in that he, as Robert Pelton says, "destroys normal communication . . . bring[s] men [sic] outside ordinary discourse, . . . speak[s] a new word and . . . disclose[s] a deeper grammar to them" (Pelton 163). He is present at moments of revelation: "at the moment of an enlargement that is also a transformation of non-sense to sense, of impasse to passage, the Yoruba see Esu" (143). Like Esu, the unknown and unnamed man "destroys normal communication." (Of course, in another sense he is behaving all too "normally" for men in our culture.) Although what he does is not desirable, he "disclose[s] a deeper grammar" and "speak[s] a new word" to Leslie. He names what has previously been unnamed, and in doing so he "transform[s] . . . non-sense to sense . . . impasse to passage" as Esu does.

And there are many Esus. To the Yoruba, each person has an Esu or inner power: "[a]n individual's Esu is an immense power to be summoned, a medicine of supernatural power" (Gates 37). Leslie, too, has her own "Esu." But she cannot summon this power within herself as yet. The experience has reduced Leslie to a state of despair. Later that evening before the revival, she slips out of the house and down the street, finding herself in front of Miss Katheryn's and Miss Renita's house. Lost in musing, she looks up and sees someone coming. She panics and darts under a hedge.

At this point, Leslie reaches the bottom of her despair and experiences a spiritual crisis: "What if I were wrong? What if I did have more than my aunt to fear?" (9). The experience Carol P. Christ calls "nothingness" has overwhelmed her: the emptiness women feel when they first encounter the definition of themselves under patriarchy

(*Diving Deep and Surfacing* 13-14; "Spiritual Quest and Women's Experience" 228-245). This experience of nothingness parallels the "dark night" that mystics of many religions have described.

Leslie's eyes rest on the house. "Dark brick with an upstairs, not different from most others on the street," it reflects the care and attention of its owners. The yard, "small and hedged" has beds of "primrose and Black Vesuvius in Geometric designs." The juxtaposition of "primrose," "Black," and "Vesuvius" suggest delicate beauty beside a hint of volcano, representing the controlled and disciplined passion of the black women who live there. Control and discipline are what Leslie needs desperately, not the repression of the church and Aunt Cynthia, but the knowledge of how to direct and focus her intense emotions creatively and meaningfully. "Vesuvius" also suggests "Venus," the Roman goddess of sexual love. This house is a shrine of the Black Venus.

Leslie's experience of nothingness reaches its nadir: "I would never go to their door now. . . . I felt tired like I had been dancing tied to the earth" (9). She hides in the hedge until she hears no more voices or cars. Then she slips around to the side of the house and peers in a window. Seeing that the women are not at home, she takes her time looking at the room. She is struck by how familiar and comfortable the room seems: "The room which faced me resembled our front-room, only here the furniture matched" (9). She gazes in admiration at the dark red color of the carpet and upholstery, the "beautiful reddish-brown wood" of a rocking chair: "[t]he quietness made things hesitate, the redness warmly pulled them in" (10).

The stages Carol Christ describes as following nothingness are awakening, insight, and naming (*Diving Deep and Surfacing* 13-26). As Leslie mentally touches everything in the room, she experiences awakening as her previous fantasy world merges with this reality: "[t]he room floated into and out of some dreamscape, I appeared miraculously in one spot and then another and the two women were there with me and then they were not; we said things to each other and laughed and then listened for the echoes in the silence" (10). At the moment when Leslie sees herself as part of the world of Miss Renita and Miss Katheryn, she experiences insight, seeing that she is like these two women and can become a member of their community. Instead of a hopeless fantasy, she envisions a possible reality. All that she longs for is there: silence and peace, order and beauty, acceptance, companions like herself. Opposites happen at the same time: she is with and not with the women; she talks with them, yet exults in the silence. Leslie has found an image of a refuge, of a community to which she can belong. The room is womblike, with its red and cream colors; it is warm, vibrant, and sensual. "Statues and objects sitting around" are objects of beauty from another world suggesting antiquity—Africa, Egypt, Greece—a pagan world that antedates Christianity and white America.

When Leslie gets home the next morning, Aunt Cynthia, always mindful of appearances, scolds her, saying, "Look at that dress . . . Lord I hope nobody saw you looking like that" (10). But Leslie is unperturbed. She has fantasized earlier that "when the starships [return] they [will] all be driven by black women, seven feet tall" (4). She imagines the "Amazons" giving "naughty winks" to "all of the church women." When Leslie fantasized about dancing with Miss Renita, she imagined that the older woman "feels just like she looks in those lean, tailored suits" (6). So now Leslie signifies upon the man's previous signifying and answers coolly, "Everybody saw me. They looked at me like I was an Amazon in a tailored suit" (10).

Leslie has claimed the man's accusation, turned it inside out, signified upon it, and used it in her own trope. In signifying, Leslie renames herself. She is no longer Kore—vulnerable and helpless, hoping for rescue by Amazons; she is herself the Amazon. She emerges from her "underworld" experience with a strengthened sense of self and purpose gained by a vision of herself as the third in a triad of women with power—her first lesbian community. She has become the signifying woman: Afrekete, the feminine face of Esu.

Similarly, the young lesbian hero of Audre Lorde's "The Beginning" also descends to an underworld and finds her way back to life. Audre's mythic journey, like Leslie's, takes her from isolation to a community of women. She too descends into an underworld where she learns to dissemble and to name herself. Her self-naming results from her meeting with her first avatar of Afrekete.

Eighteen-year-old Audre fits Zimmerman's description of the lesbian hero; she is obviously "somebody important" or is going to be. She reads constantly on her coffee breaks and likes to be "the one who [knows] some fact that everybody else in the conversation had not yet learned" (260). Her style of dress, her attitude and manner make her sexuality more obvious than she realizes. She wears blue jeans and sneakers downtown, hates nylons, comments snidely on other women's subservient attitudes toward men, and hides her shyness under a tough, knowing manner. Though young, she has learned to suppress the Kore-qualities of vulnerability and openness.

As the story begins, Audre has left home and taken a job with Keystone Electronics, a factory that processes quartz crystals for use in radio and radar equipment. This Stygian place is "too cold and too hot, gritty, noisy, ugly, sticky, stinking, and dangerous. . . . The mud covered everything, cemented by the heavy oil that the diamond-grit blades were mounted in . . . [t]he air was heavy and acrid with . . . sickly fumes. . . . Entering the plant after 8:00 in the morning was like entering Dante's Inferno" (255). Audre quickly finds a guide and companion in Ginger, a mischievous, practical young woman who flirts easily with Audre, inviting her for coffee breaks, giving advice, and calling her a "slick kitty from the city" (258). (AnaLouise Keating has noted that "slick kitty" identifies Audre with Afrekete [*Women Reading Women Writing* 248].) Through Ginger, Audre gains knowledge about African-American history that she lacked (259).

Audre and Ginger run X-ray machines that read slices of quartz to determine their electrical charges. These X-ray machines expose their operators to low but constant dosages of radiation. The women are supposed to use shields to protect their hands from the X-rays, but to save precious time, they seldom flip the shields into place: "the second that it took to flip down the hood was often the difference between being yelled at for being too slow and a smooth working relationship with the cutters" (256). In this deadly atmosphere, Ginger exudes life and warmth like a latter-day Mother Goddess. Her very presence is larger than life—maternal and sexual at once. Lorde in an evocative description boldly celebrates the beauty of an ample, voluptuous female body type not acknowledged by twentieth-century white western culture. Ginger's "gorgeously fat" body invokes the goddesses of prehistory— the "Venus of Willendorf." Her "well-buttered caramel" skin suggests both nourishment and pleasure. She has the "high putchy cheeks and great mischievous smile" of a born trickster. Her hair images irrepressible vitality with its "crinkly mass" that stands out "alive and wavy." Her pageboy with straight bangs looks like "an Egyptian headpiece" (263). Lorde's description of Ginger places the other woman as non-Western, African, ancient, in touch with life-giving forces.

Pushed by Ginger, Audre comes out to herself as well as to another person for the first time. Ginger boldly queries: "Are you gay or aren't you?" Audre is taken aback: "I certainly couldn't say I don't know. . . . I could not bring myself to deny what I had just decided to embrace." She finally answers "Yes" (262). Lorde's description of their lovemaking is both comic and lyrical. Comic because of Audre's nervousness: "I lay with my eyes closed, wondering if I could pretend to be asleep, and, if not, what would be the sophisticated and dykely thing to do" (265). As for Ginger, "[s]he sat at her little desk-table, creaming her legs and braiding her hair, humming softly snatches of songs under her breath as she buffed her nails" (265). Ginger's delay is also due to nervousness, Audre later realizes: "this wasn't just playing around. . . . This was actually going to bed with a real live New York City Greenwich Village Bulldagger" (265). When they finally touch, the experience is lyrically described: "Our bodies found the movements we needed to fit each other. Ginger's flesh was sweet and moist and firm as a winter pear. I felt her and tasted her deeply. . . . Her flesh opened to me like a peony and the richness and wonder of her woman's pleasure brought me back to her body over and over again" (266).

Ginger, the Egyptian-haired Venus, Audre's first lover, is Afrekete-like in her mischief, her knowledge and willingness to impart knowledge, her young-black-woman pride. She gives Audre the missing piece of herself that causes the rest to make sense. Ginger is Audre's first avatar of Afrekete. Yet although Ginger has been guide and lover, she cannot provide Audre with maternal nurturing and guidance or function as a role model for her any more than Audre's own mother could. For Ginger assumes that their relationship will be temporary and plans eventually to marry a man. So Audre draws back emotionally from Ginger and quietly plans her escape from Keystone Electronics. Audre's toughness keeps her from staying where she does not need to be.

Knowing that she will not be able to earn any bonuses at Keystone if she works by the rules, Audre cheats. Her job, as noted earlier, requires her to read the electrical charges in crystals, using an x-ray machine. The number of crystals a worker gets credit for reading is counted by how many she picks up, but not by how many she turns in. So Audre picks up quantities of crystals, stuffs them into her socks, goes to the bathroom, chews them up and spits them out, and then flushes them down the toilet. Kore-like, Audre ingests crystals in lieu of pomegranate seeds, but unlike Kore she spits the crystals out instead of swallowing them. By appearing to read many more crystals than she actually does, she makes extra money. Thus she enables herself to get an unheard-of $40.00 in one week as a bonus and leave the factory. Not through the intervention of a goddess but through becoming the trickster herself, Audre releases herself from the underworld.

Audre becomes Afrekete, the trickster, by learning to dissemble in order to survive. Her coming out with Ginger has revealed to her the Afrekete part of herself. Afrekete, as the feminine face of Esu, is "double-mouthed" (Gates 29); s/he represents the power of manipulating language. (Audre will, however, meet another, more definitive avatar of this goddess in the character of the same name in the concluding chapter of *Zami*.) While each person has her/his own Afrekete/Esu, or source of personal power, Audre has a special relationship to Esu. In the preface to *Zami*, Lorde writes, "I have always wanted to be both man and woman, to incorporate the strongest and richest parts of my mother and father within/into me" (7). Some critics have read this passage as indicating that Lorde wishes to appropriate male power (Brooks 271). But taking on a male identity would keep Lorde's self partial, incomplete. What she wishes is to embody *both* maleness and femaleness, as Esu does. She draws on the father within herself through the image of Esu the trickster, taking on the identity of his female aspect, Afrekete.

Afrekete, in both stories, represents the young black woman's supraordinate personality—her complete, whole self. Afrekete is daughter but not victim; in her merge daughter and mother. Afrekete, as Estella Lauter says, is "maternal in her role as guide" and "tricksterlike in her capacity to transform Audre" (405). She is the trickster, the shape-changer, the woman-loving woman of color, in whom all contradictions meet. As the feminine face of Esu-Elegbara, she bridges opposites and contains them without obliterating differences.

Audre Lorde says that "[f]or each of us as women, there is a dark place within, where hidden and growing our true spirit rises. . . . These places of possibility within ourselves are dark because they are ancient and hidden; they have survived and grown strong through that darkness" ("Poetry Is Not a Luxury" 36-37). Afrekete is that "ancient and hidden" source of wisdom. As the feminine face of Esu, Afrekete mediates between male and female, between black and white, between African America and European America. As the divine Trickster, she stirs up trouble as Esu does; she loud-talks and tells lies, she raps and plays the dozens, she "talks shit." She also mediates and translates, making alliances, laying the groundwork for reconciliation based upon mutual respect. For the power of language is hers, that bridge of bridges and veil of veils, that divider and uniter of all who are human.

WORKS CITED

Abrahams, Roger D. *Deep Down in the Jungle: Negro Narrative Folklore from the Streets of Philadelphia.* New York: Aldine, 1970.

Braxton, Joanne. *Black Women Writing Autobiography: A Tradition within a Tradition.* Philadelphia: Temple University Press, 1989.

Brooks, Jerome. "In the Name of the Father: The Poetry of Audre Lorde." *Black Women Writers (1950-1980): A Critical Evaluation.* Ed. Mari Evans. Garden City, N.Y.: Anchor- Doubleday, 1984. 269-76.

Bulkin, Elly, ed. *Lesbian Fiction: An Anthology.* Watertown, Mass.: Persephone Press, 1981.

Christ, Carol P. *Diving Deep and Surfacing: Women Writers and Spiritual Quest.* Boston: Beacon Press, 1980.

———. "Spiritual Quest and Women's Experience." *Womanspirit Rising: A Feminist Reader in Religion.* San Francisco: HarperSanFrancisco-HarperCollins Publishers, 1992. 229-245.

Dowden, Ken. *Death and the Maiden: Girls' Initiation Rites in Greek Mythology.* London and New York: Routledge, 1989.

Foley, Helene P., ed. and trans. *The Homeric Hymn to Demeter: Translation, Commentary, and Interpretative Essays.* Princeton, N.J.: Princeton University Press, 1994.

Gates, Henry Louis, Jr. *The Signifying Monkey: A Theory of Afro-American Literary Criticism.* New York and Oxford: Oxford University Press, 1988.

Jung, C.G. "The Psychological Aspects of the Kore." *The Archetypes and the Collective Unconscious.* 2nd ed. Bollingen Ser. 20. Vol. 9.1. Princeton, N.J.: Princeton University Press, 1968. 182-203.

Keating, AnaLouise. "Making 'our shattered faces whole': The Black Goddess and Audre Lorde's Revision of Patriarchal Myth." *Frontiers* 13.1 (1992): 20-33.

———. "Myth Smashers, Myth Makers: (Re)Visionary Techniques in the Works of Paula Gunn Allen, Gloria Anzaldua, and Audre Lorde." *Journal of Homosexuality* 26.23 (1993): 73-95.

———. *Women Reading Women Writing: Self-Invention in Paula Gunn Allen, Gloria Anzaldua, and Audre Lorde.* Philadelphia: Temple University Press, 1996.

Lauter, Estella. "Re-Visioning Creativity: Audre Lorde's Refiguration of
    Eros as the Black Mother Within." *Writing the Woman Artist: Essays
    on Poetics, Politics, and Portraiture.* Ed. Suzanne W. Jones.
    Philadelphia: University of Pennsylvania Press, 1991. 398-418.
Lorde, Audre. "The Beginning." Bulkin, *Lesbian Fiction.* 255-272.
———. *Zami: A New Spelling of My Name.* 1982. Freedom, Calif.:
    Crossing Press, 1994.
———. "The Master's Tools Will Never Dismantle the Master's House."
    Sister Outsider: Essays and Speeches by Audre Lorde. Crossing Press
    Feminist Ser. Freedom, Calif.: Crossing Press, 1984. 110-113.
———. "An Open Letter to Mary Daly." 1987. *Sister Outsider* 66-71.
———. "Poetry Is Not a Luxury." 1977. *Sister Outsider* 36-39.
Major, Clarence, ed. *Juba to Jive: A Dictionary of African-American Slang.*
    New York: Penguin Books, 1994.
Mitchell-Kernan, Claudia. "Signifying as a Form of Verbal Art." *Mother
    Wit from the Laughing Barrel: Readings in the Interpretation of Afro-
    American Folklore.* Ed. Alan Dundes. Englewood Cliffs, N.J.: Prentice-
    Hall, 1978. 310-23.
Ogundipe, Ayodele. *Esu Elegbara, the Yoruba God of Chance and
    Uncertainty: A Study in Yoruba Mythology.* Vols. 1 and 2. Diss.
    Indiana, 1978. Ann Arbor and London: UMI, 1982.
Pelton, Robert D. *The Trickster in West Africa: A Study of Mythic Irony and
    Sacred Delight.* Berkeley: University of California Press, 1980.
Pipher, Mary. *Reviving Ophelia.* New York: Ballantine Books, 1994.
Powers, Meredith A. *The Heroine in Western Literature: The Archetype and
    her Reemergence in Modern Prose.* Jefferson, N.C., and London:
    McFarland, 1991.
Pratt, Annis, with Barbara White, Andrea Lowenstein, and Mary Wyer.
    Archetypal Patterns in Women's Fiction. Bloomington: Indiana
    University Press, 1981.
Provost, Kara. "Becoming Afrekete: The Trickster in the Work of Audre
    Lorde." *MELUS* 20. 4 (1995): 45-59.
Reynolds, Margaret, ed. *The Penguin Book of Lesbian Short Stories.* New
    York and London: Penguin Books, 1994.
Russ, Joanna. *How to Suppress Women's Writing.* Austin: University of
    Texas Press, 1983.
Suncircle, Pat. "A Day's Growth." Bulkin, *Lesbian Fiction.* 3-10.
Zimmerman, Bonnie. *The Safe Sea of Women: Lesbian Fiction 1969-1989.*
    Boston: Beacon Press, 1990.

CHAPTER 7

Race/[Gender]

Toni Morrison's "Recitatif"

David Goldstein-Shirley

Despite being the only short story ever written by Nobel laureate Toni Morrison and a topic of her own speaking and writing, "Recitatif" has received almost no scholarly attention. This curious fact might reflect either a critical bias against the short-story genre—which, following Alastair Fowler, Michael Bérubé has suggested (322)—or the relative obscurity of the anthology in which it appeared in 1983 (the out-of-print *Confirmation: An Anthology of AfricanAmerican Women*, edited by Amiri Baraka and Amina Baraka). In any case, as Morrison herself has said, "Recitatif" puts into play the very themes and rhetorical devices for which her novels have been recognized. In fact, "Recitatif" can be viewed as a nineteen-page distillation of Morrison's grand project of deconstructing race and racism, which characterizes her remarkable oeuvre. To make the case for this story's importance, I want to discuss four principal tactics used to further its strategy of inducing the reader's involvement in its thematic goal: (1) bracketing—that is, setting aside—gender in the text; (2) "staging" within the text the "real world" debate about school desegregation and mandatory busing; (3) modeling a particularly African-American storytelling style; and (4) using cleverly ambiguous racial codes in its descriptions of the main characters. I will then describe, as evidence of the success of these textual tactics, the responses of some readers to them.

The character of Twyla narrates "Recitatif." She tells the story of meeting Roberta when both were eight years old and thrown together in St. Bonaventure, an orphanage for girls. Although it is clear from the story's first page that one girl is white and one black, the text does not indicate which is which. This omitted detail is crucial to the text's rhetorical strategy.

Despite harboring maternally taught prejudices against Roberta's race, Twyla quickly grows to like Roberta, partly because they share the shame of incompetent rather than dead mothers. During their stay at the orphanage, an incident occurs which later proves significant. A kitchen helper, a mute woman named Maggie, falls down in the property's orchard and some of the girls at the home laugh at her.

After four months together at the home, the girls separate. They reunite by chance many years later, presumably in the early 1960s, when Twyla is working as a waitress in a Howard Johnson's coffee shop and Roberta enters with two male friends on their way to California, where one friend has an appointment with rock guitarist Jimi Hendrix. The reunion immediately turns sour when Twyla reveals her ignorance of Hendrix. Roberta insults her and the conversation ends.

When the two encounter one another again in a grocery store twelve years later, Roberta has acquired the trappings of wealth. Twyla, still working-class, marvels at the ascendance of her previously poor and illiterate friend. As the two share recollections of their days together at St. Bonaventure, Roberta drops a bombshell: she insists that Maggie did not fall accidentally but was pushed by some of the girls at the orphanage. Roberta's version of the incident contradicts Twyla's and the pleasant reunion ends on a chilly note. Although she still believes that Maggie fell accidentally, Twyla expresses growing uncertainty about her memory.

A few months later, the two encounter each other again on opposite sides of a busing demonstration against the backdrop of mounting racial strife. Roberta is picketing against mandatory busing for school desegregation, and Twyla then engages in a counterprotest in favor of it. Roberta again challenges Twyla's memory of the incident with Maggie by insisting that the woman was black and, moreover, that Twyla participated in her torment by kicking her. Yelling and accusing each other of lying, they again angrily go their separate ways.

The two run into each other a final time on Christmas Eve. Roberta, slightly drunk from party-going, tearfully confesses that she is no longer certain that Maggie was black. She also acknowledges that, although she and Twyla wanted to join in tormenting Maggie, they did not. The story ends with Roberta crying and asking, "What the hell happened to Maggie?"

Although "Recitatif" epitomizes Morrison's oeuvre in its counterhegemonic attack on racial stereotypes, the story stands apart from her novels in its bracketing of gender. Just as she has said, "Racism will destroy love," Morrison has said that "the conflict of genders is a cultural illness" (quoted in Coser 104). Mary Madden (especially 586-87) argues that Morrison's fiction challenges not only stereotypes within categories of identity but the categories themselves, and not only for race but also for gender. Yet in "Recitatif," a self-conscious literary experiment in unmasking labels, Morrison focuses on race to the exclusion of gender.

Gender is severely backgrounded in "Recitatif." Both protagonists are female. They meet in a home for girls, of which the entire staff is female. The story depicts no male/female conflict, unlike every one of her novels. The only males who appear in the story at all—some police officers at the scene of the demonstration and the two young men accompanying Roberta when they enter Twyla's coffee shop—are inconsequential. Twyla's and Roberta's husbands and sons are mentioned in passing; they do not participate in the action of the story. Concentrating only on women sidesteps the social problem of sex-based Othering, which elsewhere figures prominently in Morrison's writing, and thus focuses readers exclusively on the racial issues raised in and by the story.

Not only are male/female relationships in "Recitatif," such as between the two women and their husbands, pushed into the background, but even there they pose no challenge to the hegemonic status quo. Unlike Morrison's novels, in which strong women contest male domination, "Recitatif" depicts conservative gender roles in the women's marriages. Twyla states, "Strife came to us that fall. . . . I couldn't figure it out from one day to the next. I knew I was supposed to feel something strong, but I didn't know what, and James wasn't any help" (255-56), indicating that she expects her husband to explain confusing current events and, moreover, to tell her how to feel about them. Even the more worldly Roberta suggests she has a traditional marriage in which her husband earns money and she spends it. When Twyla asks Roberta what he does for a living, Roberta replies, "Computers and stuff. What do I know?" (254). It is enough for her that her husband provides for her; how he earns the money does not concern her. These traditional gender roles for husbands and wives are atypical for Morrison's fiction. Unlike her novels, "Recitatif" is too short to tackle Morrison's dual targets of racism and sexism. By not addressing the latter, this story mounts a stronger attack on the former.

In its language usage, too, the bracketing of gender contributes to the text's task of concentrating readers' attention on race. In "Cognitive Research on Gender and Comprehension," Mary Crawford and Roger Chaffin report that readers' gender (which they view as socially defined and constructed and which is usually but not necessarily congruent with chromosomal sex [13]) affects the interpretation of language that is masculine but meant to be generic, such as the nouns "man" and "mankind" standing in for "person" and "humankind" and the pronoun "he" used to mean "he or she" (15). They cite a study by Wendy Martyna which found that men tended to interpret "he" as referring only to men, while for women the male pronoun called up neither male nor female images (15).

Crawford and Chaffin also discuss their own research that indicates differences in how men and women *remember* the content of texts that use supposedly generic—but actually masculine—language. Half of their subjects read an essay titled, "The Psychologist and His Work," which always referred to "the psychologist" as "he." The other half of their subjects read an otherwise identical essay but which was titled, "Psychologists and Their Work," and referred to a singular psychologist as "he or she" or used the plural "they" to refer to the plural "psychologists." Crawford and Chaffin state: "When they were tested for memory of the factual content of the essay, men who had read the 'generic' essay [the one using masculine pronouns in an ostensibly generic manner] recalled more than those who had read the specific version. Exactly the opposite occurred for women, who recalled better the essay form that specifically included them" (16).

With virtually no reference to men, Morrison neutralizes the problem of pronouns that ostensibly are gender-neutral but actually are not. She also disarms the potentially explosive problem of different recollections about the story among men and women. Male and female readers are not given the opportunity to respond differently. With this story, Morrison wishes to confound preconceptions of race; splitting readers by gender would not further this purpose. In contrast to Morrison's carefully ambiguous manipulation of race, which it is her purpose to demystify—or, more accurately, to lead her readers to demystify—"Recitatif" carefully brackets gender; Morrison's deconstruction of sexism is left to her other work.

The distinctively "oral" quality of "Recitatif" also contributes to the story's strategy of recruiting the reader in its mission to deconstruct racism. To analyze this aspect of the text's rhetorical strategy, Robert Stepto's model of African-American storytelling narratives is helpful. In his essay, "Distrust of the Reader in Afro-American Narratives," Stepto argues that a characteristic feature of African-American narratives is their implicit distrust of their readers, both black and white. The narratives typically feature rhetoric that resists a cavalier or "wrong" reading; instead, creative communication takes place "when the reader gets 'told'—or 'told off'—in such a way that he or she finally begins to *hear*" (202-3; emphasis in original). Stepto intentionally uses phrases ("told," "hear") that signify a storytelling paradigm. He is specifically interested in African-American authors who "choose to see themselves as storytellers instead of storywriters" (199) because he believes the prevailing reader-response theories, propounded by white critics, inadequately apply to this distinctive aspect of much African-American literature. He therefore puts forth his own model of the various forms of such narratives.

"Recitatif" exemplifies what Stepto means by an African-American storytelling narrative. Although the text is written, its structure mimics oral storytelling, a quality similar to Morrison's other works. Stelamaris Coser, citing a Morrison interview with Claudia Tate conducted in the same year in which "Recitatif" was published, states: "Storytelling was 'a shared activity between the men and women' in her family, and she attempts to write within that oral tradition. Morrison deliberately pursues an 'oral quality' in order to 'capture the vast imagination of black people'" (Coser 88). Stepto himself includes Morrison in his list of African-American writers known for telling— rather than writing—stories (207). It therefore is appropriate to apply Stepto's model to "Recitatif."

Stepto describes four variations of the basic African-American storytelling narrative, which "is fundamentally a framed tale in which either the framed or framing narrative depicts a black storyteller's white listener socially and morally maturing into competency. In thus presenting a very particular reader in the text, the basic written tale squarely addresses the issue of its probable audience while raising an issue for some or most of its readers regarding the extent to which they can or will identify with the text's 'reader' while pursuing (if not always completing) their own act of reading" (207). One variation of the framed tale, which he labels a Type B tale, features a novice storyteller who only recently has achieved competence as a listener. A consideration of the four principal characteristics of a Type B tale reveals how well the model fits "Recitatif." First, "although the story's primary narrator is a novice teller (white or black), the black master teller is fully present as the teller of the story's tale," according to Stepto (209). Twyla exemplifies the novice teller. Her tale is little more than that of the event that led to her recently achieved competence as a listener to Roberta's story, namely, grappling with her challenged memory of the Maggie incident. Stepto says that "the novice teller is seemingly still too close to the moment when competency was achieved and too overwhelmed by the teller, tale, and other features of that moment to author a story which is anything other than a strict account of that moment" (208).

It is, indeed, Roberta's story. Despite the fact that Twyla is the narrator of the framing story, it is Roberta who is the master storyteller. Although she eventually acknowledges she might be wrong about Maggie's race and definitely is wrong about kicking her, it is only with Roberta's confession that any resolution occurs. She controls the knowledge; only her telling can break the impasse. In contrast to Twyla's ignorance (e.g., her unfamiliarity with Hendrix; her confession that she failed to recognize the racial strife enveloping the nation despite nightly news reports), Roberta has had the knowledge and understanding all along (e.g., her statement, "Oh, Twyla, you know how it was in those days: black—white," and Twyla's confession to the reader, "But I didn't know" [255]).

Second, "although the novice teller may tell the tale of his or her previous incompetency to listeners situated within the tale's frame, direct address to the 'listener' outside the story (the 'outside' reader) is both possible and likely" (209). In "Recitatif," Twyla does not tell the tale to listeners within the frame, but does implicitly address the "outside" reader by speaking in first person.

Third, "although the predominating autobiographical statement is still that offered by the master teller in the tale, the novice teller's self-history also has a place, sometimes a significant one, in the story as a whole" (209). Twyla's self-history—her enlightenment regarding race— certainly is significant. Roberta's autobiographical statement, however, dominates, especially her climb from illiteracy to affluence. It is Twyla's story only insofar as she tells of her maturation into a competent listener, and it is Roberta's story that she finally hears.

Fourth, "although the story is normally a framed tale, with this type we begin to see improvisations upon that structure, especially in those instances where the story is repeated and otherwise developed for the needs and purposes of novellas and novels" (209) and, I would add, short stories. "Recitatif" is, indeed, a framed tale. Twyla is telling the story of Roberta telling a story. There is another level, though: Morrison is telling the story of Twyla telling the story of Roberta telling a story.

At this point, I need to take a step back, for Stepto actually offers two versions of the Type B story as he does for the other three types (A, C, and D) of storytelling narratives. For each narrative type that he delineates, each of which features a white listener listening to the framed tale within the framing narrative, he presents a corresponding type that differs only in the race of the listener. Thus, corresponding to narrative types A, B, C, and D are types A′, B′, C′, and D′, in which the listener is black rather than white. This dual feature of Stepto's model thus becomes especially problematic and especially interesting in relation to "Recitatif," for it is precisely the racial identity of the framed tale's listener (in this case, Twyla) that is at issue.

Is Twyla black or white? If Stepto's model fits "Recitatif" as well as I have argued it does, one must conclude that Roberta, as the master storyteller, is black and therefore Twyla is white. Corroborating this conclusion is Roberta's story of moving from illiteracy to knowledge, a well-documented African-American literary theme dating back at least as far as Frederick Douglass's *Narrative*. (See, for example, Dana Nelson Salvino's "The Word in Black and White: Ideologies of Race and Literacy in Antebellum America.") As Jan Furman notes, however, the significance of "Recitatif" lies in the open question of the characters' identities—not in its answer. The story, she says, is precisely an "experiment in communicating without using racial codes as a shortcut" (108). Morrison herself states in *Playing in the Dark* that "Recitatif" "was an experiment in the removal of all racial codes from a narrative about two characters of different races for whom racial identity is crucial" (xi). But Morrison does *not* remove all racial codes from the narrative. She only removes *explicit* racial identifications of the two characters. There are, however, plenty of codes planted in the text that the reader is challenged to interpret.

Because it takes into account not only the experiential context of each reader that approaches a given text but also the historical and social context of each reading event, Steven Mailloux's approach of rhetorical hermeneutics is a compelling one in analyzing Morrison's rhetorical tactic of using indeterminate racial codes. Readers come to the text with different assumptions and preconceptions that can best be understood in light of the "cultural conversations" about race and race relations that are both staged within the story and in which the story and its readers' interpretations participate.

In *Rhetorical Power*, Mailloux illustrates his approach by analyzing the discourse of race within and without Mark Twain's *Huckleberry Finn*. A text, he says, "can be a topic in a cultural discussion or it can be a participant motivated by and affecting the conversation" (61). "Recitatif" on its own can hardly be seen as a topic in any cultural discussion. The small number of critical references to it evidences this fact. It most certainly is motivated by a conversation about race and prejudice, however. Morrison cites the story as an example of her goal to "free up the language from its sometimes sinister, frequently lazy, almost always predictable employment of racially informed and determined chains" (*Playing* xi). This mission stems from her practical concerns as a writer: "I cannot rely on these metaphorical shortcuts [present in our language] because I am a black writer struggling with and through a language that can powerfully evoke and enforce hidden signs of racial superiority, cultural hegemony, and dismissive Othering of people and language which are by no means marginal or already and completely known and knowable in my work" (*Playing* x-xi). By coupling "people" and "language," Morrison makes clear that her deconstruction of racial codes in the language of her works, most self-consciously in "Recitatif," is, to her, akin to deconstructing racism. Her writing is the means by which she challenges the racism embedded in language and in society. Although "Recitatif" has not received the attention it deserves, it is a part of her *oeuvre*, which, as a whole, is unmistakably "affecting the conversation" about racism and racial dystopia and the power of love to overcome them. Indirectly, then, "Recitatif" does participate in and does "affect" a cultural conversation. Furthermore, Morrison's work as a whole certainly is a topic in cultural discussion, as her citation by the Swedish Academy attests.

Mailloux further argues that as a participant in cultural conversations about topics of the day, "literature can take up the ideological rhetoric of its historical moment . . . and place it on a fictional stage" within the text (61). "Readers thus become spectators at a rhetorical performance, and sometimes, as in *Huckleberry Finn*, they also become actors in the drama they are watching" (61). For all their differences, *Huckleberry Finn* and "Recitatif" share remarkable similarities. Not only are both first-person narratives by apparent innocents, but both exhibit this intriguing feature of staged debates. In "Recitatif," the debate about busing as a means of school desegregation, a topic that consumed Americans from the 1954 Supreme Court decision in *Brown v. Board of Ed.* through the 1980s (when "Recitatif" was published), is staged in the story itself. On one side of the street, literally and figuratively, is Roberta, who has joined other mothers in a demonstration against busing. "They want to take my kids and send them out of the neighborhood. They don't want to go," Roberta says (256). On the other side is Twyla, who, speaking through her car window after coming upon the demonstration, asks Roberta, "So what if they go to another school? My boy's being bussed too, and I don't mind." The argument escalates until it turns "racial": When Twyla says, "Well, it is a free country," Roberta replies, "Not yet, but it will be." When Roberta adds, "I wonder what made me think you were different," Twyla says the same thing back. As policemen pull Roberta's fellow protesters off of Twyla's car, Roberta turns her version of the Maggie incident into a verbal weapon: "'Maybe I am different now, Twyla. But you're not. You're the same little state kid who kicked a poor old black lady when she was down on the ground. You kicked a black lady and you have the nerve to call me a bigot'" (257).

Morrison does not take sides in this confrontation. Rather, by staging it—that is, by depicting the conflict like a theatrical drama in the text—she depicts the divisiveness of the issue of busing and simultaneously demystifies the racial motivation on both sides of the issue. By exposing the racial antagonism that, for Twyla and Roberta, lies beneath the surface of the busing issue, Morrison also exposes the racial prejudice for which the rhetoric for and against busing in the extratextual narrative ("real life") has become a thin veil. Readers of "Recitatif" become spectators at this scene of rhetorical performance and, in Mailloux's terms, become actors in the drama they are watching to the extent that they accept the role and get "rehearsed" in reading the debate between Twyla and Roberta about the incident with Maggie, an issue on which the success of the story as a deconstructor of racism *in the reader's mind* depends.

By withholding the critical information not only of Twyla's and Roberta's racial identities but that of Maggie, too, "Recitatif" leaves it to the reader to complete the story. To do so, the reader must decide which character is black and which is white, which woman is correct about what happened to Maggie, and what the characters' acknowledged desire to harm Maggie signifies. (Is it racism?) To the extent that the reader accepts this role, for which Twyla's maturation as a hearer serves as a training exercise, the reader confronts the problem of having to use evidence not found in the text itself—conclusive evidence simply isn't there—but in his or her own mind. If the reader recognizes this exposure of preconceptions about race, the preconceptions become problematic (e.g., "Why did I assume that Roberta's illiteracy meant she was black?" or, perhaps, "Why did I assume that Roberta's affluence meant she was white?"). When the reader acknowledges and questions these stereotypes, he or she contributes to the deconstruction of racism. To elucidate further how this and the other tactics I have described constitute Morrison's rhetorical strategy, I turn now to the readers I studied and how they responded to the text.

From late 1993 through early 1994, I recruited sixty-seven college students who read "Recitatif" and then completed questionnaires that solicited information about their demographic backgrounds and their thoughts and feelings about the story. I statistically measured associations between demographics and patterns of response and found that ethnicity proved to be a strong predictor of some aspects of readers' responses to the story. Most relevant to my argument here is the finding that readers of different ethnicities cited different clues when speculating about Twyla's and Roberta's respective races, although, ironically, I found no significant difference in the resultant speculations themselves. In other words, knowledge of readers' ethnicity did not help predict whether they speculated that Twyla is white or black or whether Roberta is white or black, but did help predict which clues they used to reach their conclusions.

Six respondents clearly missed the textual clues that indicated that the two characters were of different races. (The narrator, Twyla, complains that she had been placed in a room with a girl from a "whole other race" [243] and that they "looked like salt and pepper" [244]. She later recalls her chance encounter with Roberta: "A black girl and a white girl meeting in a Howard Johnson's on the road and having nothing to say" [253].) Five of these speculated that both characters were white; one speculated that both were black. Three other respondents ventured no conjectures about Twyla and Roberta, and one respondent conjectured only about Roberta. These respondents are the exceptions. The remaining fifty-eight respondents understood that the two were of different races, and were able to extrapolate enough from ambiguous textual clues, cross-referenced with their own experience, to conjecture which character was white and which was black.

More significant than the ability and willingness of readers to conjecture the characters' racial identities is the fact that most respondents were able to identify the elements of the text that led them to do so. The clues Morrison leaves are subtle and ambiguous, yet they led these respondents to extrapolate from them based on their own experiences. One might contend that, because these individuals came from diverse backgrounds, they attached different meanings to the clues found in the text. Yet none, so far as could be determined by their questionnaire answers, expressed an altogether anomalous set of responses—that is, falling outside the consensus regarding many aspects of interpretation. This fact suggests that the text placed parameters on (or at least guided) response while allowing differences within those parameters, or that readers approached the text with a shared set of interpretive conventions, or both. By responding to the ambiguous textual clues, most of the sixty-seven readers allowed themselves to co-create meanings along with the text. That is, they imagined something (the characters' racial identities) that was not expressly present in the text.

Nineteen of the sixty-seven respondents—more than a quarter—specifically cited as a basis for their conjectures about the characters' racial identities the characters' respective stands in the busing/desegregation issue. By ascribing racial identities to the characters on this basis, these respondents became, in Mailloux's words, "actors in the drama they are watching." While revealing their own preconceptions about racial roles, they participated in a cultural conversation about desegregation and busing by adding something to the scene—the characters' respective racial identities—that was not there originally. Like reporters who embellish the story they are covering, these readers shifted, however slightly, the discourse about the conflict.

Through this tactic of inducing readers' participation in the scene and hence in the cultural conversation about desegregation and busing, the text trains readers to appropriate for themselves Twyla's training as a critical, competent hearer. That is, Twyla, by telling of her maturation as a hearer of Roberta's narrative, helps train the reader to become a competent hearer of both Roberta's narrative (the framed narrative, in Stepto's terms) and Twyla's meta-narrative (the framing narrative). But even more crucially, the reader is trained to hear the meta-meta-narrative—that of the real-life, real-world conversation about busing, desegregation, and race relations more broadly. The text gets readers to participate in the deconstruction of racism in society by getting them to participate in the deconstruction of race in the text. This tactic of drawing the participation of the reader in meaning-making distinguishes not only "Recitatif," but all of Morrison's work. Coser, in *Bridging the Americas*, writes that Morrison's works "contain openings for the reader to fill in, invitations for a reimagining and a rewriting that should be the responsibility and the privilege of us all" (169). Morrison herself states: "My writing expects, demands to have participatory reading" (Tate 125).

By contrasting the strength of association between ethnicity and response with the weakness of association between sex and response among these readers, one can see how the text's bracketing of gender contributes to the story's strategy by concentrating attention only on race. Of nearly a dozen demographic variables in my study, sex was the only one that bore no association with the patterns of response that I was able to discern. At first, this result surprised me because feminist criticism (e.g., Annette Kolodny, "A Map for Rereading: Or, Gender and the Interpretation of Literary Texts," and Elaine Showalter, "Feminist Criticism in the Wilderness") has established that modes of reading and interpretation previously supposed as universal actually were particular to men. Feminist critics such as Judith Fetterley have argued that women have been socialized differently than men and read and interpret differently as a result. The fact that sex was the only variable in the study to show no association with response therefore merits attention. Especially when contrasted with the results of a pilot study in which sex was a good predictor of response, the finding of no difference in response between the men and the women in the primary study raises the question of what is different about the two texts that can account for the apparent contradiction. The difference is the bracketing of gender in "Recitatif." As I have argued, this tactic of the short story furthers the text's strategy of eliciting readers' complicity in deconstructing racism by concentrating their attention solely on that aspect of the story.

These collective tactics—eliminating explicit racial labels, bracketing gender to focus exclusively on race, using a framed narrative that artistically represents an African-American storytelling tradition in order to train the reader to become a competent hearer, and staging within the text the extratextual debate about desegregation—together contribute to the effective strategy of manipulating the reader to become an accomplice in the deconstruction of racism. This strategy invites readers to expose their own preconceptions, complete the narrative of the busing and antibusing demonstration, and then contribute to the greater purpose of challenging racism. That readers accept this challenging invitation testifies to the power of the text and the skill of its author.

WORKS CITED

Bérubé, Michael. *Marginal Forces/Cultural Centers: Tolson, Pynchon, and the Politics of the Canon*. Ithaca, N.Y.: Cornell University Press, 1992.

Coser, Stelamaris. *Bridging the Americas: The Literature of Toni Morrison, Paule Marshall, and Gayl Jones*. Philadelphia: Temple University Press, 1995.

Crawford, Mary and Roger Chaffin. "The Reader's Construction of Meaning: Cognitive Research on Gender and Comprehension." *Gender and Reading: Essays on Readers, Texts, and Contexts*. Ed. Elizabeth A. Flynn and Patrocinio P. Schweickart. Baltimore: Johns Hopkins University Press, 1986. 3-30.

Fetterley, Judith. *The Resisting Reader: A Feminist Approach to American Fiction*. Bloomington: Indiana University Press, 1978.

Furman, Jan. *Toni Morrison's Fiction*. Columbia: University of South Carolina Press, 1996.

Kolodny, Annette. "A Map for Rereading: Or, Gender and the Interpretation of Literary Texts." *New Literary History* 11.3 (Spring 1980): 451-67.

Madden, Mary. "Necessary Narratives: Toni Morrison and Literary Identities." *Women's Studies International Forum* 18. 5-6 (1995): 585-94.

Mailloux, Steven. *Rhetorical Power*. Ithaca, N.Y.: Cornell University Press, 1989.

Morrison, Toni. *Playing in the Dark: Whiteness and the Literary Imagination*. New York: Vintage Books, 1992.

—. "Recitatif." *Confirmation: An Anthology of African-American Women.* Ed. Amiri Baraka and Amina Baraka. New York: William Morrow and Company, 1983. 243-61.

Salvino, Dana Nelson. "The Word in Black and White: Ideologies of Race and Literacy in Antebellum America." *Reading in America: Literature and Social History.* Ed. Cathy N. Davidson. Baltimore: Johns Hopkins University Press, 1989. 140-56.

Showalter, Elaine. "Feminist Criticism in the Wilderness." *Critical Inquiry* 8. 2 (Winter 1981): 179-205.

Stepto, Robert B. "Distrust of the Reader in Afro-American Narratives." Afterword. *From Behind the Veil: A Study of Afro-American Narrative.* 2nd ed. Urbana: University of Illinois Press, 1991. 195-215.

Tate, Claudia. "Conversation with Toni Morrison." *Black Women Writers at Work.* New York: Continuum Publishing Company, 1983. 117-31.

CHAPTER 8

Playing in the Light
White Girls Dreaming in Eudora Welty's "Moon Lake"

Elaine Orr

"The text opens up a path which is already ours and yet not altogether ours." Helene Cixous

As Shelley Fisher Fishkin has observed, Toni Morrison remapped American literature with the 1992 publication of her book *Playing in the Dark: Whiteness and the Literary Imagination*. In that brief but compelling volume—one that begins in autobiography—she turned the colored world around, casting a light on the dark recesses of the white imagination as it has been manifested in our literary canon. Rejecting the idea that the traditional American canon is unshaped and unmarked by the four-hundred-year-old presence of Africans and then African Americans, Morrison argues that white American literature has relied on a dark secret: the fabrication and then subjection of a buttressing Africanist presence. Perhaps as an illustration of her preference for showing how textual worlds are invented, Morrison begins her book in first person, disclosing in personal narrative her reading of another (white) woman's autobiographical novel.

In Morrison's remapping, American literature is recognizable through "a distancing Africanism" (8). In other words, white American authors provide a marginalized Africanist presence in their texts as a sign of how far whiteness is from incivility, chaos, and bondage. White American textual independence is bought at the cost of black textual enslavement. Morrison's argument led a groundswell of critical inquiry into the natural privileging of whiteness in American literature at the same time that it contributed to the recent tendency in criticism to authorize the personal. A recent guest column in *PMLA*—"Four Views on the Place of the Personal in Scholarship"—demonstrates the new respectability extended to self-conscious analysis of the writer's own personal history of race. One potential outcome of these investigations into whiteness and blackness is that they will further divide critics along racial lines; in other words, African-American critics will have access to certain enunciating positions and white critics to others. But by invoking an autobiographical moment, Morrison provides an alternative. The inflections of autobiographical narrative within the critical essay may serve—as I hope it will here—as a footbridge across the widening chasm of white and black American discourses.

Morrison's theory appears to offer a promising avenue for reconsidering Eudora Welty's "Moon Lake," a tantalizing tale of white girlhood. The arrangement of characters seems to substantiate the argument: here we have a flock of white school girls with their counselors, set down at a summer camp on the edge of a lake, surrounded by the shadowy figures of an extended black family. The illumination of the white female plot appears to be achieved at least in part by the contrast between white agency and black stasis. Nothing happens with the black characters. Rather than actors in the play, they are part of the stage. Even Exxum, the small black boy whose prank leads to one white girl's near drowning, is merely whipped for his action. We never know what he thinks, or indeed, if he thinks.

But Welty's story complicates this reading. First, the white girls are of two antagonistic classes or statuses: middle class versus orphaned, independent versus wards of the state. The very fact that these sets do not "add up"—that middle class and orphaned are not two semantic halves of a whole—suggests an incommensurate difference within whiteness. Not only this, but the story sets in motion a dizzying number of differences: male/female; white/black; independent/guarded; youth/age; looking at/receiving the look; virginal/deflowered; written/spoken, to name a few, and these are circulated and reconstructed endlessly. Second, Welty's ironic mode of narration—the text's deviation between literal and figurative meanings—works to disclose and illuminate, rather than hide, the story's struggle over power, color, and class. Thus my title, "playing in the light." So while the text appears to employ a "distancing Africanism," the effect of the white/black dynamic in Welty's ironic voice is to show the very operations of power and identity that

Morrison says canonical American literature endeavors to hide but with an ironic distance. As Paul de Man suggests, irony allows a writer to say dreadful things because they are said by means of artful devices that provide a certain play in relation to what is being said. Thus Welty *shows* her colors with an amused self-consciousness.

"Moon Lake" does not so much comply with whiteness as it forces a recognition of the dreaming that reproduces it. This is not the same thing as saying that Welty represents the culturally imposed constrictions of white girlhood through the figurative use of black captivity. It is to say, instead, that she ironically represents a dream of captivity that emerges from the psycho/social space of a safe whiteness. In other words, she does use blackness to illuminate whiteness but her purpose is critical and her guiding trope of incommensurates—middle class/orphaned—continually defers the achievement of a satisfied white presence.

"Moon Lake" tells the story of a summer camp. The players include two sets of camp girls: on the one side, a group of county orphans, led by the tom-boyish Easter; on the other, the town girls from established families—called the Morgana girls throughout— represented by Nina and Jinny Love; Loch Morrison, Boy Scout, who occupies a tent on the edge of camp, plays reveille, and despises the feminine; Miss Moody and Mrs. Gruenwald, camp counselors, who lead the girls in songs and chants (like "Good morning, Mr. Dip, Dip, Dip, with your water as cold as ice!" [172]) and urge them into the lake for morning and afternoon swims. Living close to the camp and feeding themselves from the lake is a black family, noticed and dismissed by the middle-class white girls. Looking out of their cabin at nap time, Jinny and Nina think "there was nothing but light out there [beyond their sphere]. True, the black Negroes inhabited it" (118). The redundant marker—"black Negroes"—is one of many ironic signs in the story. While the girls think of blackness as naming something literally beyond them—and hence "nothing," the narrative hyperbole figuratively illuminates the dreamers, bringing the "light out there" to rest on Jinny and Nina.

The story is told through a series of omnisciently narrated vignettes, recording nap time and swim time, the conversations of camp, and the interactions between the orphans and the Morgana girls. For the most part, the narrator is aloof from all of the characters, but at moments, the narrative voice records the Morgana girls' imaginative visions. Always, however, one has the sense that the teller stands just behind the girl characters, almost like a ghostly counselor who has reneged on her duties and amuses herself by observing rather than directing the action. This tactic is vintage Welty, who, in the collection *The Eye of the Story*, has described her writing self as "a sort of third character along on the ride" (111) in her composing of a story.

What appears as the story's primary action comes in section five of "Moon Lake": Easter's near drowning when Exxum tickles her ankle and she falls into the lake, followed by her rescue by Loch Morrison.

Readers will remember that the story ends on the heels of this precipitous event, with Jinny Love and Nina viewing the great Loch Morrison undressing in his tent (lifeguard *Loch*!). All along he has been blowing "his horn into their presence" (172). But at last they spy a "minnowy thing that matched his candle flame, naked as he was" (212). He looked, we are told, "rather at loose ends," a description that further intones this masculine giant's diminution. Having witnessed his frenzied rescue of the drowning Easter—a rescue that looked more like a rape than anything—Jinny and Nina agree that they "will always be old maids" (212).

This ending appears sufficiently feminist since it brings Loch Morrison down more than one peg and reasserts the primacy of female/female relations. The Lacanian phallus is challenged by an originating female look that has seen the sign collapse without any damage to the linguistic universe. But surely Welty's sly wink over Loch's deflation acts, among other things, as a nod to readers to look elsewhere for the story's mystery, to take another path. And what about Easter? She is asleep in the tent, being watched by Twosie, one of the black girls in the story. While the Morgana girls look, Easter is being constituted by the gaze of a black character. While Morrison analyzes the muted "dark nurse" (61-91) in American literature, Welty's staging of a looking black nurse maid in relation to the orphaned and outcast white girl ironically signals the text's awareness of white construction and upsets "Moon Lake"'s apparently feminist closure. Throughout the story, Easter is described "darkly": "Around the back of her neck beneath the hair was a dark band on her skin like the mark a gold bracelet leaves on the arm" (177); her eyes "were neither brown nor green nor cat; they had something of metal, flat ancient metal in them" (178); her knees are "scarred and coral colored" (178).

Employing Morrison's paradigm—but with a twist—I suggest several points: first, that Easter's silencing along with her dark associations (with Twosie, for example) makes her the vehicle for an "Africanist presence"; second, that this "white Africanist" serves to destabilize whiteness in the story; and finally, that this ironic device produces *a showing*, not of masculinity or blackness primarily, but of middle-class white femininity.

"Moon Lake" simultaneously *draws attention* to and away from its poor white and black characters but the narrative effect is to *cast a light on* the middle-class girls' dreaming. Thus "Moon Lake" may be read as critiquing the very thing that Morrison says white writers try to hide: the construction of a standard whiteness in the American landscape. Furthermore, I would argue that the Africanist Easter is not entirely coopted by the dream. Because her thoughts are always implied but never revealed, she retains, even at the end, the suggestion of a selfness that the Morgana girls can never make their own. If I am right, two conclusions are plausible: either that Easter is allowed some selfness because she is "somewhat" white, or, conversely, that Easter as "Africanist presence" represents a textual awareness that the white imagination has never fully contained the blackness it finds so necessary and so disturbing.

I remember two girls who sat close to me in first grade. One, on my left, was, in Tillie Olsen's words, "thin and dark and foreign-looking," her hair wavy and long and gypsylike (12). Her dresses were a size too big and hung on her like an apology. The other girl, on my right, wore her long blond hair tightly pulled back with a hair band and barrettes. In a picture I have from that time, her perfectly pursed lips suggest a demureness I had yet to acquire. Her dresses were crisp and lacy—with lots of stand-out petticoats. I sat in the middle with my wispy blond pixie-cut hair, my hand-me-downs, which nonetheless were numerous and well- fitting. The girl on the left was quiet and kept her head lowered. So did the girl on my right. But it was the "darker" girl whom the teacher suspected of stealing some coins from my desk. And it was the "lighter" girl on my right who had to be coddled when she clung obsessively to her papers—which she believed had to be perfect—and wouldn't hand them in with the rest of us. I read these differences as differences in individual character and found both girls peculiar. It was 1960, and there were no African Americans in our school in Winston-

Salem, North Carolina. On my part, there was little consciousness of class. I credited myself with my successes and wondered at the fate of others who didn't do as well. After class, I reveled in the conversations my teacher held with my father. Speaking over me, she boasted of how bright and talented I was. But she never addressed me directly. Thus she instilled an expectation: that I need not speak; I would, nonetheless, be found.

In the center of "Moon Lake," Welty offers a sobering look at how economics furnish the white feminine romance. Although the validity of the Morgana girls' dream is later challenged, Welty makes clear the extent to which Jinny and Nina imagine selfhood and sexuality out of a middle-class position.

In the scene at hand, we find Nina and Jinny Love "run[ning] away from basket weaving" (183). Their path appears to be chosen by a desire to resist gender scripting, but in fact, their true desire *is to appear to be in danger.* "'Grand,'" intones Jinny Love when Nina makes the suggestion, "'They'll think we're drowned'" (183). To Jinny's and Nina's chagrin, they find that Easter has beaten them down the path. While Jinny and Nina know the dominant ideology—"*they*'ll think we're drowned"—they don't know what Easter thinks:

> They trudged down the slope past Loch Morrison's tent and took the track into the swamp. There they moved single file between two walls; by lifting their arms they could have touched one or the other pressing side of the swamp. Their toes exploded the dust that felt like the powder clerks pump into new kid gloves, as Jinny Love said twice. They were eye to eye with the finger-shaped leaves of the castor bean plants, put out like those gypsy hands that part the curtains at the back of rolling wagons, and wrinkled and coated over like the fortune-teller's face. . . .
>
> . . . Closer to the ear than lips could begin words came the swamp sounds—closer to the ear and *nearer to the dreaming mind.* . . .
>
> . . . The track serpentined . . . and walking ahead was Easter. . . .
>
> "Wouldn't you know!" said Jinny Love. (184-5)

The two middle-class girls dream of escape through simulated danger, but their intentions are usurped by a girl whose escape is less figurative than substantial. Easter's move to the fringes of camp accurately reflects her social marginalization and is not an enactment of a dream. In other words, Easter is not imagining her lostness or marginality; she *is* marginal. "Wouldn't you know" is Jinny Love's perfect capturing of the reality of Easter's position away from the center. Welty's ironic tone is figured in her direct suggestion of the girls' dreaming minds and in the imaging of the Morgana girls' seduction by their own imaginations: fortune-tellers and rolling wagons. Nina and Jinny have fantasized their own, ironically passive drama in running away from camp. But camp—where their white girlhood is securely established in opposition to blackness and maleness—is exactly what makes them so sure of themselves and so ill prepared to befriend Easter.

What appears to be a rather innocent description of Jinny's and Nina's escape is, in actuality, an etching of their fascination with themselves. Their dream of lostness depends on the promise of being worthy of finding. But the grounds for their difference are threatened by a girl whose liminal identity undermines the certainty of white girlhood. Easter never responds as she should, in other words, as Jinny Love and Nina expect her to. Earlier, when Nina offered Easter the opportunity to drink from her engraved collapsible drinking cup, Easter "didn't say anything, not even 'It's pretty.'" "Was she even thinking of it?" (180-81) the narrator queries. While Jinny and Nina assert their femaleness against Loch's absurd maleness, they find it difficult to maintain their dreams of selfness in the mirror provided by Easter. Rather than securing the Morgana girls position, she evokes an unhinged position, a free-floating, nonsecured middle. Through the device of the orphan, then, Welty draws our attention to the dream of danger that middle-class white girls exercise in the light of a safely shored white femininity. In the light of Easter's difference, even Twosie becomes an agent in uncovering Jinny's and Nina's fantasies.

When Jinny Love expresses a "cheerful" "hope" that she and Nina will not "meet any nigger men" (184) on their adventure, she raises the specter of the Others she knows and collapses them into one: blacks and men, black men. Employing the hobgoblin category "nigger men," she expresses the full measure of her identity as a middle-class white girl. Indeed, she reveals the overworked narrative that inspires her adventure with Nina: they flee, hoping someone *will* come find them *because white girls might be harmed* by "nigger men" in the woods. (It goes without saying that "someone" is white.) The hope of being sought reveals the girls' middle-class gendering. Unfortunately for Jinny and Nina, Easter, unlike the beloved cup, is not collapsible into "nigger men." They imagine themselves as romantic heroines, seeking danger in *order to be saved.* As we saw earlier, Jinny exclaims, "They'll think we're drowned" (183), but Easter spoils the plan.

In another scene that follows this one, Nina imagines the night as a masculine giant that enters their tent to approach the sleeping Easter: "Easter's hand hung down, opened outward. Come here, night, Easter might say, tender to a giant, to such a dark thing. And the night, obedient and graceful, would kneel to her. Easter's calloused hand hung open there to the night that had got wholly into the tent" (196). Nina envies the orphan, who is—in her projection—the beautiful and reclining recipient of a dark virile male intruder. Welty makes apparent the fallacy in the middle-class girl's fantasy when she combines Easter's "calloused hand"—a sign of actual life difficulties—with Nina's dream of genteel rape—"the night, obedient and graceful, would kneel to her." Though Easter is watched here—as she is at the story's end—the incommensurability of the dream throws a light back on Nina and provides a narrative escape for Easter. She is not there.

Like Easter, Twosie too is thought by the Morgana girls to be contained in their fantasies, but the text supplies an ironic turn that undoes the dream. Earlier, walking in the woods, the two white girls encounter Twosie: "[her] eyelids fluttered. Already she seemed to be fishing in her night's sleep. While they gazed at her crouched, devoted figure, from which the long pole hung, so steady and beggarlike and ordained an appendage, all their passions flew home again and went huddled and soft to roost" (180). Again, the Morgana girls project their dream onto another: "she seemed to be fishing in her night's sleep." But in fact, as the text makes clear ("she *seemed* to be fishing"), *Jinny and Nina* are dreaming of "her crouched, devoted figure." The passage invites a misreading—we might take Twosie for "beggarlike." But it is her pole that is so described while Twosie is "devoted," remaining steady at her task while Nina and Jinny fly "home," unstrung by the black girl's indefatigable posture.

As a young graduate student, I gave expression to a white middle-class feminine identity in a poem I titled "A Red Dress and a Pyramid."

Written in third person, the poem was to be one of a set called *Girl Tourist* and represents a moment captured on film: a photograph of me at ten, posing in front of an Egyptian pyramid.

> The spaghetti straps of the sun
> dress need to be retied.
> Studying the picture
> she remembers how the soft
> cotton gathered with
> elastic teased her small breasts.
> Halfway up
> one limestone block her
> lips are an uncertain
> smile. A bright girl knows
> she's not pretty. She thinks
> of a melodramatic
> scene: of running into
> the desert, men searching
> with flashlights like
> small suns in the night.
> Her pink arms could make
> fossils in the stone if she
> leaned there forever.

I don't have a date on the poem, but I wrote it in 1978 or 1979. At the time, I was remembering the photo, which I did not have in my possession. I got the dress wrong; in fact, I was wearing a blue, shirt-waist dress with a collar and sleeves. But apparently, my fantasy was better fitted with a red sun dress than a blue smock. The parallels between my dream and the prepubescent Jinny Love's and Nina's are numerous. I imagine myself, for example, leaning against a stone forever (could sexual passivity be given starker expression?!) at the same time visualizing men with phallic lights searching for me in the night if I were to dare an escape! Who are these men? What is their color? Are they Egyptians, "dark" men akin to Jinny Love's "nigger men"? The fossilizing image suggests a kind of drowning, with the concomitant wish—always—to be found. I was a young middle-class white girl who grew up in West Africa, the daughter of Southern Baptist missionaries (we were on a furlough the year in Winston-

Salem). And yet—or perhaps because of that—I did not escape this gendered white dream of dark danger. The poem was written twelve or thirteen years after the pose. Who knows what I was really thinking at age ten. But I project backwards on that girl-self this fantasy of sexual lost-and-found.

What Welty does not record is any hint that Easter is driven by a fantasy of lostness. Already on the path in front of Jinny and Nina, she seems less a dreamer of erotic passivity and more an active enunciator of her position. While Jinny Love and Nina can desert, assured of their place when they return, Easter's coming and going does not presume permanent residence. She is an orphan.

Morrison proposes that the true subject of the Africanist presence is the white dreamer; the subject of blackness is whiteness. But Welty's text unsettles its white middle-class dreamers by allowing the "dark" dream of rescue to be superseded by a dark agent—Easter. The safe white gendered dream of escape is punctured by the actions of an actual dark escapee, one who is tom-boyish yet clearly in need of literal protection, one whose whiteness floats free from any secure mooring.

Before Nina's and Jinny's escape, the two are enduring naptime while Easter sleeps, her "sighs and her prolonged or half- uttered words . . . fill[ing] the tent . . . like the mourning-dove's call in the woods" (182). But now Easter is already in the picture, wide awake and in control.

Both "gypsy" and "fortune-teller"—figures in the Morgana girls' dreams of self—anticipate Easter's actual presence: both are images of exotic transients. But when Jinny Love and Nina actually meet Easter face to face, she is not so exotic as they imagine. She is rather ordinary—just not ordinary enough. She who is Nina's and Jinny Love's object, or Other, is enacting their dream but differently. She does not need their symbolic rescuing and indeed appears to have no interest in the sorts of plots that Nina and Jinny were earlier dreaming about. Already on the path, she so tantalizes the girls that they follow her under barbed wire fences, through mud and muck, and into an abandoned and leaking boat. What they fail to understand, however, is that Easter is not dreaming. She really is outside the normative order that secures white female identity. The dangers she faces are not imaginary. Her moves beyond Nina's and Jinny's line of vision communicate this to the reader: "Easter was going unconcernedly on, her dress stained green behind; she ate something out of her hand as she went" (185).

Nina, a more critical thinker than Jinny but also the one more enticed with the orphan, begins to understand Easter's difference: "The reason orphans were the way they were lay first in nobody's watching them, [she] thought, for she felt obscurely like a trespasser. . . . Even on being watched, Easter remained not answerable to a soul on earth. Nobody cared! And so, in this beatific state, something came out of *her*" (185). Though Nina is unaware of what her observations say about her, she is right about Easter in many respects. As Nina observes, Easter seems to act: "something came out of *her*." Jinny and Nina are accustomed to being watched and, therefore, perform rather happily with the hope of reward, whether in learning to swim or singing camp songs, or accepting sexual passivity. Somebody cares that they are girls. Their personas come provided much like their dresses. Their sense of themselves is born out of a watching for which they happily act. Their vision of drowning is quite different from that of Tom Sawyer and Huck Finn, for example. Those two "drown" in order to get away with something else. But Nina and Jinny envision their drowning in order to be brought back, in order to be reclaimed and more desperately loved. Easter, on the other hand, never entertains any dream of drowning, as far as we know. Instead, she is the one who will literally drown, almost. Having no one to care is not exactly an enviable position even though, in Nina's mind it provides Easter with agency. But at what cost?

When Nina says nobody cares about Easter, she does not mean her words literally. She knows that orphans have rules; all the girls at camp are shuttled from activity to activity in a similar manner. In fact, it is likely that Easter, like the dark girl in my first-grade classroom, is more watched than Nina and Jinny. But she is watched differently, not to be rewarded but to be caught. And being caught is quite different from being found. Unsettled by Easter's desire to be left alone, Nina and Jinny find it increasingly difficult to sustain their own romantic drama.

So three things have happened: Jinny and Nina have escaped *into* (rather than out of) a middle-class girls' fantasy of being found. Their action emerges from the safety of middle-class white homes. But they are tripped up by a white girl who acts black, who is careless or indifferent when it comes to special cups, who refuses to swim though it's the rule, who answers questions without apparent emotion, but who is also overly protective of herself when she does not appear—to Jinny and Nina, at least—to be in any real danger. For example, she bit the hand of Mr. Nesbitt from the Bible class when he turned her around and gazed at her breasts. The reader must wonder at Easter's defense. Is she merely primitive, or is she acting wisely? Has she, in fact, received unsolicited sexual attentions from those in whose care she is entrusted? In an ironic twist, Easter's dark presence—with the added ammunition of all the story's blackness—sheds light on the Morgana girls dreaming. Because she remains outside the fold in a position of actual danger, she escapes their dreaming even as they draft her as the object of their fantasy.

When Jinny and Nina ask if they can go along with Easter, the orphan replies, "'It ain't my road'" (185). Thus the Morgana girls' assumption that Easter's only desire would be to belong to their clique is immediately critiqued. But Jinny's and Nina's fantasy is tenacious. In their imaginations, Easter "seemed very tender and very small in the waist to be trudging along so doggedly, when they had her like that" (185). Viewing Easter as their sexual conquest—"when they had her like that"—and feminizing her form in the most typical of ways—"very tender and very small in the waist," Jinny and Nina eroticize Easter's helplessness. Slipping into the role of masculine agent, the Morgana girls demonstrate the limits of their dream. With this swift shift of positions, Welty provides an ironic turn in the romantic dream, showing how the fantasy of danger and rescue depends on someone's actual conquest and bondage, and more importantly perhaps, on someone's being in *control*, in sexualized and coded ways.

But before the Morgana girls know it, Easter breaks away and darts ahead: "'There's a short-cut to the lake'" (185). Not only is Easter ahead on their path and in their dream, now the Morgana girls are left plotless. At first they were the lost girls, then the triumphant rescuers. But Easter is more outside than Jinny and Nina had imagined. Scooting under a barbed wire fence, the orphan moves courageously and knowledgeably for one so small and tender. The first thing Easter sees when she reaches the lake is a snake dropping off into the water! Nina, who has followed, misses it. But with this shorthand (the appearance of the snake), Welty makes it clear that Easter already knows the story of seduction and perhaps has not escaped unharmed: "Easter looked both ways, chose, and walked on the pink sandy rim with its purpled lip [Easter's own lips are stained with blackberries]. . . . She went around a bend, and straight to an old gray boat" (187). Given Easter's violent response to Mr. Nesbitt and the appearance of the snake, one might conjecture that Easter's purpled lip resulted from an experience of actual harm. While the Morgana girls dream of rape, Easter may have been a literal victim.

The effect of this unfolding scene is recorded on Jinny Love's face when she rejoins the other two, complaining of a twisted ankle and the odd smell of the lake: "Then she stopped with her mouth a little open, and was quiet, as though something had been turned off inside her. Her eyes were soft, her gaze stretched to Easter, to the boat, the lake—her long oval face went vacant" (188). Almost as if the movie reel has torn, Jinny's dreaming is suspended. Though the Morgana girls' eyes "gaze" at the subject before them, they cannot take it in.

The story continues to tell us what Jinny and Nina dream, so determined are they to mold a scene, force a climax. But Easter's thoughts are hidden: "Did she see the drop of water clinging to her lifted finger? Did it make a rainbow?" (188). Nina's imagined questions are not answered, so she conjures up another dream: "A picture in her mind, as if already furnished from an eventual and appreciative distance, showed the boat floating where she pointed, far out in Moon Lake with three girls sitting in the three [seats]" (188). Thus Nina once more attempts a conversion of the afternoon into the romantic adventure of helpless escape. The three girls in three seats serves not so much to record reality—this is a dream—but to up the ante of helpless femininity. In order to play out this fantasy, Nina has to follow Easter through knee-high mud, which she does, most energetically.

As Patricia Yaeger notes, the boat scene is reminiscent of the young Wordsworth in Book I of *The Prelude*. Yaeger reads gender difference in the scene since Wordsworth is allowed his self-constructive adventure while these girls are denied theirs. The boat is anchored to the shore and they cannot free it. But in my reading, the Morgana girls' escape on board would play out their feminine construction—they don't even have oars on board. In this case, their failure to leave the shore acts as an authoritative illumination, bringing to light the "dark" underpinnings of Nina's dream. The danger to Easter in the boat is real, not figurative. She can't swim.

Unhappily for Nina, "Easter only waited in her end of the boat, not seeming to care about the disappointment. . . . If this was their ship, she was their figurehead, turned on its back, sky-facing. She wouldn't be their passenger" (190). As is often the case in this story, the omniscient narration is filtered through the Morgana girls' perspective.

Failing to make Easter one thing—"their passenger"—they attempt to make her another—"their figurehead." But still there is no evidence from Easter. What is she dreaming as she lolls on the boat, her arms outstretched over her head, sky-facing?

Jinny and Nina can do nothing if not begin again, reorienting themselves in their adventure: "'—But let's don't go back yet,' Jinny Love said on shore. 'I don't think they've missed me.'" . . .

"You make me sick," said Easter suddenly.

"Nina, let's pretend Easter's not with us."

"But that's what *she* was pretending."

Nina dug into the sand with a little stick, printing "Nina" and then "Easter."

Jinny Love seemed stunned, she let sand run out of both fists. "But how could you ever know what Easter was pretending?" (190).

Like finding Easter on the path, Jinny now learns—from the more observant Nina—that Easter is already playing the game she imagines, but with a difference. Rather than attempting an escape from camp, an escape in which one might be threatened by "nigger men," Easter is attempting an escape from the Morgana girls themselves. Her disquiet is occasioned by these fanciful escapees, and she pretends them into oblivion.

When I was nine years old, living in the village of Eku, Nigeria, I read from a set of British books called *Water Babies*. I also swam often and intensely in a spring-fed river called the Ethiope. Though the landing frequented by the white missionaries was not a public one, I often saw Nigerian bathers, women doing their wash, children carrying water back to their homes, teen-aged girls washing cassava, old men in canoes selling the catch of the day. In the midst of these realities, I dreamed I was a water baby—and I would always be one. I converted one of my young schoolmates into a water baby too; he and I would always live in this river, around this river. I dove beneath the surface of this crystal clear river and imagined joining hands with a wide circle of water babies—all white and more or less nongendered. In this childish utopia, we wove wreaths of gorgeous water plants to adorn our naked bodies. My dreaming was not in the least disturbed by the presence of many black Africans whose lives were oriented so differently from my own.

What did disturb me was a playmate on the mission compound, a Nigerian girl, my age, who sometimes came over to my house. She attended the Nigerian public school while I took my lessons by correspondence from Calvert School in Baltimore, Maryland. The odd thing about Uvie was that we were alike enough in class (her father was the hospital pharmacist while my father was the business manager). But she didn't dream the way I did (of water babies and cowboys and indians and riding horses to rendezvous with other outlaws). Our games never came together.

All along, Nina and Jinny have assumed that their position is the one to be cherished, the point of leaving and returning. But Easter will not confirm their belief. To pretend to be in danger is not her fantasy, and she will not join them. This resistance is played out in her refusal to learn the true spelling of her name.

In the standoff on shore, Easter spies Nina misspelling her name in the sand. While the orphan's name is spoken "Easter" (and spelled so throughout by Welty), the orphan herself spells it as "Esther." Wiping the sand "and with a formal gesture, as if she would otherwise seem to reveal too much, [she] wrote for herself . . . 'Esther'" (190). A debate about the spelling of Easter ensues, Nina taking the position of compassionate counselor and teacher—she only wants, she explains, for Easter to "spell it right" (191). But again Easter will not oblige. She is not the grateful student even when Nina, alarmed, exclaims, "'Spell it right and it's real!'" (191). Easter, the girl, will not allow a unification of her name's signifier (the sound image) and its sign (the word). Indeed, she makes as plain as day the arbitrariness between the two, thus disrupting the experience of security that furnishes Nina's dream of danger.

As with her attempts to insert Easter in her fantasy, Nina's attempt to teach is also an attempt to colonize the orphan, to create the same dreams in her. In the colonialist drama, one incorporates the outsider who will save you. This drama allows one to imagine one's own vulnerability because one is, in fact, always in control. In the Morgana girls' fantasy, the Easter story of sacrifice better befits the orphan than does the nomenclature of queenliness suggested by Esther, the sign the orphan claims. The fact that Easter is comfortable with the slip between Easter and Esther infuriates Nina because it suggests that the differences she finds remarkable isn't the one that counts in someone else's imagination. Resisting through silence and noncooperation, "Easter

never did intend to explain anything. . . . She just had hopes. She
hoped never to be sorry. Or did she?" (191).

The narrative demurring continues the mystery surrounding Easter.
Hoping never to be sorry could mean hoping never to be down and out,
or hoping not to be chagrined about one's own crimes. Or it could
mean hoping never to be as middle class and white as Jinny and Nina,
feeling sorry for someone else. A slight inversion of words in the
sentence "she just had hopes" resolves into "she had just hopes." In
other words, what Easter may hope is not to be condescending while
pretending to be sympathetic, a feminine middle-class pose if ever there
was one. Or it could mean that she hopes not to be an object of
injustice.

When Easter offers the other girls a smoke, they moralize in
sympathetic condescension: "it stunts [your] growth" (192). To the end,
the Morgana girls weave Easter into their dreams: "Jinny Love's gaze
was fastened on Easter, and she dreamed and dreamed of telling on her
for smoking while the sun, even through leaves, was burning her pale
skin pink, and she looked the most beautiful of all: she felt temptation.
But what she said was, 'Even after all this is over, Easter, I'll always
remember you" (192). The "temptation" of this scene as well as the
sublime imagery—"most beautiful of all"—suggests the Last Supper
recorded in the New Testament. Jinny Love's promise is easily made
and easily broken. When the girls hear Loch's horn, Nina declares, "'It's
time to go. I reckon they've worried enough'" (193). For Jinny and
Nina, the afternoon is a success. But what about Easter? How will she
turn or return to the safety implied in the other girls' fantasies?

If we return to the climactic ending of the story from this rereading
of the girls' afternoon escape, we must read Easter's near drowning and
rescue differently. Readers have commented amply on Loch's rescue-as-
rape. Out of the depths of the water, he "snatch[es] the hair of Easter's
head, the way a boy will snatch anything he wants. . . . Under the
water he joined himself to her. He spouted, and with engine-like jerks
brought her in" (200). With Easter spread out on the picnic table, "the
Boy Scout . . . lifted up, screwed his toes, and with a groan of his own
fell upon her and drove up and down upon her, into her, gouging the
heels of his hands into her ribs again and again" (202).

But what if Welty's description here constitutes the most ironic
moment in "Moon Lake"? What if, as I have surmised, Easter has
already been hurt? What if the symbolic rape—viewed through the
Morgana girls' eyes—points to Easter's real life of actual harms?

Wouldn't we read this tableau differently if it were something other than a satirical extension of the Morgana girls' dream of rescue? Who, exactly, is punishing Easter for her transgressions? All along, we have seen the camp world primarily from the Morgana girls' point of view. The figurative rape scene is also theirs, isn't it? Gathered up in the watching presences of Jinny Love's mother and Mrs. Greunwald, the girls watch with fascination: "there was a sigh, a Morgana sigh, not an orphans'. The orphans did not press forward, or claim to own or protect Easter any more" (202). Easter is now, finally, where Nina and Jinny want her, within their grasp, the mute and abused sign of their protected lives. As it turns out, then, their dream of rescue depends not only on their actual safety but on someone else's (potentially) actual rape.

But perhaps, even in the last words of the story, Easter still retains a power to dislodge. In the last spoken sentence, Jinny remarks to Nina, "You and I will always be old maids." While this comment appears to refer to the girls' shared disgust at the sight of Loch disrobed, it may also refer to a lingering awareness of Easter and the afternoon on the path. "Old maid" may mean spinster but it may also mean a woman who lies outside the dream of romance. In the second case, Easter is an old maid. Once again, her position speaks of a surviving and resisting presence that Nina and Jinny have only begun to imagine.

Isn't it the case then, that Welty facilitates a reading of whiteness through the marginalization of blackness? The seduction becomes a betrayal, but not of the Africanist presence. Instead, the white middle-class girl dreamer betrays herself. She, like Loch, is disrobed to the seeing eye. Perhaps in hoping to be old maids, Nina and Jinny have begun to have those seeing eyes in regard to themselves, to hope for a space and a consciousness outside the romance of danger. One can hope that such a self-critique is possible, even for those of us who grew up dreaming ourselves in the light of day.

WORKS CITED

de Man, Paul. "The Concept of Irony." *Aesthetic Ideology*. Ed. Andrzej Warminski. Minneapolis: Univ. of Minnesota Press, 1997. 163-184.

Fishkin, Shelley Fisher. "Four Views on the Place of the Personal in Scholarship." *PMLA* 111.5 (Oct. 1996): 1063-1079.

———. "Interrogating 'Whiteness,' Complicating 'Blackness': Remapping American Culture." *American Quarterly* 47.3 (Sept. 1995): 428-466.

Morrison, Toni. *Playing in the Dark: Whiteness and the Literary Imagination.* Cambridge: Harvard University Press, 1990.

Olsen, Tillie. "I Stand Here Ironing." *Tell Me a Riddle.* New York: Dell, 1989.

Welty, Eudora. *The Eye of the Story: Selected Essays and Reviews.* New York: Random House, 1979.

——— "Moon Lake." 1947. Rpt. in *Eudora Welty: Thirteen Stories.* Ed. Ruth M. Vande Kieft. San Diego: Harcourt, 1965. 171-212.

Yaeger, Patricia. "The Case of the Dangling Signifier: Phallic Imagery in Eudora Welty's 'Moon Lake.'" *Faith of a Woman Writer.* Ed. Alice Kessler-Harris and William McBrien. Westport, Conn.: Greenwood. 253-271.

CHAPTER 9

Ruth's Journey into the Fields
Feminism in Ozick's "The Pagan Rabbi"
Kathy Rugoff

Cynthia Ozick is deeply committed to a central tenet of Judaism, Rabbi Hillel's statement, "love the stranger," a view also expressed, with some variation in emphasis, by several twentieth-century existentialists such as Martin Buber and Simone de Beauvoir. In addition, some of Ozick's fiction lauds a defining characteristic of Judaism, namely, the extensive consideration of texts: the Bible, the rabbis' discussions of it, and their intepretations of these discussions; pages from the Talmud, for example, include eleven blocks of print, eleven interrelated texts. Finally, some of her fiction critiques a dimension of Judaism, its patriarchal bias. Roles, expectations, and responsibilities of men and women have been separate and not equal as outlined by male rabbis over the centuries.

In a remarkable short story, "The Pagan Rabbi" Cynthia Ozick contends with the irony of sexism in Judaism in light of Hillel's statement. At the same time, the complex, multilayered text of the story affirms and celebrates the fascination with text and its interpretation in Judaism. While critics have discussed Jewish themes in the story, they have not recognized its feminist perspective. In perhaps the author's most complex fiction to date, Ozick ponders what it should mean for a man to love his neighbor, the stranger, the existential Other, especially when she happens to be a woman, perhaps even his lover.

Ozick has addressed the subject of women's equality explicitly in various essays. For example, in "Against Modernity: Annals of the Temple, 1918-1922" published in the collection, *Fame and Folly* (1996), she treats the stunted view of the American Academy of Arts and Letters, and she notes the "tirades" and "gloating" as members dismiss the idea of admitting women (240, 263). In the 1970s, Ozick had supported *classical feminism*, namely, the equality of women and men, and opposed it to *liberation*, a facile solution, in her view, that merely serves to define men and women in separate terms. Her essays advocate change in two areas: one is to dismiss limited views applied to women as artists and writers; the other is to reform aspects of traditional Judaism that maintain separation and inequality based on gender.

Ozick's fiction, in varying degrees, has also responded to sexism. "Virility," included in the collection *The Pagan Rabbi and Other Stories* (1971), is an outstanding example of a satiric tale attacking double standards applied traditionally to the work of male and female authors. The main character, Elia Gatoff, has escaped Russian pogroms and eventually becomes a published poet in the United States. He changes his name to Edmund Gate and plagiarizes the work of his aunt, "'[a]n old Jewish immigrant lady who never even made it to America'" (263). Critics hailed the poetry, calling it "'[t]he Masculine Principle personified, verified, and illuminated.' 'The bite of Pope, the sensuality of Keats'. . . . 'Seminal and hard.' 'Robust, lusty, male.' 'Erotic'" (254); the books of poetry are titled *Virility* and *Virility II* through *V*. But the last series of poems, *Flowers from Liverpool*, is published under Gate's aunt's name; critics write, "'[a] lovely girlish voice reflecting a fragile girlish soul: a lace valentine.' 'Limited, as all domestic verse must be. A spinster's one-dimensional vision.' 'Choked with female inwardness. Flat. The typical unimaginativeness of her sex.' 'Distaff talent, secondary by nature. Lacks masculine energy'" (266). Ozick herself employs a male narrator, further eroding the notion that women authors are only able to write from a perspective based on their gender.

In other fiction, Ozick presents third-person omniscient narrators who convey the mentality of either male or female characters, and she often creates portraits of men. For example, *The Cannibal Galaxy* (1983) focuses on the consciousness of Joseph Brill, and *The Messiah of Stockholm* (1987) presents the perceptions of Lars Andemening. Both protagonists have limited perspectives. For example, Brill, a school principal, is intelligent but lacks imagination; he finds himself at a loss and ensnared by the insight of Hester Lilt, one of the mothers, and by the artistic talent of her daughter, Beulah.

It is the feminist perspective in Ozick's Puttermesser stories that has received attention from critics. In "Puttermesser: Her Work History, Her Ancestry, Her Afterlife," "Puttermesser and Xanthippe," and "Puttermesser Paired," an iconoclastic woman, at thirty-four, forty-six, and finally at fifty-five, has affairs, becomes mayor of New York, and finally marries a much younger man. "Puttermesser and Xanthippe," steeped in urban American-Jewish culture, is a fanciful fiction about a woman in a dead-end job; she has a vision, "an immigrant's grandchild's dream of merit" and justice: a dream of "New York washed, reformed, restored" (*Levitation* 85, 121). Her professional salvation and her Jewish spiritual drive to repair the world are brought about and undone not by a boss, a husband, or children, but by her golem, a magical, animated clay figure; in Ozick's story the golem is female and created by a woman, both contrary to centuries of Jewish myth and lore. Through the humorous, anachronistic juxtaposition of a golem and Gracie Mansion, Ozick merges feminism with Jewish culture and tradition.

"The Pagan Rabbi," which predates these stories, also abandons realism, refers extensively to both Jewish and classical Greek myth and lore, employs a complex multidimensional narrative, and suggests a feminist reading. Feminism is not dealt with in most critical discussions of this story, which are guided, first, by several themes in Ozick's early novel *Trust*, and second, by several of her essays discussing how Judaism differs from Greek myth and pantheism. This approach is not entirely valid because *Trust*, a long realistic novel, has little relationship stylistically to the story, and many of Ozick's other essays also have some bearing on interpreting it. In addition, few critics fully consider various themes that emerge in "The Pagan Rabbi" as a result of its multifaceted narrative and its layers of images; thus, critical discussion of the story has not fully accommodated Ozick's complexity, wherein the connection between her engagement with Judaism and her predilection for feminism is manifest.

"The Pagan Rabbi" is composed of a series of texts, including a notebook and letter written by Isaac Kornfeld, a rabbi who had committed suicide. These texts are framed by a first-person narrative in the voice of Kornfeld's friend, who recounts his visits, soon after the death, with Sheindel, Kornfeld's widow, an orthodox Jew. The narrator reveals early on that he and Kornfeld were the sons of rabbis who had had an unpleasant relationship, marked by competition and envy. In addition, he confesses that he is divorced, having had an unloving relationship with his wife, a Gentile. Finally, he reveals that part of his motive for visiting Sheindel is that he has hopes for a romantic involvement. The frame of the story hinges on a narrator with a less than ideal Jewish past as he describes his visit to the rabbi's wife and provides the reader with a summary of—and quotations from—her husband's notebook.

The story is further complicated when the narrator visits the rabbi's wife a second time and goes on to quote himself and her while they take turns reading aloud and commenting on the rabbi's last letter; within the text of the letter, the rabbi included quotations from a conversation he was having near the time of his death. Thus, passages of "The Pagan Rabbi" include a series of punctuation marks—double quotation marks around a single quotation mark that surrounds another double quotation mark. It is also worth noting that the three texts—the framing narrative, the notebook, and the letter—share images that play off one another. This rich fabric of quotations and intertextual connections parallels Jewish biblical exegesis, which includes quotations from scripture, commentaries on them, and commentaries on the commentaries.

Unlike a narrator in conventional fiction, who serves as a guide to the reader, the narrator in "The Pagan Rabbi" is perplexed. He is trying to fathom what possessed his friend, a gifted rabbi, to quote Byron and Keats in his diary, to write "Great Pan Lives," and finally to hang himself by his prayer shawl from a young oak tree in a city park. In addition, the narrator is confronted by Kornfeld's own account of his final experience in the park. It is a bizarre tale describing his coupling with a wood nymph, her rejection of him, his grasping for her, and his sudden death suggested by the fact that his letter, describing these events, comes to an abrupt end.

Several critics, including David Zucker, Lawrence Friedman, Josephine Knopp, Sara Blacher Cohen, Elaine Kauvar, and Vera Keilsky present similar readings of "The Pagan Rabbi" based on the epigraph to the story, a quotation from the *Pirkei Avot*, the *Ethics of the Fathers*, part of the Talmud traditionally read on the Sabbath. In the epigraph, Ozick quotes Rabbi Jacob who said, "He who is walking along and studying, but then breaks off to remark, 'How lovely is that tree!' or 'How beautiful is that fallow field!'—Scripture regards such a one as having hurt his own being" (3). These critics conceive of "The Pagan Rabbi" as a modern-day Midrash—that is, an imaginative commentary on scripture or on rabbinic responses to the Bible; thus, "The Pagan Rabbi" illuminates Rabbi Jacob's warning. Since Rabbi Kornfeld wandered off into secular poetry and into the park away from the Law and toward pantheism, he suffered great harm and died.

Zucker, in "Midrash and Modern American Jewish Literature," points out that the passage from the epigraph was "in its historical context . . . an attempt to dissuade Jews from becoming involved in the Hellenistic culture of the Greco-Roman world around them," and he maintains that the wood nymph "serves as a metaphor for the idolatry of hellenistic [sic] thought and philosophy" (13, 16). Similarly, Friedman argues, "What is central . . . is not Isaac's sexual liaison with the dryad but its religious implications. Sexual union with what is essentially a tree becomes the abomination that seals his abandonment of Judaism and his confirmation in pantheism" (68). Knopp contends that Ozick "is in deadly earnest about the theological conflicts and ultimate transformation that take place within Isaac" (28); Cohen, on a lighter note, observes the story's playfulness and departure from realism, and she points out that it is Ozick's "most inventive amalgam of the whimsical and moralistic" (*Comic Art* 64). "The Pagan Rabbi," writes Cohen, is one of "her most effective stories," a contemporary parable "grounded in Judaic teachings" ("Prophet" 285). "Just as the prophets reproached the Israelites for worshipping nature deities and foreign idols, Ozick, through this story, warns modern-day Jews of the injurious effects of choosing pagan aesthetics over Jewish ethics and spirituality. . . . Ozick chastises Isaac Kornfeld for wanting to be a creature of nature, leading a life of ease and spontaneity," Cohen argues ("Prophet" 287). Focusing to a greater degree on theology, Kauvar contends that Kornfeld "attempts to bring paganism into accord with Judaism." Since they are "asymptotes and can never meet," Isaac has entered into "an act of moral self-cancellation" (46-47). Finally, with a stronger sociological focus, Kielsky concludes, "In Rabbi Isaac Kornfeld, Cynthia Ozick found an excellent image to exemplify what the results of yearning for and worship of beauty bring, to emphasize her thesis that the Gentile culture with its attraction to physical and aesthetic pleasures is the strongest destructive power for the Jews. . . . She stresses particularly that by hovering unrestrained, a Jew will only find disillusionment and extinction" (114).

All of these readings, thus, are variations on the theme that "The Pagan Rabbi" is a moral tale illustrating the devastating results when one is seduced by the lure of paganism and idolatry. Joseph Lowin points out this dimension of the story but goes on to discuss the tale and how it is affected by its context in the depiction of Ozick's narrator (69-73). Although Sandford Pinsker observes that Kornfeld "has abandoned his Jewish soul in obsessive pursuit of the pagan body," he goes on to argue that the story has some sympathy for the pagan rabbi; it addresses "the old charges against 'Jewish writing'—that everything not Torah is levity. . ." (36, 39). Similarly, Janet Burstein maintains that while it treats the Jewish prohibition against idols and art, it also suggests the dilemma this poses for the artist. "The Pagan Rabbi," according to Burstein, "discloses not only Ozick's familiar anxieties about imaginative freedom, but also her awareness that life may turn bitter, cold, and sterile in its absence" (92). Victor Strandberg discusses the "Pan-versus-Moses dichotomy" and argues that the rabbi's death is not a punishment in that he "chooses to join his dryad-lover, hanging himself from the tree with his prayer shawl" (83).

A good deal of evidence supports the view held by the majority of critics; but like Burstein, I sense there are other dimensions to the story. It intimates the possibility of multiple readings, including a reading that is opposed to the one that is widely accepted. The critical consensus is based upon Ozick's essays, which in one respect support this interpretation of the "The Pagan Rabbi." For example, Ozick in "Metaphor and Memory" (1986) pits Jewish monotheism against Hellenistic pantheism. She argues that in Greek pantheism with its gods in beasts and in brooks, there is no metaphor; she writes, "metaphor is one of the chief agents of our moral nature" (270). Finally, she associates metaphor with memory and compassion. Ozick argues that the ram in the story of Abraham and Isaac becames a metaphor for sacrifice, a result of God's compassion and that references in the Bible to the bondage in Egypt assume the role of metaphor, reminding the Jewish people to love the stranger. "Metaphor," she observes, "is the reciprocal agent, the universalizing force: it makes possible the power to envision the stranger's heart" (279).

As a result, I believe that "The Pagan Rabbi" is not only a moral parable warning of the dangers of straying from the Law but a highly fanciful fiction advocating a major tenet of Judaism. This view, similar to one of the foundations of twentieth-century existentialist thought, is the moral imperative of reciprocity and dialogic relation—the principle of maintaining a reciprocal relationship with the not I, the Other, and in "The Pagan Rabbi," the not I is female. Ozick's fiction, thus, advocates what de Beauvoir maintained in *The Second Sex*. For example, de Beauvoir, whom Ozick has written about, claims that while men and women "remain for the other an *[O]ther*" they should be "mutually recognizing each other as subject" (439). This view is suggested in "The Pagan Rabbi" in the outcome of the relationship between the rabbi and the dryad and in the portrayal of the other characters within the context of a series of images of nature.

In their focus on pantheism pitted again monotheism, many critics have not considered the fact that images of nature carry much symbolic freight in the Bible, in Jewish lore, in various mystical texts, including *The Book of Splendor*, and in Jewish holiday observances such as Sukkot, a holiday based on Leviticus 23:40-43, which draws heavily on plant symbolism to celebrate God and God's relationship to humanity. The same is true of Shovuot, a summer harvest festival during which The Book of Ruth is read and, traditionally, homes and synagogues are decorated with plants and flowers. The holiday also celebrates the marriage between God and humanity. In various Jewish texts and traditions, then, images of nature have associations both with God and with a female force in God's divinity. These dimensions of Judaism have not been incorporated into the arguments of the critics cited above, and they pay too little attention to Ozick's complex narrative with its theologically significant nature imagery, which appears in several textual layers and fuses several plots.

In "The Pagan Rabbi" images of trees, plants, and streams in a park are opposed to images of the city, including highways and sewers. At the beginning, for example, the narrator writes that he went to the place in the park where his friend had committed suicide. Isaac had hanged himself on a limb "of a delicate young oak, with burly roots like the toes of a gryphon. . . . " This image of nature is followed by a repugnant one related to human beings: "The tree was almost alone in a long rough meadow, which sloped down to a bay filled with sickly clams and a bad smell. . . . I knew what the smell meant: that cold brown water covered half the city's turds" (4). Ozick introduces other signs of violence to nature: "At the margins of the park they were building a gigantic highway. . . . The bulldozers had bitten far into the park, and the rolled carcasses of the sacrificed trees were already cut up into logs. There were dozens of felled maples, elms, and oaks" (4). The odor and carcasses suggest impurity, loss of innocence, and death.

These images in the expository section of "The Pagan Rabbi," which resonate through the story in other allusions to nature, have associations with Jewish texts. For example, the union of God and humanity before the Fall is depicted in that famous garden. The Song of Songs—viewed in *The Book of Splendor* and other medieval texts as a celebration of God's presence in the world—is rife with images of plants, animals, and streams. The image of the tree, as Gershom Scholem, the celebrated scholar of Jewish mysticism, points out, is central to Kabbalistic cosmology. God is thought of as a mystical tree. On a less heady note, Deuteronomy warns, "When you beseige a city for a long time—. . . / You shall not destroy its trees" (20:19-20). The late eighteenth-century Hasidic Rabbi Nahman of Bratslav also warned, "If a person kills a tree before its time, it is like having murdered a soul." Finally, in Proverbs 15:4 "a healing tongue is a tree of life" and in 3:18 wisdom is called "a tree of life to those who grasp her." Thus, the image of the tree is associated with the Torah itself (Stein, 86, 91, 70).

The image of the tree is also found in the philosophy of Martin Buber, the Jewish existentialist, whose work Ozick knows well. His description of a tree is an important passage in his book *I and Thou*. In it, Buber claims, "[r]elation is reciprocity" and love "is responsibility of an I for a You: in this consists . . . the equality of all lovers" (67, 66). Buber calls for human beings to have dialogic relations; this reflects and parallels the human relation with God. Thus, Buber calls for human beings to respond to the sanctity of God and of one another. This is symbolized in his description of a tree in which he invokes his reader to enter into a relation with the tree, to respond to it for its uniqueness and not to categorize the tree and consider it as merely an object. By entering into a dialogue with the tree, we may enter into a cosmic relation with God, suggests the existentialist, who also had a strong interest in Jewish mysticism.

The sacredness of the world in many mystical Jewish texts is also symbolized by the union of male and female. In Kabbalistic cosmology, the *Shekhina* is the female force in God, the presence of God in the world. This presence is stressed in prayer on the Sabbath, the holiest day of the week. Traditionally, it is a husband and wife's duty to couple on this day, thereby paralleling the connection between God and the world. In this respect, the rabbi's coupling with the dryad whom he calls "loveliness," the English equivalent of his wife's

Yiddish name, Sheindel, is not an abomination but rather an act of holiness.

Unfortunately, it seems, though, that the dryad in "The Pagan Rabbi" rejects the rabbi and claims that his soul "denies all our [nymphs'] multiplicity," and that when they had coupled, she complains, "your soul in its slow greed kept me close and captive" (34). Thus, this coupling was not satisfactory to her; he had tried to possess her rather than respond to her. The rabbi's subsequent death appears to be the result of his inability to value the nymph's otherness, to respond to her sexuality because he treated her as the mere object of his sexuality. The problem with the rabbi is not in his obsession with nature and the out-of-doors but is in his effort to possess the dryad.

The story seems to conclude with this feminist perspective; but "The Pagan Rabbi" further suggests that the rabbi's wife and the narrator fail to accept the otherness of Isaac; his wife makes cold, unkind comments throughout. It ends with the narrator following the lead of the widow, who had thrown away her houseplants in disgust after she had seen her husband's notebook and letter. The narrator writes, "I remembered her earlier words and dropped three green house plants down the toilet; after a journey of some miles through conduits they straightway entered Trilham's Inlet, where they decayed amid the civil excrement" (37). This passage is in sharp contrast to the images of nature in the rabbi's notebook, which were reminiscent of Jewish holidays and mystical texts celebrating holiness and the connection between God and humanity. In this context, throwing the plants into human excrement is an abomination. Since it is the result of a woman's suggestion, Ozick thereby presents a highly flawed female character.

In both her stories and her essays, Ozick avoids oversimplication; with tremendous patience she considers labyrinthine questions and their nuances. Thus, to make broad generalizations about Ozick's world view has pitfalls. For example, in "What Has Mysticism to Do with Judaism," an article published in 1978, she is highly critical of mysticism. She says that "[my]stical ideas are, like having a pair of feet, humanly universal, and are not especially Jewish" (70-71). Yet two years later she wrote an article celebrating the life and work of Gershom Scholem, who perhaps more than any other twentieth-century scholar, has written about the history of Jewish mystical tradition. She observes that his "reclamation of Kaballah, empowered intellectual-

rationalist Judaism to reharness the steeds of myth and mysticism, and
to refresh the religious imagination at many wells and springs along the
way" (*Art* 144).

Similarly, her view of rationalist Judaism—embodied in Rabbinic
Judaism with elaborate discussions of Jewish Law in the Talmud—is
no simple matter. In "Torah as the Matrix for Feminism," Ozick offers
a new perspective on the biblical figure, Hannah, Samuel's mother. She
is traditionally celebrated because "she was a barren woman who prayed
to have a child and got one." But she was, according to Ozick, a heroine
for a very different reason: Hannah "invents, out of her own urgent
imagining, inward prayer." Ozick contends the Torah is not sexist and
"that the rabbis are obliged to serve the Torah, not that the Torah is to
serve as an instrument of the rabbis . . . " (47-48). It appears then that
Ozick finds the Bible exemplary rather than the interpretations of the
rabbis.

Several years earlier, however, in a long and involved essay, "Notes
Toward Finding the Right Question," Ozick pointed out that the Torah
is sexist in a profoundly significant respect. It presents the possibility
for humans to live morally so that "the salient meaning of Torah [is] to
give precepts against the-way-the-world-ordinarily-is." But there is "one
tragic exception. With regard to women, Torah does not say No to the
practices of the world as they are found in actuality: here alone Torah
confirms the world. . . ." Consequently, the "status of women under
Torah is not remarkably or radically different from the status of women
in the world at large" (58-59, 57). The age-old rationale for the
difference in the treatment of and expectations of men and women is
based on men's views of biological difference. Here the novelist argues
that biology does not determine the person.

She maintains this in her essays on Judaism, on women in
American society, and on women as artists. In each context, Ozick
stresses the personhood of women and celebrates the freedom of the
individual woman to think and do as she wishes; Ozick disputes the
claim that women are limited by their bodies or should be praised
because of their capacity to bear children. As in her celebration of
Hannah, noted above, her focus is on consciousness, on what can be
willed, on what can be thought of, on what can be imagined, not upon
involuntary instincts and actions.

Ozick's predilection is for the world of the mind and the
imagination, so that she is a strong advocate for the writer's freedom.
"When I write," she observes, "I am free. I am, as a writer, whatever I

wish to become. I can think myself into a male, or a female, or a stone
. . . or the leg of a mosquito" ("Does Genius" 56). In "The Pagan
Rabbi" she weaves the narrative from the point of view of Kornfeld's
fellow rabbinical student, presents the intimate notes of Isaac Kornfeld,
and finally expresses the sentiments of a wood nymph who is fed up
with him. The story reflects Ozick's celebration of freedom.

Ozick's fiction, in several respects rejects a sexist definition of the
artist and the muse, as fostered by the poet Robert Graves and other
writers and artists. Graves even titled a book, *Man Does, Woman Is*; for
him the artist is a visionary male, a genius who is inspired by his
muse, a beautiful woman. "If she cannot hear the Muse," Ozick
satirically paraphrases Graves in the essay "Women and Creativity,"
"what does it matter? She *is* the Muse." The essay continues, if "we are
expected to conclude from this that woman is an It rather than a Thou
(to use Martin Buber's categories), why deplore it?" Her sarcastic
response to Graves is simply, the "Parthenon too is beautiful, passive,
inspiring. Who would long to *build* it, if one can *be* it?" (312).

In "The Pagan Rabbi," the novelist suggests through narrative
technique, characters, and plot what she says explicitly in the essay.
Monolithic, stonelike, and immovable are qualities least like the tree
nymph in "The Pagan Rabbi," whom the rabbi embraces, desiring
inspiration and transformation; and she will not be his muse. In
addition, the novelist as an artist breaks the bounds of gender. She
creates a male narrator and thereby writes from the point of view of a
man, and she also imagines and presents another male character's sexual
desire.

Where and what are her roots as a teller of stories? The oldest
stories she knows are biblical; the oldest interpretations of them are
rabbinical. Both her essays and "The Pagan Rabbi" consider issues
concerning gender and Rabbinic tradition. In an essay on "The Book of
Ruth," contrary to what is traditionally stressed, Ozick celebrates
Ruth's vision, Boaz's kindness, and Ruth's generational relationship to
David. The essay opens with a vivid image tied to gender: "There were
only two pictures on the walls of the house I grew up in." One was of
her grandfather, a *melamed*, a scholar. "His eyes were severe, pale,
concentrated. There was no way to escape those eyes; they came after
you wherever you were." He had eyes that "drill through bone." The
other picture, a print, was, according to her mother, "Ruth gleaning in
the fields of Boaz" (*Metaphor* 240, 244, 241). "[W]hat is the connection

between this dusty indoor *melamed* and the nymph in the meadow, standing barefoot amid the tall campanula?" asks Ozick. And she answers, "Everything, everything. . . . The track her naked toes make through spice and sweetness, through dodder, vetch . . . and scabious, is the very track his forefinger follows across the letter-speckled sacred page" (244). For Ozick, Judaism is an on-going dialogue in the marriage of scholarship and imagination.

The imagery in the essay "Ruth," published in 1989, is reminiscent of the imagery in "The Pagan Rabbi." In it none of the characters, male or female, tolerates freedom in the nymph, freedom for Ruth's gender, nor understands the qualities she embodies. The nymph is cursed by the Rabbi's wife, who is very religious but unkind. The narrator, convinced by Sheindel and appalled by the demise of his friend, throws out his house plants. Finally, Kornfeld, the pagan rabbi, denies nymphs' multiplicities and makes a nymph the object of his sexuality.

This remarkably imaginative tale with its multiple layers of narration and interplay of imagery suggests that Ozick has thought about the two pictures in her home for a long time, and she refuses to privilege one over the other; it also suggests that traditional assumptions concerning the role of men as opposed to that of women are highly suspect. Ozick advocates a dialogic relation between men and women, and this is the result of her thoughtful and thought-provoking consideration of Jewish texts, culture, and tradition. Finally, her vision of justice and equality in regard to women, despite some of Judaism's patriarchal attitudes, is also very much part of a Jewish perspective, namely, in the desire to help repair the world.

WORKS CITED

Buber, Martin. *I and Thou*. Walter Kaufmann, trans. and prologue. New York: Charles Scribner's Sons, 1970.

Burstein, Janet Handler. "Cynthia Ozick and the Transgressions of Art." *American Literature* 59. 1 (1987): 85-101.

Cohen, Sarah Blacher. *Cynthia Ozick's Comic Art: From Levity to Liturgy*. Bloomington: Indiana University Press, 1994.

———. "Cynthia Ozick: Prophet for Parochialism." *Women of the Word: Jewish Women and Jewish Writing*. Ed. Judith R. Baskin. Detroit: Wayne State University Press, 1994. 283-298.

de Beauvoir, Simone. "The Second Sex." *Existentialism and the Philosophical Tradition.* Ed. Diane Barsoum Raymond. Englewood Cliffs, N.J.: Prentice-Hall, 1991: 426-439 [excerpt].

Friedman, Lawrence S. *Understanding Cynthia Ozick.* Contemporary American Literature. Columbia: University of South Carolina Press, 1991.

Kauvar, Elaine M. *Cynthia Ozick's Fiction: Tradition and Invention.* Bloomington: Indiana University Press, 1993.

Kielsky, Vera Emuna. *Inevitable Exiles: Cynthia Ozick's View of the Precariousness of Jewish Existence in a Gentile Society.* New York: Peter Lang, 1989.

Knopp, Josephine Z. "Ozick's Jewish Stories." *Cynthia Ozick.* [1975]. Ed. and Intro. Harold Bloom. Modern Critical Views. New York: Chelsea House Publishers, 1986.

Lowin, Joseph. *Cynthia Ozick.* Twayne's United States Authors Series. Boston: Twayne, 1988.

Ozick, Cynthia. *Art and Ardor: Essays.* New York: Alfred A. Knopf, 1983.

———. *The Cannibal Galaxy.* New York: Alfred A. Knopf, 1983.

———. "Does Genius Have a Gender?" *Ms.* 6 (Dec. 1977): 56+.

———. *Fame and Folly: Essays.* New York: Alfred A. Knopf, 1996.

———. *Levitation: Five Fictions.* New York: Alfred A. Knopf, 1982.

———. *The Messiah of Stockholm.* New York: Alfred A. Knopf, 1987.

———. *Metaphor and Memory: Essays.* New York: Random House, 1991.

———. "Notes toward Finding the Right Question." *Forum* 35 (Spring/Summer 1979): 37-60.

———. *The Pagan Rabbi and Other Stories.* [1966]. New York: Penguin Books Inc, 1983.

———. "Puttermesser Paired." *The New Yorker* 8 Oct. 1990: 40+.

———. "Torah as the Matrix for Feminism." *Lilith* 12/13 (Winter/Spring 85): 47-48.

———. *Trust.* New York: E. P. Dutton, 1983.

———. "What Has Mysticism to Do with Judaism?" *Sh'ma* 17 (Spring 78): 69-71.

———. "Women and Creativity: The Demise of the Dancing Dog." *Woman in Sexist Society: Studies in Power and Powerlessness.* [1969]. Ed. Vivian Gornick and Barbara K. Moran. New York: Basic Books, 1971. 307-322.

Pinsker, Sanford. *The Uncompromising Fictions of Cynthia Ozick.* A
    Literary Frontiers Edition. Columbia: University of Missouri Press,
    1987.
Scholem, Gershom G. *Major Trends in Jewish Mysticism.* [1941]. New
    York: Schocken Books, 1974.
Stein, David E. *A Garden of Choice Fruits: 200 Classic Jewish Quotes on
    Human Beings and the Environment.* Wyncote, Penn.: Shomrei
    Adamah, 1991.
Strandberg, Victor. *Greek Mind/Jewish Soul: The Conflicted Art of Cynthia
    Ozick.* Madison: University of Wisconsin Press, 1994.
Zucker, David J. "Midrash and Modern American Jewish Literature." *Studies
    in American Jewish Literature* 11. 1 (1992): 7-21.

CHAPTER 10

Reconstructing the Native-American Woman

Louise Erdrich's "Fleur"

Corinne H. Dale

In Louise Erdrich's short story "Fleur," the plot centers on the Chippewa woman Fleur's gang-rape by three German-American butchers, yet that event is never actually described. More than exposing Fleur, the story reveals the narrator Pauline, whose subjective positions determine her shifting constructions of Fleur. Pauline reads the mysterious young woman Fleur first from the standpoint of an integrated Chippewa and next as an Indian woman marginalized in the German-American culture. But Pauline comes to resist both the Indian construction of Medicine Woman and the white construction of Squaw. She develops her own story of Fleur as avenging Mother (Nature) in spite of the material reality of Fleur's rape. In the end though, Pauline's own representation of Fleur as transcendent Mother is critiqued by her final view of Fleur as "the girl [who] smiles boldly in her sleep" (14)— an unknowable individual. Erdrich thus posits storytelling itself as a way of negotiating the postmodern dilemma of reconstructing history: Pauline's narrative demonstrates that storytelling reveals subjective truth, not objective history. In fact, the narrator Pauline's subjective constructions of Fleur reflect Pauline's own transformations as an individual and as a storyteller.

Critics have analyzed Pauline's character in the context of the novel *Tracks*, but neglected her development in the short story "Fleur." The second chapter of *Tracks* consists of an alternate version of the short story "Fleur," but the Pauline who is developed there and in the rest of the novel is quite different from the Pauline of the short story. Like the short story "Fleur," the second chapter of *Tracks* is narrated from the point of view of Pauline, but later in the novel she goes mad as she attempts to deny her Native-American heritage and her female sexuality, both represented by Fleur Pillager. Critics point out that Pauline adopts the white gaze in the text by negatively valuing herself as nonmale and nonwhite (Castillo 230-235); consequently, Pauline's loss of subjectivity, her internalization of hegemonic white values, leads to her attempt to make herself invisible, to erase herself (Tanner 116-120). So critics of the novel read Pauline's early experience with Fleur as a prelude to her loss of identity and subsequent madness, both of which are later developed in the novel.

The novel *Tracks* was the first manuscript that Erdrich finished, but she then divided it up and re-used pieces of it elsewhere—"It has become the old junked car in the yard front, continually raided for parts"—until it was revised and appeared in 1988 as Erdrich's published novel (Chavkin 238). The short story "Fleur" was one of the re-used pieces published as the first-place winner of the O. Henry Prize in 1987, a year before its alternate version appeared incorporated into the novel *Tracks* as the second chapter "Summer 1913: Miskomini-geezis: Raspberry Sun." The story "Fleur" remains free of the novel's context in anthologies, where many readers encounter Erdrich's fictional world for the first time. Moreover, "Fleur" differs in some important ways from "Raspberry Sun"—the most significant being the portrayal of the narrator Pauline. In *Tracks*, for example, Pauline degenerates to a crazed nun and psychotic murderess. But at the end of the story "Fleur," Pauline has left the town of Argus, gone home to the reservation, and re-envisioned herself as a Chippewa woman, modeled on her perception of Fleur. In the story "Fleur," then, Pauline successfully negotiates both the Chippewa and the German-American constructions of woman, making a space for herself as a storyteller within her tribe.

For these reasons, I propose to examine "Fleur" as a separate story—outside of the context of the novel *Tracks*. Nevertheless, I must heed the postmodernist warnings that commonly appear in the criticism of Erdrich's longer fiction: warnings about the subjective construction of history—the impossibility of knowing historical actuality and the danger of overdetermining meaning from the reader's own subjective position.

Wary of interpreting Native-American experience from an Anglo perspective as Other, white critics like myself must consider Native-

American and in Erdrich's case, Anishinaabe (the original name for the Chippewa tribe) traditions as well as acknowledge European codes. At the same time, we must recognize that Native Americans develop constructions of whites and of white culture also. For example, just as the Chippewa tribe is marginalized by the local white culture in Erdrich's fiction, the German Americans are also a tribe who are constructed as Other by the Native-American narrator Pauline. Equally pertinent is the recognition that gender too is not monolythic. Individual lives are not fully determined either by gender or by ethnic codes; yet both ethnicity and gender are constructions that influence characters within the text as well as guide the reader's reactions.

In "Fleur," Pauline's readings of Chippewa culture and of German-American culture are the keys to her own behavior: her strategies for survival in the white town of Argus and her resistance to both Indian and white male constructions of Woman. In both surviving and resisting, Pauline demonstrates her development as an individual who belongs to a community but is not subsumed by it.

Louise Erdrich herself is German American on her father's side and French American and Anishinaabe on her mother's side; both parents worked as teachers in the boarding schools run by the Bureau of Indian Affairs. Erdrich grew up in a small German and Norwegian town and often visited the nearby Turtle Mountain Chippewa reservation, which was led by her grandfather, a great storyteller and traditional powwow dancer. Erdrich describes herself as "bound to my own [ethnic background], as anyone would be—both trapped and enriched" (*Publishers Weekly* 22). Living herself in two cultures, she writes about characters of different ethnic backgrounds—some are full-blooded Indians; some are white; some mixed.

Like all marginalized peoples, Erdrich's Chippewas learn the values, perceptions, and language of the dominant culture, even as they resist in order to retain their native culture. Catherine Rainwater claims that Erdrich's texts represent conflicts of these Native-American and European-American codes. In *Tracks*, for instance, Pauline's failure to resolve the shamanic code with the Christian code leads to her maginality as a crazed Indian nun (408-409). In addition, Rainwater argues, the reader's own failure to resolve the ambiguity leads to "the marginalization of the reader by the text" (407).

Storytelling, however, is a way of negotiating these conflicting codes, just as it is a way of negotiating the postmodern dilemma of reconstructing history. Erdrich herself observes that traditional Chippewa stories "have incorporated different elements of non-Chippewa or European culture as they've gone on, so that sometimes you see a great traditional story with some sort of fairy tale element added to it" (Jones 4). In "Fleur," the storyteller Pauline resists ethnic codes—both Indian and white—as she develops a strong sense of self within the Chippewa tribe. Further, the storyteller Pauline gives an account of the past that is filtered through her own consciousness and thus dependent upon her own ethnic and gender identity.

Though in *Tracks* Pauline is identified as a half-breed, in the story "Fleur" there is no sign that she is not full-blooded Chippewa. Pauline and her Chippewa mother were brought to the town of Argus from the reservation by Pauline's step-father Dutch, a German American. A year later, her mother is dead, and Pauline takes her place as housekeeper and worker in the local butcher shop. Critics of the novel stress Pauline's alienation from her tribe and denial of her Chippewa identity, but in the first seven paragraphs of "Fleur," and in *Tracks* as well, Pauline reveals herself clearly to be well integrated with the tribe.

In those beginning paragraphs, Pauline asserts the tribal understanding of Fleur as indicated by such phrases as "it was clear" and "we noticed," and " we knew for sure" (2). In the space of two paragraphs, she uses "we knew" three times "and "we thought" three times. Pauline specifically identifies with the Chippewa girls for whom Fleur's story is told as a cautionary tale. She quotes her grandmother with respect, "It went to show, my grandma said. It figured to her, all right" (1). And the first person plural becomes more specific: "our mothers warn us [the young girls]" (2). While writing *Tracks*, Erdrich discussed point of view with her husband/collaborator Michael Dorris, who claims that in the self-conception of native peoples, there is no "I," only "we" (Peterson, 992-993). The first-person plural pronoun and the certainty expressed by the verbs thus mark Pauline as an integrated young girl of the tribe.

Speaking with the voice of the tribe, Pauline tells in the present tense the story of the water monster who has claimed Fleur, a story told as a compelling warning to Chippewa girls, including herself. The water monster seduces and then drowns girls, and Chippewas cannot survive death by drowning—with the exception of Fleur. The story retells a well-known Anishinaabe tale of the lake monster who has the power to drown or to save, and the story is told specifically as a warning to girls to beware of seductive strangers. Reinforcing Pauline's use of the first-person plural "we," Pauline's present tense narrative further demonstrates her identification with other Chippewa girls, her own presence within Chippewa life.

Throughout Erdrich's fiction, Fleur is feared and avoided by the tribe. The water monster, called Misshepeshu, is described in Chippewa stories as instigator of both good and evil deeds, often drowning people and causing stormy waters (Sergi 281). These stories counter the more commonly known positive stories of ritual sexual encounters between humans and spirits of nature in Native-American literature. For instance, Paula Gunn Allen and Patricia Clark Smith explain that the sexual act between human and spirit beings "ultimately yields benefit for their people" (178). But in "Fleur" this relationship is feared by the tribe: incorporating a Christian element, Pauline calls the water monster a "devil" (2), and Fleur's sexual relationship with the water spirit brings death by drowning to George Many Women and Jean Hat. Fleur is ostracized rather than celebrated by her people.

For the reservation people, Fleur is the Other: the unknown, the feared; she has gone "haywire, out of control" (2). Moreover, the tribe's rejection of Fleur seems to reflect their specific anxiety about her refusal to conform to the Chippewa construction of female. No man courts Fleur. "She messed with evil, laughed at the old women's advice, and dressed like a man" (2). It follows that she also takes on the bodies of animals. Pauline tells us that we know for sure "because we followed the tracks of her feet and saw where they changed where the claws spread out . . . " (2).

The word *track*, reinforced by the novel's title, suggests that knowledge is subjective. People (like other animals) are known by their tracks: their identities are constructed from signs. The Chippewas have tracked Fleur and found that she is Other—literally an animal: powerful, magical, fearsome. They are ready to run her off the reservation when she leaves on her own for the summer. So before Fleur reaches the German-American town of Argus, she has already been rejected by her tribal community, which includes Pauline, as a dangerous and powerful individual who has violated the tribal construction of woman.

Although Pauline has participated in the community's fearful rejection of Fleur as Other, when she describes Fleur's entry into Argus, she identifies with Fleur to the point of telling the reader what Fleur must have seen and reacted to as she entered the town. Now Pauline empathizes with Fleur as a representative Chippewa marginalized by white culture, a member of a hunting and gathering tribe that is being forced into capitalism (see Peterson 986). In fact, Pauline constructs Fleur's history as the experience of a precontact Chippewa. Imaginatively, Pauline confronts with Fleur the white culture as if for the first time, and she proceeds to empathize with Fleur's (imagined) reactions to capitalism, sexism, and violence, the lessons of loss learned by native Americans (Peterson 988). Indeed, Erdrich has said that "longing is as much a part of 'Fleur' . . . as is the setting itself" (Chavkin 242).

Pauline presents Fleur at this point as a stereotypical pre-(European)-contact Indian. Yet even Fleur's name is evidence that her parents had contact with Europeans. As Erdrich has pointed out, the Turtle Mountain Chippewa people "are heavily mixed with French and Cree, and so the language that they speak . . . is called Michif, which is a combination of all those. . . . The traditional music in Turtle Mountain is fiddle music and there are a lot of French names in there" (Coltelli 21).

Gloria Bird argues that Erdrich writes "colonialist" literature because she reifies Indian stereotypes in Fleur's characterization as a "Savage," a solitary hunter, a childlike, innocent pagan who is corrupted by civilization and thus doomed to extinction (40-44). Bird especially faults Erdrich for equating the savage with evil and notes that Erdrich's refusal to allow Fleur a voice means that she is seen only from a colonialist view (45). Indeed, Pauline does reinforce these traits in her initial presentation of Fleur. On the reservation, Pauline reflects the tribal view of Fleur as evil Savage; in Argus, Fleur becomes the innocent Savage. But as she tells the story of Fleur's rape and her own revenge, Pauline implicitly questions these preconceived ways of knowing.

Pauline as narrator and Fleur as imagined traveler together enter the alien culture of whites, where both are constructed as marginalized Squaws. Pauline's description of the town reflects her tribal response to the colonialists themselves: she presents Argus as a stereotypical white community, focusing on what is alien to Chippewa sensibility and reinforcing stereotypical European values. Argus, she tells us, is laid out in a grid—a linear structure alien to Chippewas: with a railroad depot, two elevators, two stores, and three churches. Pauline's details reinforce the Chippewa construction of whites: the grain elevators mark white agriculture; the stores, commerce; and the churches, Christianity. The railroad depot connects all of these to the larger white world.

Significantly the houses that must have sheltered the three hundred inhabitants of Argus are absent from Pauline's description: she does not present the town as a community of homes. In particular, Pauline marks the tall steeple of the Catholic church, twice as high as any other buildings or trees, as a "sign of pride" (3). And she supposes that the steeple offended and drew Fleur.

Here the certainty that Pauline shared with the reservation in their estimation of Fleur as Other is transformed to Pauline's certain knowledge of Fleur's shared vision of Argus ("No doubt, she saw ...."). Yet when Pauline considers Fleur's motive, she hesitates: "Maybe" she says twice, it was the Catholic steeple, that "sign of pride ... that marker" (3), that drew Fleur and began the chain of events that brought destruction on the town. Despite the sense of shared ethnicity here, Pauline reveals her incomplete knowledge of Fleur. As she describes their shared past in Argus, Pauline does not presume to "know" completely the medicine woman Fleur. These "maybe's," then, signal a separation from the tribal certainty in its knowledge of Other, and reflect Pauline's later experience in an alien culture: as a displaced person herself, Pauline acknowledges that the individual woman Fleur cannot be known with certainty.

Pauline's narrative next focuses on the butcher's shop, where at least a thousand animals have been carved up and stored and sold. Pauline does not mention the effect on the nearby reservation, but of course this mass butchering of game contributes to the impoverishment and starvation of many Chippewas (later described in *Tracks*). Presumably, Fleur comes to Argus because she no longer can live off the land. The storehouse, in particular, is described as "a marvel" (4), constructed of sawdust and lumber from the woods, bricks, and earth, and containing ice from the lake. Thus, Pauline implies again the white exploitation of nature and the subsequent effect on Chippewa lives. For Fleur there is a personal connection with the exploitation since the ice is taken from Lake Turcot, the home of Fleur's monster lover, the same water that refuses to drown her.

So far, Pauline's construction of the ethnic community of Argus fulfills stereotypes of whites as rapists of nature; the butchers who rape Fleur reinforce Pauline's perception of whites. As marginalized Squaws, Fleur and Pauline transcend their earlier alienation from one another within their tribe. Indeed, between Fleur and Pauline an intimacy develops like that of mother and child. Fleur speaks to Pauline for the first time in the butcher shop; on the reservation, she has been silent. She carries Pauline to a safe closet for sleeping, and Pauline afterwards follows Fleur around, no longer afraid. Pauline thus comes to accept Fleur as Mother, rejecting her earlier tribal view of Fleur as Other. Pauline's new relationship to Fleur signals a dramatic change to a new phase of awareness. Rainwater contends that this sort of shift in family structure is characteristic of tribal kinship systems and significant in Native-American narratives (420).

In other ways too gender exerts a counterforce to ethnic conflict. In fact, Erdrich suggests a sort of female solidarity, even a community, that resists ethnic identification. The German-American woman Fritzie, who works alongside Fleur cutting up the animals, resists to some degree at least the German-American construction of Fleur as Squaw. For example, when Fritzie and Pete return after the tornado, Fritzie asks first of all about Fleur, then about the missing white men. This female solidarity is especially emphasized in "Fleur" as opposed to *Tracks*, since the story "Fleur" does not include the Chippewa boy Russell of *Tracks*. In "Fleur," it is Fritzie, rather than Russell who knows the secret of where Fleur sleeps, just as it is Pauline rather than Russell whom Fleur mothers.

Furthermore, Pauline's narrative does not completely validate the construction of female as negative value; for Fritzie is not victimized by the men. Pauline tells us that Fritzie does not tolerate talking from her husband Pete when she is not around. Even in her absence, she censors Pete so that he talks only of weather and business. Since Pauline has just revealed that the men talk about women when Pete and Fritzie are both absent, we understand that Fritzie's censoring is aimed at sexist conversation. Fritzie acts as a protective force for the other women, establishing a community of women that transcends ethnic identity. Fleur's rape occurs only when Fritzie has temporarily left Argus. In the butcher shop at least, the women seem to stand together against the men.

Gender is addressed in other ways by Pauline, who continues to transform her earlier fearful responses to Fleur as Other into admiration of her as a forceful woman who defies gender constructions. Significantly, Pauline continues to perceive Fleur as manlike, but she now praises the differences that earlier offended Pauline as an integrated Chippewa woman. Pauline comments on Fleur's strength, her broad shoulders, her narrow hips, and her half-tamed aspect. Her wildness, or uncontrollability, is especially marked by her hair: her braids are half-tamed; later, her braids unravel more, and finally during the assault on Fleur, her hair is completely loose. Since Native-American culture does not mark gender by long hair, Pauline's description of Fleur's long hair does not counter her new admiration for Fleur's masculine-marked traits.

At the same time, a conflict of codes is apparent: for in European-American culture, loose hair traditionally suggests sexual abandon, but in Chippewa culture, it signifies mourning. Rather than proving frustrating, though, as Rainwater suggests (406), these codes reinforce meaning: Pauline's celebration of Fleur's freedom and, at the same time, Fleur's grief. At this point, then, Pauline no longer reveals an unalloyed fear of Fleur as "out of control" because unfeminine; instead, her fear of the consequences of Fleur's boldness is mitigated by a new admiration of Fleur as a transcendent woman: strong, bold, free, and in (her own) control.

Fleur's bold behavior directly contrasts Pauline's own fearfulness among the whites. Pauline constructs the German-American men as sexual threats. She tells us that her stepfather Dutch has brought her to Argus, "to take her [mother's] place." She immediately continues, "I kept house . . ." (3) as if to counter the reader's unspoken question about sexual abuse. But the reader perceives a gap in the text. Do Pauline's duties include serving Dutch sexually? Pauline does not say, but the issue of sexuality has been raised, and Pauline is certainly aware of her own vulnerability. Her behavior in the butcher shop is more than discreet; she erases herself so effectively that even the dog ignores her. In this way, Pauline is silenced and made invisible.

Tanner argues that in *Tracks* Pauline internalizes essentialist assumptions about race and gender. She describes Pauline's effort to become invisible as her own negation of self, like her negation by the men, who are unable to read her as woman since Pauline's thin body is not conventionally marked as woman (118-119). Yet Fleur's broad shoulders and narrow hips do not protect her from being read as woman and inscribed as rape victim by these butcher rapists. Like Fleur, Pauline is not necessarily safe because of a body that is perceived as unwomanly.

Pauline's construction of the white men as potential rapists is later proven accurate. In fact, she reads the men more accurately than Fleur does. Thus, Pauline makes herself "invisible" in response to a material danger rather than because she internalizes German-American negative

views of Indian and women. Pauline's plaintive regret for her
appearance: "my dress hung loose and my back was already curved, an
old woman's. . . . I was not much to look at, so they never saw me"
(6) along with her abililty to act—to avenge the rape—indicates that her
invisibility has been temporary and reversible rather than internalized.

The rape itself is described by Pauline as a stupid attempt by white
men to know and control a force of nature. Throughout the story, Fleur
is linked to nature, especially by her name, her wildness, her mystical
connection to the lake and to the storm. Fleur is of the bear clan, and
the revenge of Fleur as representative of nature is suggested by the fact
that the men are later found wrapped in bearskins frozen to death in the
meat locker. The men are characterized as blind, stupid, drunk, and
angry. Pauline comments on the men, "they were blinded, they were
stupid, they only saw her in the flesh" (5). In other words, Pauline
believes that the white men, unlike the tribe, cannot perceive Fleur's
mystical power: for them she is a "squaw" (7)—a white construction of
powerlessness and victimization, just as Pauline herself is. Though
Fritzie transcends ethnic codes to develop a relationship with the
Chippewa woman, the whites cannot perceive Fleur's mystical power
as Pauline does, and as the Chippewas in general do.

Even though the Chippewas recognize Fleur's power while the
white men do not, both seem to be most offended by Fleur's
unconventionality as a woman. The Chippewa people believe they
know Fleur as a Pillager (her family name) and the water monster's
lover. But the butchers of Argus do not have an explanation for Fleur.
Pauline is at pains to point out that Fleur's crime against the white
men is not that she is Indian or Woman, but that she defies their
knowledge of her as Squaw. Certainly, they are shocked by a woman
playing cards—here their construction of Woman is in direct conflict
with the Chippewa construction; for gambling games are popular
among Native Americans in general, and certainly among Pauline and
Fleur's tribe. But again the gambling itself is not what angers the men.

Fleur does not enact the white male construction of the Indian
woman as powerless. Like the Chippewas, the German butchers are
offended by Fleur's being out of (their) control. Instead, she is
mysteriously in (her own) control: each night she wins exactly $1, "too
consistent for luck" (7). The men are offended by her failure to lose, to
be victimized, and they cannot fathom why she wins only $1 each
night. They want to know her, and they want to know her specifically
as victim. Laura A. Tanner explains that "hegemonic culture . . .

constructs the woman of color, like the rape victim, as a featureless absence" (116). By forcing the men to acknowledge her presence, Fleur violates their construction of her as woman of color, so they rewrite her as rape victim, that is as "a text on which his will is inscribed, a form that bears the mark of his subjectivity" (115). In spite of Pauline's vision of Fleur's power, the rape inscribes Fleur for the men as powerless, erasing her subjectivity. Through rape, they believe, they can at last know her as Squaw.

Pauline's description of the attack on Fleur is abbreviated; she refuses to perceive Fleur as an absence, closing her eyes and hearing only Fleur's voice crying out in the old language and calling Pauline's name, "so loud it filled me" (11). Rather than becoming absent herself, then, as Tanner argues (120), Pauline is "filled" with Fleur's presence, and it is this presence, represented in Fleur's cry, that later causes Pauline to retaliate against the men. On the reservation, Fleur's voice was not heard; in Argus, Pauline notes that Fleur speaks to her for the first time as a caring older woman; during and after the rape, Pauline hears Fleur's cry as a full-filling call, echoed in the sow's scream and in the storm's shriek. So it is true that Fleur as an individual ends up silenced "by the writing itself" as Peterson claims (990). For as Pauline retells the story, she transforms Fleur's voice by describing it as a cry for vengeance from the transcendent voice of Woman, of Nature, and of Native Americans rather than as an individual cry of despair.

Instead of participating in the gang rape by witnessing it and representing it, Pauline tells in detail about Lily's brief encounter with the sow who has been penned outside waiting to be slaughtered. This episode is told as a grotesquely humorous dance: The sow "sank her black fangs into his shoulder, clasping him, dancing him forward and backward through the pen. Their steps picked up pace, went wild. The two dipped as one, boxstepped, tripped each other. She ran her split foot through his hair. He grabbed her kinked tail. They went down and came up" (10). A surrogate for Fleur, the sow in Pauline's story becomes a grotesque dance partner rather than a victim. Rejecting the sight and sound of Fleur as victim/object, Pauline transforms the material reality of tragic assault into a subjective and comic episode, an episode that will end not in tragedy for the women, but in triumph.

After the rape, an avenging storm, as Pauline describes it, rips off that prideful Catholic steeple, demolishes the shed in which Fleur has been raped, and generally plays havoc with the town. The bankers and shop owners appropriately hide in their safes and behind their cash registers. The butchers too seek shelter in the marvelous meat locker. But Pauline obeys the shrieking voice she hears in the wind and lowers the bar that locks the men in the freezer. Pauline justifies her own action of locking the men in the freezer as obedience to the storm and thus to Fleur. Even though the reader may be troubled by this vengeful act, this murder demonstrates Pauline's own transformation from Squaw-victim.

The revision of the short story for inclusion in the novel diminishes the issue of gender by including the Chippewa boy Russell as an accomplice to Pauline, both in her victimization and in her empowerment: in fact, in the novel it is Russell who first grasps the bar to imprison the men in the meat locker where they soon freeze to death, vainly covered by the skins of bears that they have slaughtered. In "Fleur" however, Pauline acts alone, empowered by the shriek in the wind that she hears as an echo of Fleur's cry and the sow's scream. "The storm screams like the sow, a shrill scream that . . . spoke plain so I understood that I should . . . slam down the great iron bar that fits across the hasp and lock" (11). And the tornado becomes a "fat snout that nosed along the earth and sniffled, jabbed picked at things sucked them up, blew them apart, rooted around as if it was following a certain scent, then stopped behind me at the butcher shop and bored down like a drill" (12).

The description of the storm as avenging sow in Pauline's story connects the storm to the rape and, imagistically, to Fleur. Moreover, the water monster is known to cause storms. But since it is Pauline who locks the men in the freezer, she now acts as a powerful Indian woman in league with nature and in resistance to white male brutality—like her image of Fleur. Moreover, as she avenges Fleur, her surrogate mother, Pauline also avenges her biological mother since one of the rapists she kills is her white stepfather. Pauline's mother died within a year of that marriage and her removal to Argus, a fate that evokes the colonization and genocide of the American Indian.

Rainwater explains that "Native American individuation occurs in close relationship with nature" rather than in terms of "psychological essence or individual psychology" (421). Clearly, Fleur is characterized as individual through the many associations with nature—the lake, her name, her legend, for instance. When Pauline hears the shriek of the avenging tornado and obeys by lowering the bar to the meat locker, she allies herself not only with Fleur, but also with nature itself. In terms of Native-American tradition, she thus establishes herself as an individual in concert with Nature. At the same time, her plight as Squaw among brutal white male master/rapists reinforces the symbolic connection with the white colonialist construction of Native-American and European-American relations. Again in contrast to European tradition, Native-American individuation does not entail rejection of or separation from the community. Thus, Pauline emerges as the champion of nature, of her people, of women, and of her mother. In fact, soon after, Pauline goes "home" to the reservation.

As she narrates the story, which now features Pauline as the principle agent, Pauline continues to focus on Fleur's power rather than representing her as a victim. Pauline constructs Fleur as a powerful Mother allied with nature, although Fleur cannot protect herself and even challenges the men foolishly by winning that $1 night after night—forcing them to see that they do not really know her. In Pauline's narrative, the material fact of Fleur's rape is absent, replaced by the dancing sow, and Fleur causes the storm that destroys the town, avenging her own rape.

Perhaps even more important for Pauline is Fleur's ability to survive: "the upshot of it all was that Fleur lived" (3). The Chippewa tell stories about Fleur's ability to revive after drowning, the death that no other Chippewa can withstand. She resists death by assigning her place to a substitute: Jean Hat and George Many Women. Fleur's experience in the town is akin to those earlier stories, for the men who assault her die, but Fleur survives. This ability is especially meaningful to Pauline, whose real mother has not survived the town of Argus nor her white husband. Yet Pauline admires Fleur for more than simply surviving. Erdrich says in an interview that women "are taught to present a demure face to the world and yet there is a kind of wild energy behind it in many women that is transformational energy, and not only transforming to them but to other people" (Bruchac 101). Fleur possesses this wild energy that transforms Pauline.

Pauline's recognition of Fleur's transcendent power reaffirms Pauline's own Chippewa identity—but now individuated within the tribe—and Pauline returns "home" to the reservation shortly thereafter. At this point, Pauline uses the present tense again, as she suggests an ethnic determination of selfhood: "the blood draws us back" (14). Erdrich has said that the women in her books are heading home, but also that "going home for most people is like trying to recapture childhood. It's an impossible task" (Pearlman 153). When Pauline goes home, she is no longer a child: she now resists the tribal construction of Chippewa woman and the warning to Chippewa girls, claiming spiritual kinship with Fleur and positively valuing Fleur's power. Both live quietly now, and their intimacy continues to develop; though before Fleur acted as Pauline's mother, now Pauline acts as midwife to Fleur's actual child.

In her dreams, Pauline's transformation is confirmed: "I look straight back at Fleur, at the men, I am no longer the watcher on the sill, the skinny girl" (14). This direct look, which is impolite in the Chippewa culture, marks Pauline's resistance to her tribe as well as a general assertion of self in terms of her representation of Fleur; for the gaze she adopts is that of Fleur's bear clan. In white materialist readings, Pauline's forceful stare is minimized because it is dreamed. For example, Tanner argues that because Pauline's resistance occurs only in her dreams (123), Pauline does not actually affirm her own presence. She points out that in Pauline's narrative, it is sometimes difficult to distinguish between what is imaginary and real, that is, between what is Pauline's subjective construction and what is material reality.

The lack of separation between the material and spiritual does not prove Pauline psychotic though, nor does it diminish her newly found assertiveness in spite of her presently quiet life. Rainwater reminds us that the valuing of material over spiritual (including dreams) is a European-American value (417). The blending of the imagined and the material is typical in Native American, and for that matter most, oral storytelling traditions. Thus, if we conceive of Pauline's narrative as a story told in her Chippewa oral tradition rather than simply written down as in European-American written tradition, we must value the dream positively as a story that presents Fleur's individual experience as a transcendent tale of Native-American and nature's revenge on whites. Pauline's subjective sense of self-worth balances Fleur's rape in the material world and is in fact precipitated by it. Thus, Pauline's avenging murder of the white rapists acts out in the material world her own sense of worth as a Chippewa woman. Fleur herself retains her own transcendent wildness in spite of the rape. Just as Fleur smiles boldly in her sleep, Pauline stares boldly in her own dreams.

Within the Chippewa reservation, Fleur has constructed a space for a woman who smiles boldly and who bears a green-eyed, coppered-colored child. Within Argus, Fritzie occupies the space of the forceful, self-actualized woman, a place reserved for white women only. In narrating the story, Pauline celebrates Fleur as a powerful Chippewa woman, in spite of the material reality of Fleur's gang-rape and in violation of both Indian and white expectations of women. In this way within her narrative, Pauline invents her own newly assertive self. In the dream world Pauline looks boldly, and in the material world she lowers the bar to the meat locker.

It is true that in the novel *Tracks*, Pauline attempts to erase both her Chippewa and female identities, accepting the hegemonic negative valuing of her gender and ethnicity. But in "Fleur" the outcome is quite different. Pauline transcends the constructions both of the tribe and of white Argus, not through psychosis, but by retelling her story and claiming her own worth. Pauline shifts from dissolving herself within the tribe's "we" to differentiating herself from "them," the Chippewa people. This process has been catalyzed by her experience in Argus, where Pauline learned to identify herself as "I" and to resist the codes of those around her. At one point, Pauline ironically describes how "we" looked for the men (13), suggesting a false sense of community with Argus: Pauline of course knows where the men are, since she has locked them in the fatal meat locker. So this ironic use of "we" serves to underscore her secret resistance to the codes of the dominant white community in Argus—her developing sense of self outside the constructions of others.

Individuality itself, however, is a problematic value. Within the male-dominated European-American tradition, the individual tends to be celebrated in his or her difference from the community. But community is more positively valued within Native-American tribes, as it also tends to be in female-centered texts. In the story "Fleur," Pauline creates herself as a woman who defies the certainty of the tribe as a whole, yet this space is specifically within the tribal tradition. Tribal stories are told in order to approach a truth; often the narrative transcends ordinary material experience in order to approach spiritual reality. A greater community truth rather than individual experience results, paradoxically through the stories of transcendent individuals. The stories change depending on the narrator, on the occasion, and on the listener; for above all, stories are a way of seeking. The stories of the old men who seek what they do not know illustrate: their stories are the ways in which they seek to know Fleur. They try out, in narrative alternatives, Fleur's way of living and the father of Fleur's child. "The old men talk, turning the story over. It comes up different every time and has no ending, no beginning. They get the middle wrong too. They only know that they don't know anything" (14).

"Fleur" begins with Pauline's reporting the tribe's certain knowledge of Fleur; by the end of the story, knowing has become problematic. The Chippewa women ostracize Fleur, telling her story as a warning to young girls to beware seductive strangers. The Argus men believe they know Fleur through rape as Squaw. When faced with mystery, they attack it and attempt to fix (control) it through inscribing Fleur as rape victim. In this way, they themselves are destroyed. Both cultures construct Fleur as Other, and both at least initially punish Fleur's failure to enact their expectations. But at the end of Pauline's narrative in "Fleur," the Chippewa people accept Fleur, if only on the outskirts of their community. Recognizing Fleur's mystery, the Chippewa men seek Fleur through storytelling, but do not presume to know her. The difference is underscored by Pauline: while the rapists "know" Fleur as Squaw, "the old men [of the tribe] only know they don't know anything . . ." (14).

Like the old men, Pauline has become a storyteller, abandoning the voice of the tribal women and developing her own in concert with the old men. Still, on the margin of the tribe, she has made a place for a female storyteller who creates a narrative rather than echoing the stories she has been told. In her story, Fleur is absent as Squaw, and present as Other, as transcendent Mother and finally as "the girl [who] smiles boldly in her sleep" (14)—the individual whose mystery is inevitable. Participating in the Native-American oral tradition, she tells Fleur's story to create meaning rather than to record physical events. Pauline thus frustrates materialist white readings of the text. She also demysticizes the tribal wisdom by re-authorizing it—that is, by exposing the fact that tribal stories are told by individuals and reflect individual seeking.

The unresolvable question of Pauline's own understanding remains: when she recognizes the limitations of the old men, does she mean to vaunt her own certain knowledge? Or does she recognize the inherent mystery of the individual and the limitations of narrative? Perhaps she combines the two: aware of her own superior knowledge of Fleur, does she yet accept her own subjectivity as storyteller? The story raises these questions rather than resolving them.

In an interview with Chavkin, Erdrich was asked if Pauline is a reliable narrator in *Tracks*. She replied: "I think it is me, the writer, who in the end is unreliable and continually searching for the truth of an imagined story, a truth which changes with each consciousness and each point of view. . . " (224). In this statement, Erdrich addresses the purpose and nature of storytelling, making a point that holds true for her storytelling characters as well as for herself as writer: stories are told by seekers and truths reflect the teller. "Fleur" demonstrates that the point of view of the teller depends on ethnic and gender identities, but is not determined by them. To come to terms with the truth of the story, we must recognize the place of the storyteller—and also of the reader: like the old men of the tribe, we need to know that we do not know.

WORKS CITED

Bird, Gloria. "Searching for Evidence of Colonialism at Work: A Reading of Louise Erdrich's 'Tracks.'" *The Wicazo SA Review: A Journal of Indian Studies* 8.2 (Fall 1992): 40-47.

Bruchac, Joseph "Whatever Is Really Yours: An Interview with Louise Erdrich." *Survival This Way: Interviews with American Indian Poets.* Ed. Joseph Truchac. Tucson: University of Arizona Press, 1987. 73-86. Rprt. in *Conversations with Louise Erdrich and Michael Dorris.* Ed. Allan Chavkin and Nancy Feyl Chavkin. Jackson: University Press of Mississippi, 1994. 94-104.

Castillo, Susan Perez. "The Construction of Gender and Ethnicity in the Texts of Leslie Silko and Louise Erdrich." *Yearbook of English Studies* 24 (1994): 228-36.

Chavkin, Nancy Feyl, and Allan Chavkin. "An Interview with Louise Erdrich." (Sept. 1992- Apr. 1993). Rprt. *Conversations with Louise Erdrich and Michael Dorris.* Ed. Allan Chavkin and Nancy Feyl Chavkin. Jackson: University Press of Mississippi, 1994. 220-253.

Coltelli, Laura. "Louise Erdrich and Michael Dorris." *Winged Words: American Indian Writers Speak.* Lincoln: University of Nebraska Press, 1990. 41-52. 19-29.

Jones, Malcolm. "Life, Art Are One for Prize Novelist." *St. Petersburg Times,* 10 Feb. 1985: 1D, 7D. Rprt. in *Conversations with Louise Erdrich and Michael Dorris.* Ed. Allan Chavkin and Nancy Feyl Chavkin. Jackson: University Press of Mississippi, 1994. 3-9.

Erdrich, Louise. "Fleur." *Prize Stories 1987: The O. Henry Awards.* Ed. William Abrahams. New York: Doubleday, 1987. 1-14.

"Louise Erdrich." *Publishers Weekly* 237.1 (1990): 22.

Pearlman, Mickey. *Inter/View: Talks with America's Writing Women.* Ed. Mickey Pearlman and Katherine Usher Henderson. Lexington: University Press of Kentucky, 1989. 143-148. Rprt. in *Conversations with Louise Erdrich and Michael Dorris.* Ed. Allan Chavkin and Nancy Feyl Chavkin. Jackson: University Press of Mississippi, 1994. 151-156.

Peterson, Nancy J. "History, Postmodernism, and Louise Erdrich's *Tracks.*" *PMLA: Publications of the Modern Language Association of America* 109.5 (Oct. 1994): 982-94.

Rainwater, Catherine. "Reading between Worlds: Narrativity in the Fiction of Louise Erdrich." *American Literature* 62.3 (Sept. 1990): 405-22.

Sergi, Jennifer. "Storytelling: Tradition and Preservation in Louise Erdrich's *Tracks.*" *World Literature Today: A Literary Quarterly of the University of Oklahoma* 66.2 (Spring 1992): 279-82.

Smith, Patricia Clark, with Paula Gunn Allen. "Earthy Relations, Carnal Knowledge: Southwestern American Indian Women Writers and Landscape." *The Desert Is No Lady: Southwestern Landscapes in Women's Writing and Art.* Ed. Vera Norwood and Janice Monk. New Haven: Yale University Press, 1987. 174-96.

Tanner, Deborah. "'Known in the Brain and Known in the Flesh': Gender Race, and the Vulnerable Body in *Tracks.*" *Intimate Violence: Reading Rape and Torture in Twentieth-Century Fiction.* Bloomington: Indiana University Press, 1994. 115-141.

Contributors' Notes

M. Charlene Ball has published on women's coming-of-age fiction in *Journal of the Short Story in English*, on women's utopias in *The Women's Studies Encyclopedia*, and on lesbian writing in *The Encyclopedia of Continental Women Writers* and *The Lesbian Review of Books*. She has also published fiction and poetry and is the author of several plays. She is working on a study of women's coming-of-age narratives, specifically how myth in these narratives intersects with race, class, and sexuality. She is the Administrative Coordinator of the Women's Studies Institute at Georgia State University in Atlanta.

Marta Caminero-Santangelo is an Assistant Professor of English at the University of Kansas. She is the author of *The Madwoman Can't Speak: Or Why Insanity Is Not Subversive* and of articles on Margaret Atwood, Eudora Welty, and Shirley Jackson.

Nancy L. Chick teaches multicultural American literature at the University of Georgia. She has published articles on Marita Bonner in *The Langston Hughes Review* and on Jamaica Kincaid in *The CLA Journal*. She is currently completing her dissertation on Toni Morrison, Louise Erdrich, Maxine Hong Kingston, and Judith Ortiz Cofer.

Corinne H. Dale is Professor of English at Belmont University and Associate Editor of *Journal of the Short Story in English*. She has published articles in such journals as *Southern Quarterly*, *Southern Literary Journal*, *Mississippi Quarterly*, *Journal of Narrative and Life History*, *JSSE*, and in the collections, *Courage and Tools: The Florence*

Howe Award for Feminist Scholarship, 1974-1989 and *Walker Percy: Art and Ethics.*

David Goldstein-Shirley holds a Ph.D.in comparative culture from the University of California, Irvine. He has published several articles and book chapters on ethnic American literature and is completing a book on Toni Morrison. He teaches in the Liberal Studies Program at the University of Washington, Bothell.

Lakshmi Holmström is a freelance writer and translator who studied at Madras and Oxford. She is the author of *Indian Fiction in English: The Novels of R. K. Narayan*, editor of *The Inner Courtyard: Short Stories by Indian Women*, and coeditor of *Writing from India*, a collection of stories from India for readers aged 14 to 16. She has translated and edited Asokamitran's novel, *Water*, and several collections of short stories by contemporary Tamil writers (including *A Purple Sea* by Ambai, *Neermai* by Na Muthuswamy, and most *recently Mauni: a Writers' Writer*). Her retelling of the fifth-century Tamil narrative poems *Silappadikaram* and *Manimekalai* was published in 1996.

Deborah L. Madsen holds the Chair of English at South Bank University, London. She is author of *The Postmodernist Allegories of Thomas Pynchon, Rereading Allegory: A Narrative Approach to Genre, Postmodernism: A Bibliography, 1926-1994, Allegory in America: From Puritanism to Postmodernism, American Exceptionalism*, and editor of *Visions of America Since 1492.*

Elaine Orr is Associate Professor of English at North Carolina State University in Raleigh, North Carolina, where she teaches American Literature and Women's Studies. She is the author *of Tillie Olsen and a Feminist Spiritual Vision* and *Subject to Negotiation: Reading Feminist Criticism and American Women's Fictions*. In addition, she has published essays in *South Atlantic Review, Modern Language Quarterly, Journal of Narrative Technique*, and *Journal of the Short Story in English*. She is currently at work on a memoir titled *Bamedele: A White Girl's History of Nigeria.*

J.H.E. Paine, Professor of Literature at Belmont University, is Advisory Editor of *Journal of the Short Story in English* and a Founding Editor of *The Tennessee Review*. He has published *Theory and Criticism of the Novella* and teaches courses in modern fiction and literary criticism.

Kathy Rugoff, an Associate Professor in English at the University of North Carolina, Wilmington, has published essays on the relationship between history and modern and postmodern poetry, on poetry and feminism, and on connections between modern literature and music. She teaches several interdisciplinary courses.

Veronica C. Wang, Associate Professor of English at East Carolina University, teaches Asian-American Literature, Women's Studies, and nineteenth-century English and American Literature. She has published essays on Basho, Yukio Mishima, John Cheever, Chuang Hua, Walt Whitman, and Maxine Hong Kingston. She is currently working on a book of critical essays on Kingston.

Index

—A—

Abrahams, Roger D., 88, 95, 159
Alarcón, Norma, 23, 32
Alcoff, Linda Martín, 19, 20, 32
Alvarez, Julia, 23, 32
Anaya, Rudolfo A., 21, 22, 32
Anzaldúa, Gloria, 21, 22, 32, 33, 49
assimilation/ist, xiii, 53, 54, 62

—B—

Bardeleben, Renata von, 17, 18
Bérubé, Michael, 97, 109
Bhabha, Homi K., 37, 50
Bildungsroman, 82
Bird, Gloria, 148, 159
Braxton, Joanne, 85, 95
Brooks, Jerome, 94, 95
Bruchac, Joseph, 155, 159
Buber, Martin, 129, 136, 139, 140
Bulkin, Elly, 95, 96
Burstein, Janet Handler, 134, 140

Burton, Robert S., 32

—C—

Calderón, Hector, 17, 18
Campion, Thomas, 37, 48, 50
Castillo, Ann, 4, 17, 28, 30, 32, 144, 159
Castillo, Debra A., 4, 17, 28, 30, 32, 144, 159
Castillo, Susan Perez, 4, 17, 28, 30, 32, 144, 159
catachrestic space, 37
Chan, Jeffery Paul, 78
Chávez, Denise, 5, 11
Chavkin, Nancy Feyl, 144, 148, 158, 159, 160
Cheung, King-Kok, 68, 75, 77, 78
Christ, Carol P., 89, 90, 95
Cixous, Hélène, 20, 22, 111
Classen, Constance, 39, 50
Cohen, Sarah Blacher, 132, 133, 140
colonial/ist/ism, 19, 38, 42, 43, 55, 125, 148, 155
Coltelli, Laura, 148, 159

Coser, Stelamaris, 99, 101, 108, 109
Crawford, Mary, 100, 109
Crow, Charles L, 77, 78
cuento, 36, 40, 44, 45, 46

—D—

Davis, Cynthia J., 22, 33
de Beauvoir, Simone, 129, 135, 141
de Man, Paul, 113, 127
de Vries, Ad, 42, 50
Demeter-Kore, xiv, 81, 82, 83, 84, 85, 95
dialectic/al/s, 4, 14
dialogic/al, xv, 134, 136, 140
diaspora/ic, xiii, 54, 55, 56, 57, 58, 59, 60, 62, 64
discontinuous narrative, xii, 6, 10, 11, 14
Dowden, Ken, 83, 95

—E—

ensayo, xii, 36, 37, 40, 46, 48
essentialist/ism, 20, 151
Esu-Elegbara, xiv, 81, 84, 85, 89, 91, 94, 96
ethnic/ity,
    and difference, xiii, 22, 64
    and gender, vii, ix-xvi, 68, 84, 150-152, 159
    and narrative, xiii, 5-6, 13, 149,159
    and reader, xvi, 20, 22, 106-108
    definition of, ix-xi
    influence of, xii, 16, 145, 149, 155, 157
    multiethnicity, vii, xii, 35, 38, 48-50, 64
    resistance to, xiv, 27, 48, 64, 146

ethnocentric/ism, 38, 84
Eurocentric, 38, 81, 84
existential/ist, 129, 134, 136

—F—

Felman, Shoshana, 76, 78
feminism/t,
    and Jewish culture, xv, 129, 130-137
    and narrative, 14-16, 114, 131, 137
    and racism, 5, 7, 17
    and reader, 20-22, 68, 82, 84, 108
    and whiteness, x, xii
    narrative, xii, 3, 14-16
Fetterley, Judith, 108, 109
Fishkin, Shelley Fisher, 111, 127
Flores, Juan, 37, 41, 50
Foley, Helene P., 82, 95
Friedman, Lawrence S, 132, 133, 141
Furman, Jan, 103, 109

—G—

Garcia, Cristina, 23, 33
Gates, Henry Louis, Jr, 84, 88, 89, 94, 95
gender,
    and Catholicism, 49
    and colonialization, 38, 42, 120, 124
    and determinism, 145-147
    and ethnicity, vii, ix, xi, xiii-xiv, 49, 97, 100, 108, 120, 124, 150, 159
    and Judaism, xv, 130, 139-140
    and narrative, xiv, 5-6, 10-11, 13, 15, 49, 97, 99, 102,

108-109, 130, 139, 141,
154, 159
and reader, x, 20-22, 102,
108-110
and tradition, xiv, 13, 40, 99,
116, 118, 120, 123
androgyny, 85
definition of, x-xii, 25, 40-
41, 46-47, 151
female community, xiii, 10,
16, 47-49, 150
oppression, 6, 9, 10-11, 16,
56, 75
resistance to, xii-xvi, 5, 25,
40-42, 46-49, 54, 70, 75-78,
116, 130, 139, 141, 150,
157
Graves, Robert, 139
Grewal, S. J., 58, 65
Gutiérrez, Ramón, 48, 50, 51

—I—

imperialism/ist, xii, 35, 42

—J—

Jameson, Fredric, 77, 78
Jones, Malcolm, 43, 96, 109,
146, 159
Jung, C.G., 82, 83, 86, 87, 95

—K—

Kanellos, Nicolás, 24, 33
Kauvar, Elaine M., 132, 133,
141
Keating, AnaLouise, 84, 85, 92,
95
Kielsky, Vera Emuna, 133, 141
Knopp, Josephine Z., 132, 133,
141
Kolodny, Annette, 108, 109

Kristeva, Julia, 39, 50
Künstlerroman, 13, 15

—L—

La Llorona, 21, 27, 31
Lacan, Jacques, 114
Lauter, Estella, 94, 96
lesbian/ism, xiv, 22, 81, 82, 83,
84, 85, 86, 88, 91, 161
Low, Gail Ching-Liang, 64, 65
Lowin, Joseph, 134, 141

—M—

Madden, Mary, 99, 109
Mailloux, Steven, 104, 105,
107, 109
Major, Clarence, 88, 96, 142
margin/al/ity/ization,
and dominant culture, x, 16,
60, 145, 148
and exile, 40, 54, 59, 60, 64
and narrative, 5-6, 11, 15,
17, 158
and reader, 22-23, 82, 104,
145, 158
gender and race, x-xi, xv, 6,
15, 26, 104, 111, 117, 127,
143, 145, 148-149
material/ism/ist/istic, 62, 156,
158
matriarch/al, 41, 82
melting-pot, 60, 62, 64
misogyny/ist/istic, 8
Mukherjee, Bharati, xiii, 53, 54,
55, 61, 62, 63, 64, 65
multicultural/ism/ist, ix, x, 22,
31, 62

—N—

negotiated identity, 22

Novas, Himilce, 35, 43, 50

—O—

Ogundipe, Ayodele, 85, 96
Olsen, Tillie, 115, 128, 162
Ortiz, Laureano, v, xii, 35, 36,
    37, 38, 40, 42, 44, 45, 48,
    49, 50, 51, 161
Other/ing,
    and black men, 117
    and community, xiii, 147-
    150
    and critics, 19-22, 31-32,
    144, 153
    and language, 104
    and Self, x, xvi, 23
    and women, x, 99, 147, 150
    as enemy, 25, 29-30, 74,
    145-147, 158
    as love object, xv, 120, 129,
    134
    challenge to, xiii, xvi, 23,
    25, 32, 158
    definition of, ix-x, xv

—P—

pantheism/ist, 131, 133, 134,
    135
patriarch/y/al,
    and Judaism, 129, 140
    defining the feminine, x-xi,
    6, 11, 13, 15-17, 22, 38, 57-
    59, 73, 76, 78, 81, 82, 87,
    89
    discourse, xii, 6-7, 10-12,
    15, 17, 72, 84
    nurturing, 86
    oppression, vii, x, xii, xiv,
    7, 9, 11-13, 16, 17, 54, 57,
    67, 69, 70, 71, 73, 83-84
Pearlman, Mickey, 156, 160
Pelton, Robert D., 85, 89, 96

Penelope, 46
Perera, Padma, 53, 65
Persephone, 81, 82, 83, 95
Peterson, Nancy J., 146, 148,
    153, 160
pigmentocracy, xii, 48, 49
Pinsker, Sanford, 134, 142
Pipher, Mary, 83, 96
positionality, 22
postcolonial/ist/ism, 19, 20,
    50, 55, 64, 65
postmodern/ist/ism, xvi, 19, 22,
    64, 65, 143, 144, 145, 160,
    162, 163
Powers, Meredith A., 82, 83, 96
Pratt, Annis, 82, 96
Provost, Kara, 85, 96

—Q—

Quintana, Alvina, 5, 18

—R—

race/racial/ist/ism, xii, xiii, xiv,
    5, 6, 7, 9, 11, 13, 15, 16, 22,
    25, 26, 27, 43, 49, 67, 77,
    83, 84, 97, 98, 99, 100, 101,
    102, 103, 104, 105, 106,
    107, 108, 109, 112, 151,
    161
Rainwater, Catherine, 145, 150,
    151, 154, 156, 160
rape/rapist, 63, 88, 114, 118,
    123, 126, 143, 148, 149,
    150, 151, 152, 153, 154,
    155, 156, 157, 158
Reynolds, Margaret, 81, 96
Rich, Adrienne, 13, 15, 18
Ríos, Alberto, 5
Rivera Quintero, Marcia, 45, 51
Rocard, Marcienne, 18
Rosaldo, Renato, 5, 18
Roy, Anindyo, 63, 65

Rushdie, Salman, 58, 65
Russ, Joanna, 81, 96

—S—

Saldívar, Ramón, 4, 17, 18
Salvino, Dana Nelson, 103, 110
Sandoval, Chela, 22, 33
Scholem, Gershom G., 136, 137, 142
Sergi, Jennifer, 147, 160
Showalter, Elaine, 108, 110
Smith, Patricia Clark, 147, 160
Spenser, Edmund, 37, 48, 51
Spivak, Gayatri Chakravorty, 23, 37, 51
Stein, David E., 136, 142
Stepto, Robert B., 101, 103, 108, 110
Strandberg, Victor, 134, 142
Suleri, Sara, 19, 20, 33

—T—

Takaki, Ronald, 77, 78
Tanner, Deborah, 144, 151, 152, 153, 156, 160
Tate, Claudia, 101, 108, 110
Tatum, Charles, 36, 51
Thomson, Jeff, 18
Thorne, Barrie, 25, 33
trickster/s, xiv, 45, 81, 84, 85, 86, 88, 92, 94
Trimmer, Joseph, 32, 33
Trinh T. Minh-ha, 31, 33

—V—

Vaid, Krishna Baldev, 62, 65

Valdes, María, 11, 18
Venus, 90, 92, 93
Virgin, the, 38, 39, 40, 44, 46, 47, 48, 51

—W—

Walcott, Derek, 58, 65
Warner, Marina, 38, 39, 51
white/ness,
    America, xii, xiv, 28, 43, 58, 77, 91, 94, 102, 155
    and feminine identity, xi, 37, 38, 45, 48, 49, 87, 92, 94, 97, 115-121, 124, 143, 146, 150, 152, 157-158
    and literature, 6, 31, 111
    critics/readers, xvi, 5, 19-21, 25, 32, 84, 101-103, 106-107, 112, 114, 156
    definition, ix-xii, xv, 25, 26, 112-114, 119, 127, 145, 148-149
    white patriarchy, 13, 16, 43, 66, 144, 148, 149, 151, 152, 154, 155
Wong, Sau-ling Cynthia, 71, 78
Woolf, Virginia, 36, 46

—Y—

Yaeger, Patricia, 123, 128
Yogi, Stan, 70, 79

—Z—

Zimmerman, Bonnie, 82, 83, 91, 96
Zucker, David J., 132, 133, 142

For Product Safety Concerns and Information please contact our EU
representative GPSR@taylorandfrancis.com
Taylor & Francis Verlag GmbH, Kaufingerstraße 24, 80331 München, Germany